Wofford's Blood

All the time I was growing up, I heard stories about James D. Wofford. As an adult, I began collecting everything I could find about him—from family stories, Cherokee records, and articles in books. Because he was able to read and write both English and Cherokee fluently, he was often chosen as a translator. His tombstone says, "He translated the Bible for the Cherokees." He is buried in a Wofford family cemetery, on land that my family still owns, in Delaware County, Oklahoma. The family is honored that Donna Coffey Little chose James D. as the central character of this novel. The events in this story fit with what we know about his life.

—Marsha Mullen, great-great-granddaughter
of James D. Wofford

It takes a diligent writer to develop conversational dialogue and intertwine it with facts and names from history, all based on extensive research. Making the characters come alive in fictional settings has made this book one well worth reading.

—Leslie Barker Thomas, Georgia Chapter of the Trail
of Tears and Gilmer County Historical Society

With the heart of a poet and the tenacity of a researcher, Donna Coffey Little brings fresh perspective on Native American heritage in North Georgia. In *Wofford's Blood*, Little focuses on the legacy of the tiny lost town of Wofford's Crossroads, now known as White, Georgia. She draws you in with deep research and a diary hidden in the National Archives. Little composes this tale using the notes of James Mooney when he interviewed James Daugherty Wofford in 1891. We are privy to a conversation that explains the journey of the Wofford's. We might have never heard of J.D. Wofford and his journey to many tearful trails. This historical fiction feels like a documentary.

—Lisa Russell, author of *Lost Towns of North Georgia,*
Lost Mill Towns of North Georgia, and
Underwater Ghost Towns of North Georgia

Wofford's Blood

A Novel

Donna Coffey Little

MERCER UNIVERSITY PRESS
Macon, Georgia

MUP/ P698

Published by Mercer University Press
1501 Mercer University Drive
Macon, Georgia 31207

28 27 26 25 24 5 4 3 2 1

Books published by Mercer University Press are printed on acid-free paper that meets the requirements of the American National Standard for Information Sciences—Permanence of Paper for Printed Library Materials.

Printed and bound in the United States.

Maps on pages 28, 118, and 214 are from the Library of Congress.

This book is set in Adobe Garamond.

Cover design by Burt&Burt.

ISBN 978-0-88146-940-0
978-0-88146-941-7 eBook

Cataloging-in-Publication Data is available from the Library of Congress

This novel is dedicated to the memory of
James Daugherty Wofford and to the Cherokee Nation,
past, present, and future.
Long may you thrive!

MERCER UNIVERSITY PRESS

Endowed by

TOM WATSON BROWN
and
THE WATSON-BROWN FOUNDATION, INC.

Author's Note

This is a work of fiction, but with a few minor exceptions, all of the characters are actual historical persons. All of the places, larger historical events, and Cherokee customs mentioned in the book are authentic and based on primary source materials. James Mooney was a Smithsonian ethnologist who interviewed James Daugherty Wofford in 1891. The reader can easily find Mooney's *Cherokee History, Myths, and Sacred Formulas* (1900). The transcripts of those interviews do not exist, to my knowledge. I have created a fictional version of them as a way to tell J.D. Wofford's story, based on over a hundred references to Wofford (Mooney spells it Wafford) in Mooney's book. I have also used primary source materials like wills, land deeds, maps, court documents, and Cherokee Nation documents to reconstruct the lives of these characters as accurately as possible. The family trees in the Appendices are accurate, to the best of my knowledge, except where I have indicated they are speculative or fictional.

However, the personalities and personal interactions of the characters are all pure fiction. I beg pardon of their descendants if I have done injustice to any ancestors in my speculations.

I woke down-country
In a quandary of ways:
Where shall I go?
And how do I get there?
When the country is marked
But not both ways,

And the third is a gamble
Whether up or down?
Is there no rough
Arrow fixed for crows,
Some point at the center
Where all ways are none?

George Addison Scarbrough
"A Dream of Summer Crossroads"

Contents

Prologue:
National Anthropological Archives, Smithsonian Museum, 2022

We don't know where we live. Whose feet walked the land beneath our own feet. Who labored here, who gave birth here, who died here. Whose bones lay buried beneath our very houses.

That was the thought that led me to this poorly lit room in the basement of the Smithsonian's National Anthropological Archives, waiting for the fussy clerk to bring out a box.

I live in a little north Georgia town called White. It used to be called Wofford's Crossroads. And I began to wonder: who were the Woffords? The town is at the foot of Pine Log Mountain, the southernmost mountain in the Appalachian chain. I knew there'd been a Cherokee village nearby. I'd hiked the mountain many times, trying to picture the people who lived here until they were removed on the Trail of Tears in 1838.

I started digging around in the files of the local historical society, looking for information on the Woffords. And what I discovered astounded me. The Woffords were part Cherokee. They were a notorious white Intruder family who had intermarried with Cherokee women. When the Removal came, some of them embraced their Cherokee identity and went on the Trail. Others passed as white and remained in Georgia. One brother went, and another brother stayed. One cousin went, other cousins stayed.

One of the Woffords who left was James Daugherty

Wofford, who led a detachment on the Trail of Tears, and who in 1891 was an informant for Smithsonian ethnologist James Mooney. Mooney's *Myths of the Cherokee* (1900) is considered the seminal collection of Cherokee lore. Mooney was the son of poor Irish immigrants, a self-taught journalist who earned the trust of several Native American tribes and produced detailed catalogues of their languages and cultures. In 1887 and 1888 he interviewed several Cherokee elders in the Cherokee Nation East in North Carolina—the remnant of Cherokee who stayed behind when most were forced to walk the thousand miles to Oklahoma. In 1891 he traveled to the Cherokee Nation West in Oklahoma and interviewed only one elder—James Daugherty Wofford.

Mooney's famous book provides hundreds of tantalizing references to J.D.'s life and personality. It was clear that he had a deep knowledge of the sacred stories and rituals, and he had also been part of the dramatic events of the 1820s and 1830s, leading up to the Trail.

I also found out something else about the Woffords, something that stunned and fascinated me. The great African-American novelist Toni Morrison was born Chloe Wofford, and her father George Wofford was from Georgia, a descendant of the slaves of the same Woffords who founded Wofford's Crossroads.

What was the story of these intertwined white, Cherokee, and Black Woffords? What kind of lives had they lived, here in Georgia prior to the Removal, and then out in Oklahoma in the Cherokee Nation West?

I discovered that the Smithsonian National Anthropological Archives had a collection of James Mooney's papers, and I flew from Georgia to Washington, D.C. to look at them. I carefully filled out the request slip for file 2497, the "Cherokee Notes" of James Mooney.

The clerk emerges from the secret labyrinths of the archives not with a box, but with a cart loaded with six or seven boxes. He wheels it over to the table where I wait.

"There's a lot," he says, pushing his glasses back on his nose. "I think this will take you more than a day."

He hefts a box off the cart and onto the table. I pull on those white cotton gloves they make you wear in archives, so you don't smudge anything. I lift the gray cardboard lid, and that mildewy smell of old books and papers fills the air. I have the feeling that I am the first person to open this box in over a hundred years.

I pull out the first leather-bound journal. On the very first page, Mooney has scrawled: *Interview with James Daugherty Wofford. March 13, 1891; Tahlequah, Oklahoma, Cherokee Nation West.*

Part 1

The Valley Towns

Cherokee Nation East,
Smoky Mountains near North Carolina

March 1812

Chapter 1

The Ghost Dance

Interview One: James Mooney and James Daugherty Wofford
March 13, 1891; Tahlequah, Oklahoma, Cherokee Nation West

[Mooney's Notes: J.D. Wofford is eighty-nine years old. Born in 1802 in Franklin County, Georgia, at Wofford's Settlement to a Cherokee mother and a white father. A leader in the anti-Removal movement and a Conductor on the Trail of Tears. A traditionalist and an abolitionist, affiliated with the secret Keetoowah Society. Fought for the Union in the Civil War. A close friend of Baptist missionaries Evan Jones and his son John Buttrick Jones. Speaks perfect English and has often served as a translator.

Wofford is a small man, short and wiry. He wears a European-style white collared shirt, dark trousers, and dark jacket. A bowler hat with a single white feather, the tip dyed red. A sash around his neck with traditional Cherokee beadwork, red, blue, and white, curlicue designs, almost like a question mark, with cross designs at each end. On his left lapel, a pair of crossed pins. Thick, wavy white hair spilling down his shoulders, bushy white eyebrows, droopy white moustache, and spade-shaped beard. Nut-brown skin creased like a map that has been folded and unfolded many times. Eyes heavily lidded, almost closed, like a sleeping turtle. But when he looks at you, his eyes are a startling blue.

I am interviewing the subject in his home. From the outside, it is a rough log cabin. But the inside is like a museum. The walls are lined with art objects, old tools, old weapons. A dozen turkey fans, the feathers artfully spread. Shelves hold rows of gleaming ceramic pots. Tools hanging on pegs: an axe, an awl, mallets. Baskets. Two muskets, several bows, blowguns, stickball sticks. On the table are a clay pipe and a cane flute.

Wofford shuffles over to the hearth of a big stone fireplace and throws a log on the fire.]

I keep the fire. Someone has to. I carried this same fire all the way from Kituwah to Oklahoma. My wife died on the Trail, her mother died, my niece died. So many died on that journey. The only thing I saved was the fire. That, and the stories. As long as the fire burns, and the stories are told, there will be a Cherokee people.

I think the Creator kept me alive to tell this story. *Who will tell this tale*? He asked, in that booming God-voice of His. *Send me*, I said. *I'll go*. And He seared my tongue with the living coal. I've been left here to witness that these things really happened. And my testimony is true.

If you want to know where the Trail started, it started for me with the Ghost Dance. That was 79 years ago, the year eighteen and twelve. I was ten years old, living with my mother and my stepfather Ebenezer in a cabin on a hill above the Valley River. That's North Carolina now, but in 1812 that was the heart of the Cherokee Nation.

I never liked Ebenezer much. The man was a drunk, and he turned my Mama into a drunk. Or maybe she already was, I can't say. My father was also fond of his liquor. Ebenezer farmed a few acres of corn, but really it was her that worked it. He found himself a good Cherokee woman, a farming woman, and she worked for him. And at night they drank from that jug. And I went outside and studied the stars.

It was about dusk one day in March. Ebenezer and Mama were inside, and I'd been going my solitary way, hunting squirrels and whatnot in the foothills. I roamed all over those mountains by myself. The forest was thick there, chestnut trees so big that ten people holding hands couldn't reach all the way around. Stands of spruce so tall you couldn't see the top, thickets of rhododendron along every creek. So many birds that the sky grew dark with the great cloud of wings and the air was loud with the thunder of their flapping.

Everywhere I went, I carried my blowgun and my dagger and the flute my uncle made for me. I was a good shot with a blowgun. Any meat in that cabin came from me, the rabbits and possums I shot or the fish I caught in the river.

I'd climb Peachtree Bald, trying to catch a glimpse of the Nûñnĕ'hĭ, the Spirit People who lived in the mountains. Sometimes I'd hear their songs and drums. And I'd try to match their melodies on my flute as I went my lonely way. Sometimes I'd catch a quick glimpse of them, before they faded into the trees.

Such a green place. So alive, the Seen and the Unseen. The rocks sang and the trees whispered secrets. The wolves gave us music every morning from their high dens.

The stories that I will tell you, they are not just the stories of the people. They are the stories of the land. Everything about the land has spirit. We call them the Tree People, the Rock People, the Animal People. That is why we say *Nigada dedadanilvgi*. Respect all things.

When we were torn from the land, from everything that made us who we are, we were allowed only what we could carry on our back or in a wagon. But it was the weightless things that were the heaviest: songs and prayers and dances, and the embers of the sacred fire. From this, we have remade ourselves, like a pruned tree that grows back, even when you've cut it to the nub.

The day of the Ghost Dance, I'd been off in the woods somewhere, and when I got back to the cabin, I looked down the road, and here came a great band of people walking up the hill, some still crossing the river at the ford.

I'd never seen so many people in my life. That cabin was on the only road in the gap between the mountains that we called *Gu-li-se-tsi-yi*mountains of blue mistand the whites called the Smoky Mountains. You took that road to the sacred placesKuwahi, Kituwah, Nikwasi, Cowee. We were used to a few travelers coming through, but never anything like this.

I called to my mother and Ebenezer to come out and see, and Ebenezer stumbled out with his musket, a musket that never hit anything, except maybe a wall when he was drunk.

There had to be a hundred people, and they were wearing deerskin tunics and breechcloths, even though it was Windy moon, *Anuyi*, still cold. Sometimes you saw mountain Cherokee wearing deerskin, but most people I knew wore white clothes, even if they didn't speak a lick of English. I was wearing a wool shirt and breeches, and I was still cold.

They were coming from the southwest, and the sun was setting over the river, pink and purple, and the first trees were blooming, the peach trees my mother had planted near the cabin, and the white sarvis and the purple redbuds. When you saw those trees bloom, that was when you knew there'd be no more snow and it was safe to cross the mountain roads. Safe to bury the winter dead.

It was a sight, those people, climbing the hill, wet and singing in the cold dusk. They walked with a dance in their step. At the front walked a man with the confidence of a chief, but not dressed like a chief. He wore only a deerskin breechcloth. Like many who followed the old ways, his head was shaved except for a long topknot with a red eagle feather attached. That usually meant a war chief, but he led a band of men, women and children, not warriors.

The people were singing a song I'd never heard before, and I knew a lot of songs. Even though I'd lived with my father's people in the Wofford Settlement until I was seven and my mother ran off with Ebenezer, I always spent the winters hunting with my mother's uncles. They taught me the old ways. My grandfather's cousin, Yonaguska, he was a medicine man. He'd learned it from his father. And he taught me the medicine ways.

This song I'd never heard. They were singing something like,

On Kuwahi he will meet us!
Dressed in light he comes!
The old ways are restored,
the land is ours; the land is ours!

I knew what Kuwahi was, what the whites call Clingman's Dome, the tallest mountain in the Smokies. Yonaguska had told me stories of the bears that hold council there, and the enchanted lake, Atagahi. But I didn't know who they thought would meet them on the mountain, unless it was the Great White Bear.

Ebenezer was griping, asking "What are they carrying on for?" He didn't speak Cherokee, even though he'd lived among us for many years and was married to a Cherokee woman. Ebenezer always spoke in anger. The world seemed to exist to make him mad.

I explained it to him, that they were singing about Kuwahi, and a god who would come and bring back the old ways.

Ebenezer just grunted and said, "Fat chance of that." He was clinging to that old useless musket. "Are they dangerous?" he wanted to know. He was wearing that moth-eaten beaver hat of his, and his beard looked like a bird might have nested in it.

"They don't have any weapons," I told him. "It's women and children. Nothing to worry about."

My mother tried to pull me close to her, like she always did, and I pulled away, like I always did. I was her only child, didn't look like she'd ever have another one, and she wanted to keep me a baby long past when I was one. She used to call me *tsisdu*, rabbit. I guess because I was small and tricky and never stopped talking, like the rabbit in all the stories.

She was short, and I must have got that from her, because the Woffords were tall. She had pock marks on her face from childhood smallpox. I know it's wrong but I was always a little ashamed of her. She was short and round and drank too much. Her two front teeth stuck out and even though her name was Nancy, a lot of people called her *Doya*, beaver. She was *Ani'-Wâ'di*, Red Paint Clan, so that is my clan, too. A child belongs to their mother's clan. It's a clan to be proud of. Many medicine men come from Red Paint Clan. Maybe it was in my blood to seek the medicine ways.

My mother had a lot of famous relatives. Chief Young Tassel Watts was her uncle and Chief Doublehead was her great uncle. Both great warriors. And because she didn't have any brothers, I was close to her cousins, but I called them uncles. On her mother's side, Agili and Sequoyah. On her father's side, Yonaguska. They taught me the Cherokee ways, but she did, too. She told me some of the stories I am telling you. I didn't respect her like I should have, not until I got older.

When the group reached the cabin, the leader turned and waved his hands, and the song stopped. He called out to us, *Osiyo*, and the people smiled happily like they had a good secret we didn't know.

"I am Tsali," the leader said, in Cherokee of course. "We are on the road to Kuwahi. I ask permission to camp on your land."

He was formal like that, like everything was a ceremony. He took himself pretty seriously, old Tsali. I saw that he had a red scarf around his neck, and a weasel skin pouch, dyed white, hanging from a leather cord. I knew the *adawehiyu,* the powerful magicians, carried white quartz crystals in a pouch like that. The most powerful was an *Ulvsata*, the white star from the forehead of the *Uktena*, the great serpent. A man had to fight with the *Uktena* to get it, pluck it from his head. Only very holy men had such a stone.

Tsali had a tattoo of a water spider on his arm, very big and fancy, and face paint, black and red around his eyes, a smear of white on his cheeks. He had a long beak of a nose and his eyes were dark and bright at the same time, lit from within. The eyes of a true believer.

Red meant war and white meant peace, and I wasn't sure which one he was bringing. He could be a War Chief, with the red eagle feather and red scarf. Or he could be a Peace Chief, with the white pouch for crystals. We'd heard rumors that another war was coming between the Americans and the British. I knew that most of the Cherokee had sided with the British in the last war, and most of the whites with the Americans. My father and grandfather had fought with the Americans against my mother's people. I didn't know who I was supposed to side with. I didn't want to have to choose.

My mother stepped forward, her arm around my shoulders. "We welcome you. I am Nancy, daughter of Elizabeth Watts and Alickee Natchez. We are Red Paint Clan, my son and I."

I saw Tsali studying her, maybe trying to figure out her story, just as we were trying to figure out his. He certainly knew the Watts name—Young Tassel Watts had been a famous War Chief. Yet here she was living with Ebenezer, a raggedy settler. She was dressed plainly in a rough linen shirt, a woolen wrap skirt, and deerskin leggings. But her earrings were made from tiny ocean shells, and she always wore a copper necklace with a medallion engraved with concentric circles, like the ripples when you throw a rock in water. This kind of jewelry didn't match our poor cabin and her ne'er-do-well husband.

Of course, my mother spoke to Tsali in Cherokee, and Ebenezer didn't understand a word. I was always the one to explain things, because my English was better than my mother's, even though she'd been married to two white men. Or married might be too strong a word. I've spent most of my life now being a translator, and it started when I was just a boy. A linkester, that's what we used to call an interpreter. And I was the link, a rusty broken link holding together chains pulling in two different directions.

"He's a prophet," I told Ebenezer, "Like Tecumseh and Tenskwatawa." We'd all heard the stories of the Shawnee medicine men who predicted the comet, and the earthquakes, and the drought. I'd seen the silvery streak the comet painted across the sky. I'd felt the solid ground tremble when the earthquakes came, not just one, but several, the last one only about a month before. It cracked the sloppy stone chimney that Ebenezer had built, and the whole cabin rattled. A sinkhole opened near the spring, and you could look down and see the innards of the earth. The land was cracking open beneath our feet.

Later I learned these were called the Madrid earthquakes, not Madrid in Spain, but New Madrid, Missouri. At that time, we thought it had to be an omen, maybe the *Uktena*, that giant horned snake thrashing around under the ground, causing trouble.

It was a bad time. Hunters came back empty handed. Because of the fur trade, the game was scarce. Because of the drought, last year's corn had withered in the field. It didn't take a prophet to see that the earth was out of balance, that the *tohi*, the right way for things to flow, was gone.

Now here was a man who thought he'd seen a god, and people who would follow him.

"Tell them to go back where they came from," Ebenezer growled. "Tell them this is a load of horseshit. No one is coming to meet them." Ebenezer walked closer to Tsali and shook his head back and forth and pointed back down toward the river and made sweeping motions with his hand as though he could shoo the band like a flock of unruly chickens. Ebenezer thought Indians were stupid.

Tsali was not stupid, and he frowned back at Ebenezer.

"I can't tell them that," I said. "They wouldn't listen if I did. We should offer them hospitality." I didn't like disagreeing with my stepfather. It could earn me a wallop. But I wasn't about to start some trouble with Tsali and his group.

My mother agreed with me. It was terrible manners to mistreat a guest. "We need to give them our hominy," she told Ebenezer. “Let them sleep in our field.”

“I won’t stop them,” Ebenezer said. “But I ain’t lending a hand. You two are the Indians around here, you can help them if you want to.” He went back in the cabin and left me and my mother to deal with the guests.

“He says you are welcome,” I told Tsali. I was lying and Tsali knew it, but we both pretended I was telling the truth. “He says he is honored to host a prophet on his land.” I was laying it on thick. “Our field is yours for the night, and my mother will bring you hominy.”

I led them to a fallow field where soft grass was coming in. They smiled and thanked me as they pulled blankets from their packs and spread them on the cold ground. The children were peering at me shyly from behind their parents’ backs.

My mother went into the cabin and came back out carrying the heavy kettle full of *ganohenv*, what the whites called hominy. It was corn cured in ashes, to make it keep, and we always had a big kettle full hanging in the fireplace.

“This is not enough,” my mother said, “but it is something.”

A few women stepped forward and scooped out shares and carried them to the resting people.

My mother went back inside to be with Ebenezer, and it made me sad. These were her people. I knew what she and Ebenezer would be doing, what they did every night, drinking from that jug until they turned stupid and clumsy. Sometimes angry and sometimes rough, but mostly just stupid.

It wasn’t how I ever wanted to be. I decided to stay outside and watch the people, figure out what they believed and what they wanted.

Night was falling as the people ate the hominy with some

hardtack and dried meat they carried in their packs. Some boys gathered branches to make a fire. Tsali knelt down and opened the basket where he kept the embers of the sacred fire. You'd think you couldn't carry embers in a basket, but inside the basket was a clay pot with a lid. It stayed hot all the time. He pushed some coals onto that clay lid and slid them beneath the branches, then put his chest to the ground and blew gently until the small twigs caught fire. Then he pulled from the basket a few splinters of cedar and put them in the fire, and as the fire grew the smoke had the sharp holy smell of cedar.

Tsali stood up and wailed, high-pitched like the cry of a wolf, and the people rose and gathered in a circle.

And old Tsali gave a speech.

"Now! Ha, then! We are *Ani-Yunwiya*, the Real People! We are the *Ani-kitu-hwagi*, the Kituwah people! You know of my vision on the mountain, the spirit messengers that came to warn me. You know of my dream, the man who wore the robe of leaves, and the crown of leaves. He told me that *Yowah*, the Creator, is angry that we have turned from his ways. We have broken the road that was given to our fathers at the beginning of the world, the *tohi*. The earth shakes and stars fall from the sky."

"Now! Ha, then! We must return to the old ways. We must pound the corn with the *kanona*, not mill it like white men. The millstones have broken our mother's back. Our mother is not pleased with us. The corn withers. The deer are gone, the buffalo are gone. We killed them for their fur, to buy guns and tools and clothing from the whites."

"Now! Ha, then! We must reclaim the Beloved Towns the whites have destroyed, Kituwah and Tugaloo, the mother towns. Currahee Mountain and Toccoa, sold by that traitor

Doublehead to the Wofford Intruders. And we killed him for it. We will give away no more land."

The people whooped and hollered. "He speaks!" they were yelling. "Listen to him speak!"

I was scared. Doublehead was my mother's uncle, and Wofford was my father, my grandfather, my uncles. Wofford was me. I'd grown up in Wofford's Settlement, still spent my summers there. I'd climbed Currahee Mountain many times, swam in the pool at the base of Toccoa Falls. What if the prophet found out I was kin to the traitor, or worse, kin to the Intruders? Would they kill me, or kill my mother?

Tsali went right on. "Now!" he said. "Ha, then, now! A terrible hailstorm is coming, with hailstones as big as hominy. It will destroy the whites and the traitors. We have left behind our beehives, our orchards, our slaves. Our white clothing, our white tools, and guns. The Great Spirit will meet us on Kuwahi. We will dance the ancient dances where the bears hold council. Where the Great White Bear heals the wounded in his magic lake."

A couple of the men had pulled drums from their packs, and they started to play. And the people danced the Ghost Dance. It wasn't about ghosts, although you might say it was about calling on the ancestors. It wasn't the same dance the Lakota and Arapaho and Kiowa are doing now. It was a dance Tsali learned from the Shawnee prophets. Tsali back then was like Wovoka now. He was a prophet, trying to call the people back to the old ways, before it's too late.

The moon was full and huge and yellow as an egg yolk, and the fire was yellow and blazed in the center of the dance. Round and round they went, stomping and twirling, swinging into the center and out to the edge. The women had tied tortoise shell rattles to their legs, and they made that swishing sound, almost like water. The drums were pounding, the drummers chanting. I took out my flute and joined their song.

[Mooney's note: Here Wofford picked up the cane flute from the table and played a song both eerie and haunting, more like a dirge than a song of hope.]

This is the same flute, and that was the same song. This flute has walked a thousand miles and seen so many fires, so many dances. So many deaths. Yet it still plays, and my fingers still remember, my breath remembers.

The faces of the people in the moonlight that night were eager and sure. They were looking at something I couldn't see, but I recognized the longing. Like when the moon shines on still water and that Other world in the water looks more real than the Seen world, and you want to go there. But you can't, you're trapped in this world, this in-between place. There's a window but there ain't no door.

And I rose and danced with them, and they welcomed me into the circle. A dance is a way of knocking on the door, and sometimes going through the door. You have to leave your mind behind and let your body say the things that words can't say. *Here, now. Here, now.* You don't know what you're going to do until you do it. I went to the center and gathered some ash and smeared it across my face. I was just a skinny little boy, but I knew, even then, I'd be a mourner. I couldn't see what they were seeing, but my feet were always the feet of a dancer. I leapt not in faith, but in endless longing.

Chapter 2

The Leech of *Tlanusi'yi.*

Interview Two: James Mooney and James Daugherty Wofford March 13, 1891; Tahlequah, Cherokee Nation

[Mooney's Notes: Wofford has dragged a large leather trunk next to his chair and is rifling through it. The leather is inlaid with intricate designs and studded with large brass tacks. The big brass hasp and two brass buckles hang loose. The trunk looks and smells like an old saddle. I can see a couple of blankets in there, some clothing, some deerskin satchels.]

I brought this all the way from the East, Mooney. It was a gift from my cousin Jimmy, before I left for Oklahoma. It rode on the back of a wagon for a thousand miles. Everything I was allowed to keep fit in a box smaller than a coffin.

[Mooney's note: Wofford runs his fingers along the tooled leather designs.]

Jimmy's hands worked this leather, that's why it means so much to me. And Alfie's hands touched it too, rubbed in the oil.

But I am getting ahead of my story. I suppose you want me to finish telling you about Tsali?

The next morning the people rose before dawn and went down to the river, and I went too. The Valley River, we called it *Konehetee*, comes down from the mountains, and it was still high and cold from snow melt and spring rains. The water is calm in that valley. At that time of year, the banks were thick with flowers -- trillium, violets, trout lily, irises. And the warblers and thrushes had returned and sang in the dawn.

Tsali had to cross the river so that he could face east, where the sun was just rising red above Peachtree Bald. If you did not grow up near mountains, you would not understand that the mountains are a part of you, as much as your arms or legs, as much as the shell of a turtle or a snail. And the rivers are like the blood that runs through your veins. *Nigada gusdi didadadvhni*, that is what we believe. *We are all related.*

I had hunted on Buzzard Roost and Snowbird to the north, Brushy Head and Peachtree to the southeast, and I swam and fished all along Valley River. I knew every rock, every bend, and swimming hole.

The high water rippled and murmured around the rocks, talking to us. It was up to Tsali's chest, but he walked right in, and the people followed, carrying the smaller children. I followed too, and that water was cold as ice, up to my neck. We stayed in the water, while Tsali climbed up on the far bank. I looked back toward the cabin and saw my mother scurrying down the hill. When she walked into the river, it was up to her shoulders.

"*Etsi*," I said. *Mother.* She found my hand under the water and gave it a squeeze. I was so glad to see her, glad she didn't miss this chance.

I had practiced going to water many times, not with her, but with my uncles. This felt more solemn, though, because there were so many people and because Tsali was leading them. He stood on the shore, dripping but not shivering, and chanted the prayer:

"And this is to go to water, early in the morning.

Yunwi Gunahita, Long Man. You hold all things in your hands.
O helper of men! You let nothing slip from your grasp!
We bathe in your body!"
He stooped down and scooped up water in his palms, then splashed it on his face, and said:
"I will stretch out my hand.
Water, you slide, the white foam washes us.
It will cling to our heads as we walk the path.
We listen to your voice. You make us new."

The people in the river turned to the east and plunged beneath the water, seven times down, and seven times up. I plunged with them. When you're under the water, holding your breath, feeling the current pull on you, you don't belong to yourself anymore. You dissolve. What seemed important, doesn't anymore. And that time, with a hundred people plunging and rising, I felt for a short time like I was part of something that wasn't already broken.

When we turned back to look at Tsali, he was pulling something out of his pouch, and it was beads. I'd seen this before with my uncle Yonaguska. There are red beads, black beads, and white beads. The *adewehiyu* use them for conjuring. The spirits speak through them and tell the future. He was praying again:

"When we are stopped by wizards and have given up,
when everything has gone wrong,
when we are covered with the Great Black Loneliness,
this will break the grip, this will rid us of evil."

He rolled the beads around in his palms and between his

fingers and thumbs.

I knew all about the Great Black Loneliness. I'd been alone so much living with my mother and Ebenezer. Even when I stayed in the Settlement I'd wander off by myself sometimes and stare at the clouds or the tree tops or the water, with a hole inside me that felt black and deep. I thought for a second there that Tsali might show me how to fill it.

He closed his eyes and lifted his hands with the beads. "Show me," he chanted, "Show me the end of the journey."

As he opened his eyes to look at the beads, the ground began to shake. It was just a small tremor that time, but we were standing in the river and the water sloshed toward one bank and then the other, foaming and boiling, sending up a column of white spray. Now all of us knew about the great leech that lives in a deep hole in the Valley River, and we were only a few miles upriver from its hiding place at *Tlanusi'yi.* That leech is red with white stripes, big as a house, and it's greedy for human flesh. It makes the river overflow so it can carry people away, suck them to the bottom. Later they're found dead, their ears and noses eaten off.

So when the water began to heave and foam, everyone scrambled out of the river, parents holding their children above their heads.

One woman was screaming, "My son, my son." She had lost hold of him and he'd been swept under. I didn't think. I went back in. I was the only one who knew the river. The water was still heaving and all the commotion had churned up the riverbed. It was almost impossible to see in the brown, mucky water. I was trying to keep my eyes open but the grit stung. I groped along the bottom, running my hands over the slick rocks and tangles of river weed. Holding my breath, holding my breath, tasting the river. I swam downstream, figuring the current would pull him along.

In my teeth I clutched the dagger my father had given me. I was a boy. I'd been waiting all my short life to save or kill someone. I thought I could conquer any monster.

Now I tell you this, and you won't believe me, but out of the corner of my eye I saw that leech. Curled up in a dark hole, slimy and slithery, waiting, biding its time. I saw its twisted teeth, its sucking greed, its stubby feet. Its lidded eyes blinked in the murk. Here is something nobody knows: that leech has wings, like the wings of a bat, skin stretched over knobby bones. They were slack at its sides, but I knew that it could fly.

Sometimes I wonder what would have happened if I had killed it then, when I was a boy with a dagger. Before the shadow of its hairy wings spread across the land. Maybe all of the things that happened later wouldn't have happened.

At that moment I saw the boy lying still at the bottom of the river. I saw him and dove. Pulled him up just as my lungs burst.

I had been down so long, the people had given us both up for dead. When I surfaced, thrashing and choking with the boy in my arms, a couple of the men rushed in and dragged us both out, me coughing and vomiting, the boy lifeless. They laid the child on the bank, not breathing. Tsali knelt next to him and prayed. He opened his medicine pouch and pulled out a small bundle of *tso la*, Indian tobacco. With a flick of flint, he lit the leaves and waved the smoke over the boy's body.

Then he placed both hands on the boy's chest and pushed hard, pounded on the boy like a drum. One, two, three, four, five times. Suddenly a spurt of water came out of the boy's mouth, then he breathed and coughed and his eyes flew open. He was alive.

The people cried out in joy. The mother cradled her son and wept. My mother embraced me and just this once I let her. "My *tsisdu*," she said, squeezing me. "It is lucky that you swim like an otter."

Tsali stood and turned his burning eyes on me, standing shivering on the bank. "What is your name, boy?"

I could not make any words come out of my mouth. Finally I said, "James Daugherty Wilcox."

I lied to the prophet. Wilcox was Ebenezer's last name. I could not tell him my name was Wofford. I could not tell him who I was. I did not have my Cherokee name yet, only the baby name my mother called me. I glanced at my mother, and she nodded ever so slightly.

"James Daugherty Wilcox," he said, and he looked at me with those eyes that seemed to bless and damn. He handed me the singed bundle of tobacco. "May your life be long upon this earth," he said.

That was the only prophecy he got right that day. Because here I am.

[Mooney's note: Here Wofford paused and rummaged in his trunk. He pulled out a small deerskin pouch, loosened the drawstring, and brought it to his nose to sniff it, then handed it to me. Inside the bag were crumbled leaves of Indian tobacco. I inhaled the faint, acrid smell. When I handed it back to him, he reached his fingers in the bag and rubbed his fingers together. He smudged the ashy residue on his forehead and resumed his story.]

I kept it all these years. It has the power of life and death. When you smell this, you should make a prayer in your mind.

About a month later, I was working in the field with my mother when Tsali and his people came back down the road. They were skinny and dirty, still singing, but weaker. Tsali strode in front, the only one who still held his head high.

I stood at the edge of the road and watched. When he saw me, Tsali walked up to me and grabbed the front of my shirt. He put his face close to my face and looked deep into my eyes with those crazed eyes of his.

"Yowah has spoken," he said. "He told me things I cannot say. He showed me the Unspeakable Road that we must travel. I saw *you* on this road. I saw you in the snow and you were weeping."

"What could this mean?" I said, for I was a boy and dearly loved. I knew no sorrow.

"We will meet again," Tsali said. "*Wofford.*"

Part II

Wofford's Settlement, Georgia

Spring/Summer 1812

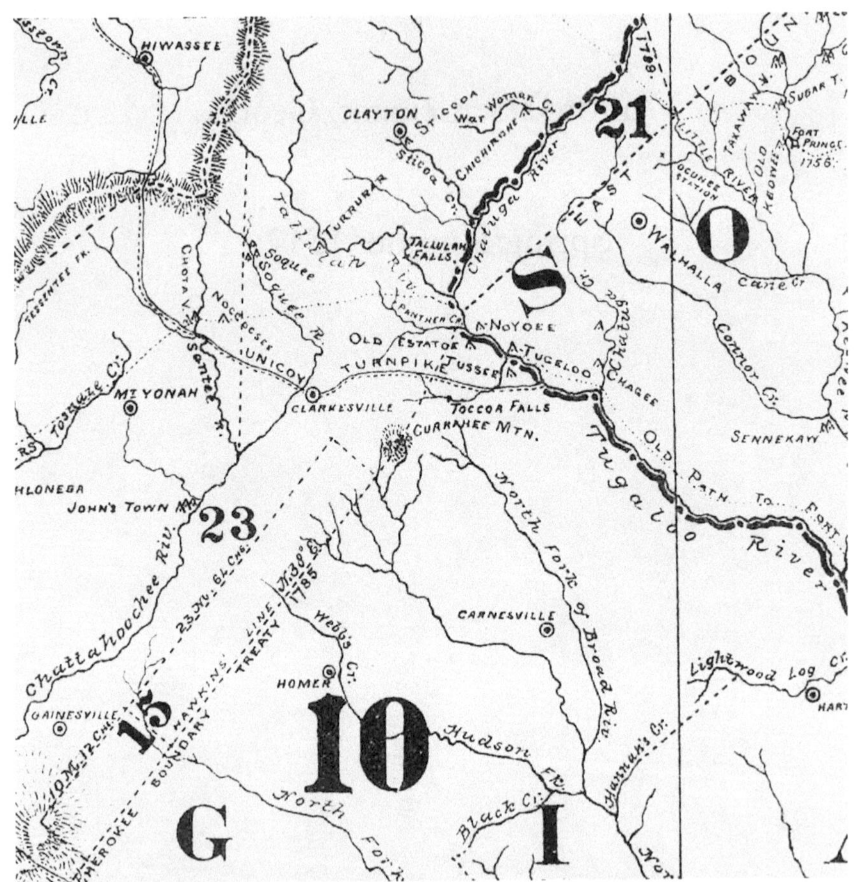

Former territorial limits of the Cherokee, 1884:
Section 15, Wofford's Settlement, Georgia.

Chapter 3

The Green Birds

Interview Three: James Mooney and James Daugherty Wofford
March 14, 1891; Tahlequah, Cherokee Nation

[Mooney's Notes: A large, colorful map is spread across Wofford's table. I have seen this map many timesRoyce's Map of the former Cherokee Nation in the East.]

Every year when spring came, it was time to return to Wofford's Settlement. That spring of Tsali's visit, my mother let me take the old swayback mare we used for plowing. As I rode to my father's house, I pondered Tsali's prophecy. The road I traveled then was green and lush. I could not fathom the Unspeakable Road.

The road from the Valley Towns to Wofford's Settlement later became the Unicoi Turnpike. It was about sixty miles, a two-day journey, so I had to stop and camp along the way. Here, I'll show you on Royce's map. Everything on this map used to be the Cherokee Nation. Now it's North Carolina, South Carolina, Georgia, and Alabama. All of this territory was given away, or should I say stolen, in treaty after treaty, until finally they sent us all to Oklahoma, except for the small band that stayed in North Carolina.

Right here, where the map says Murphy, North Carolina, that's where my mother lived. Royce changed most of the Cherokee names to settlers' names. See, here's the Valley River. And this road right here that says Unicoi Turnpike, that was the route I took the from the Valley Towns to Wofford's Settlement, only it wasn't called that 'til later. It goes down into Georgia, and right here where it says Clarksville, that's when I left that road and headed here, where this long pink rectangle is, number 15. That's the Four-Mile Purchase. That's Wofford's Settlement.

The Settlement was on the border between Georgia and the Cherokee Nation. All this to the west of it, the rest of north Georgia, stayed in Cherokee hands until they removed us in 1838. In fact, Wofford's Settlement *was* Cherokee land. It was famous because a surveying mistake in the 1780s placed it within Georgia, but when Benjamin Hawkins surveyed it again in 1797, it turned out that it was part of the Cherokee Nation. My grandfather and the other settlers petitioned the U.S. government, and the Four-Mile Purchase was born. For 5,000 dollars, a strip of land four miles wide and twenty-three miles long was sold by the Cherokee to the state of Georgia. James Vann, the richest Cherokee there ever was, was part of those negotiations, as was my great-uncle Doublehead. Doublehead profited from this deal, and that's why Doublehead was killed.

And the Woffords became known as the worst of the white Intruders.

Every year when I returned to the Settlement, I paused at the famous Chopped Oak, *Digälu'yätûñ'yï*, "Where it is gashed with hatchets." It stood where the Unicoi Turnpike crossed the north-south trading route, right here near Clarksville on the map. You can see Currahee Mountain from there. The Chopped Oak was scarred with notches that stood for a scalp that had been taken. It was some kind of meeting place or law ground on the boundary between the Cherokee towns to the east and the Creek towns to the west. The Cherokees and the Creeks had been at each other's throats for a hundred years. That's why my uncles were so eager to fight when the Americans decided to fight the Creeks. We were all equally doomed, we just didn't know it yet.

At the Chopped Oak, I turned south on the trading route toward Chenocetah Mountain and the Settlement. I walked across the barren borderland between the Settlement and the Nation. They'd cut down the trees to mark the border and left great stumps no one had ever bothered to grub out, so high weeds and scrawny saplings were taking over. It wasn't just the border between Wofford's Settlement and the Cherokee Nation, or between Georgia and the Cherokee Nation. It was the border between the United States and the Cherokee Nation. Two different countries, and I was a citizen of both. Which side was home? That was a question it took me a long time to answer.

My grandfather's house was inside the stockade he built back in 1793, when the white Intruders were under attack from both Cherokees and Creeks. It sat on a knoll above where Nancytown Creek and the Middle Fork of the Broad River came together, in the foothills of the Currahee Mountains. The Wofford fields spread over many acres below the homestead. My grandfather owned more than 10,000 acres that used to be Cherokee land.

As I rode up that spring, I saw my father and grandfather and uncle in the fields along the river. Small flocks of sheep and cows grazed in the distance. I saw my grandfather had felled more trees to create new ground for planting. My father, my grandfather, and my uncle Nathaniel were standing by the new fields watching Tom, Tony, and Carolina, my grandfather's slaves, plow and plant.

"J.D.," my father shouted when he saw me. I slid off my

horse and into his hug. He put his hands on my cheeks and studied me like something that he'd lost and finally found.

My father Benjamin was shorter than the rest of the Woffords, and stout. His round face must have come from his mother, who died long before I was born. He had big bushy eyebrows, a red nose, and thick, curly hair, already white, escaping from its queue. He had a thick white beard and he always had a pipe in his mouth. My father was quick for a laugh, a drink, a smoke, a woman. He was less ambitious than either my grandfather or his brother Nathaniel. He brewed good moonshine and he drank it, too.

He looked so different from my uncle Nathaniel that you wouldn't know they were brothers, but they were close. Wherever one went, the other soon followed. Nathaniel was tall and gaunt, with my grandfather's long nose, the same one that had skipped over my father and landed on me. He was clean-shaven and neat, the curly Wofford hair slicked back and tightly braided. But his eyes were restless, always looking out to the horizon for the next thing, whether it was a new woman or a new frontier.

Nathaniel, like my father, had a liberal understanding of the institution of marriage. He stayed married to my aunt Lydia, who was half Cherokee, but he kept a second household with another mixed blood Cherokee woman named Elizabeth Terrell. Nathaniel had a daughter with Betsy named Meley Jane, and she was as much a part of the family as his children with Lydia.

You have to understand that in those days it was very common for white men to marry Cherokee women, and we had a very different view of marriage than whites. Whites believed marriage was for life. A Cherokee woman, if she tired of a man, could just divorce him and move on to another man. By the same token, a Cherokee man at that time could have more than one wife.

My father was married to a white woman, Mary Hollingsworth, and never divorced her, but did not live with her. He had a series of romances with Cherokee women, my mother just one of them. This never bothered folks on the frontier, but as white culture took over, it became a source of shame and something to lie about and cover up.

That spring, Nathaniel embraced me as well. "Look at you, lad," he cried, pulling back and holding onto my arms. He squeezed my upper arm. "The muscles on this boy, Benji!"

I grinned up at my uncle. Our families had always lived together. His son Jimmy, like me a James Wofford, was born the same year as I was, and we had grown up like twins.

As my grandfather strode toward me, I called out, "It's late to plant the corn, grandfather."

My grandfather was tall and lean like Nathaniel, in his 80s but age had not slowed him down. A pair of spectacles rested on his hawkish nose, and his white hair was long and thick as a horse's tail. Everyone, even his family members, called him the Colonel, from his Revolutionary War service.

He put his hands on my shoulders and kissed my forehead. He always did love me best, of all his grandchildren. Everyone knew it. I might have been half-Indian, but I was *his* Indian. Just like I'm *your* Indian now, Mooney.

"It's not corn," my grandfather cried that day. He was always shouting, even if he was right next to you. "It's cotton! This crop will make our fortunes, my boy!"

We all turned to watch the men working in the new field. Tony, who was my age, guided a plowshare pulled by two mules. Carolina, his father, came behind him with a hoe, scooping out small holes every six feet or so. And Tom, Tony's grandfather, who was getting old now, followed behind, dropping seeds from a sack and kicking the dirt over them with his boot. Tom was probably the same age as the Colonel, but life had been harder on him, and he walked with a hitch in his step as he sowed the corn.

"Can Tony stop for today?" I asked. For he was one of my two best friends, him and my cousin Jimmy. The Thunder Boys, we called ourselves. That was a butchering of the Cherokee story, because there are really only two Thunder Boys. Plus, the Thunder Boys killed their own mother, Selu, and were banished to the Darkening Land. So maybe it wasn't the best thing to call ourselves.

It sounded strong and brave and that's what we three wanted to be. We had climbed every mountain, swum every river, hunted every critter, within ten miles of the Settlement. Oh, to be a boy again, in the woods with my two best friends!

We made up names for our Thunder Boy adventures. I was *tsisdu*, Rabbit, just like I was to my Cherokee family. Small and fast and full of mischief. Jimmy was Bear, because he was big and solid. And Tony was Crane, because he was tall and skinny. It never mattered to us that Tony was a slave. In fact, Tony was Jimmy's cousin through his mother Lydia. Lydia and Carolina were first cousins. Lydia's Cherokee mother Susannah had a brother named Red Fern who was in love with the Colonel's slave Izzy. I never met either one of them, but Lydia and Carolina both remembered them well.

Carolina was tall and his hair fell in long waves. His cheek bones and hair said that a Cherokee man had loved an African woman. You could see it in Tony, too, in the tilt of his eyes and wave of his hair.

So, the Thunder Boys were not just friends but cousins.

Bound by blood *and* friendship. We'd even done that little ceremony all boys do, cutting our fingers and pressing them together, mingling the blood. We swore an oath of loyalty.

The Colonel fancied himself an enlightened slave owner who treated his slaves like part of the family. In the past, the Wofford men had always worked alongside the slaves in the fields. So I was surprised that year when I saw Tom, Carolina, and Tony working while my grandfather, father, and uncle looked on. Before this new cotton crop, the Settlement had only grown tobacco and corn, just enough for food and fodder, and the whiskey my father brewed.

The Colonel had owned Tom and Carolina since his time in North Carolina, where they helped him clear the trees on his property on the Catawba Road. He also owned Tom's wife Peggy, and their daughter Rachel, who was married to Carolina.

"Why are they doing all the work?" I blurted out.

My grandfather wouldn't look at me. "Times change," he said. "Cotton is the new king. You can't stop progress." For once he wasn't shouting. "Look at all this land, J.D. All Wofford land, as far as your eyes can see. It's been wasted up until now, but we'll make it yield, every inch of it."

Even then, I knew there was something wrong with this. The land owned itself, no matter what a piece of paper said, or a surveyor with chains, measuring the boundary lines.

I reached in my pack for the conch shell my cousins and I used to call one another. The sound carries at least a mile, and I used it with Jimmy and Tony so that we could always find each other. It was the call of the Thunder Boys. Here, I have it still.

[Mooney's Note: Wofford rummages in his trunk and pulls out a large pink conch shell. It seems out of place in Oklahoma, so far from any ocean. He traces his fingers along the ridges of the shell.]

The Colonel gave me this shell. He told me it contained the sounds of the ocean, all its waves and tides, and when you put it to your ear, you can hear the rush of the sea. When you put it to your lips and blow, if you know how to do it, it bellows like an angry animal.

[Mooney's Notes: Wofford blows into the shell. The deep boom is startling in the small cabin.]

It carries far. When Tony heard it, he looked over from the field, not sure what he was supposed to do. The Colonel nodded, and he dropped the plow and ran to greet me. He'd grown even taller in the months since I last saw him. His face was dripping with sweat from the work he'd been doing, but his smile was still a boy's.

"Crane," I yelled.

"You old Rabbit," he yelled back. "I'm gonna cook you for dinner!"

"Not 'fore I snap your long legs like a twig," I cried. Tony had long skinny legs, like small saplings, even as a man.

I heard shouts in the distance and saw three figures splashing across Nancytown Creek. It was my cousins Jimmy and Meley Jane, and our neighbor Altha McCracken. We called her Alfie. She and Meley Jane were the same age as Jimmy and me. They couldn't be part of the Thunder Boys because they were girls, but we let them tag along, and we even gave them special names. Alfie was Redbird because of her bright red hair. Meley Jane was Little Dove because she was gentle and timid.

They were laughing and hooting as they ran, water flinging from the bottom of Jimmy's trousers and Alfie's and Meley Jane's dresses.

"Will you look at him, Jimmy," Alfie said. "A real live Indian! We come in peace, oh mighty Rabbit!"

Alfie was always silly like that, always joking. They were mountain people, the McCrackens. Scotch-Irish. They'd followed the Woffords from Burke County, North Carolina, the lot of them. All the families in the Settlement were either people the Colonel knew from North Carolina, or fellow soldiers in the Revolution, or both. The McCrackens spoke with a mountain lilt, while the Woffords, who came from Maryland and South Carolina, spoke with more of a drawl. Alfie's mother was a Wofford, the daughter of my grandfather's brother John, so I guess Alfie was actually our second cousin. Their homestead was just a mile down the road.

Alfie was red-haired, like all of her family, freckled, with eyes the blue of late cornflowers. The blue at the base of a flame. She was a lively one, my Alfie. *Our* Alfie. Quick to laugh, quick to anger.

"Thunder Boys!" Jimmy yelled. And he shoved me, and I shoved him, and we both shoved Tony and punched each other in the shoulder. That was how we greeted each other.

Jimmy was the closest thing I had to a brother, since my half-brother Will was ten years older than me, and I was my mother's only child. Jimmy looked mostly white but had his mother's dark brown Cherokee eyes, while I looked Indian but had the blue Wofford eyes, like a spooky blue-eyed wolf. Jimmy had a high forehead and a narrow bony face. He looked a bit like President Abraham Lincoln, tall like him, but not as skinny. He always had a hank of brown hair falling on his face, even when he was older. He'd push it back and it would fall again. Jimmy had his father Nathaniel's hard work habits, but not his wandering eye. He was solid as a rock. He was practical and never believed my stories, but he loved to hear me tell them. In our group, he was the quiet one, the careful one, and the fair one. He was the truest friend I ever had.

Meley Jane was dark like me, but her black hair fell in spiraling curls from the Wofford side. She was a beauty. You couldn't help but love Meley Jane. She was gentle with animals and had a healing touch. If a dog or a horse was hurt, she could calm it and doctor it. Her spirit was so still that I'd seen wild birds perch on her like a branch. She was smart as a whip, and when my grandfather ran his school for us under the trees, she was the one who read all the books and knew all the answers.

The Colonel said, "Go on, Tony," and the five of us took off down the road.

Alfie grabbed my arm and said, "J.D., you have to come see the birds." She pulled at me, and we all ran up the hill and through the open gate of the stockade. My grandfather had long ago replaced the original log cabin with a two-story frame house. When my mother lived with my father, I always stayed with my parents. After she left, I often stayed with my grandfather.

The house was painted white, with a two-deck porch on the front. Over the front door were small glass panes in the shape of a square horseshoe. The door was what used to be called a "Christian door," with the top carved in the shape of a cross, and the bottom carved to look like an open Bible.

The inside of this house was paneled with wide boards of

knotless forest pine. There was a wide front hall, and my grandfather, who was an excellent artist, had painted on the wall a beautiful sailing ship. The ocean beneath was crashing blue waves, and the ship itself had great white sails and a long, pointed keel. Why he chose a ship I do not know, since I don't think he had ever been on one, although he'd travelled to Charleston and seen them. I guess that's where he got the conch shell. The crashing waves in the painting reminded me of the rolling Currahee hills, and the ship was our homestead, balanced on the top of a wave.

That day we didn't enter the house. We went around the back, passing the barn and kitchen and chicken house. Behind the house, there was a vegetable garden and a small orchard of apple, peach, pear, and pecan trees. The apple trees were in bloom, the sweet scent filling the yard, and the first green shoots were pushing up in the garden.

Next to the garden stood a wooden platform with a small roof, and on top of the platform sat a large, bell-shaped cage with two bright green birds inside. They were Carolina parakeets. I'd seen them many times in the wild. They were the most colorful birds in the Nation, greener than spring's first green, with orange and yellow around their heads. They perched on wooden dowels, peering out between the thin brass bars of the cage. A tiny brass door with a little door pull was all that stood between them and freedom.

"Aren't they glorious?" Alfie exclaimed. "Have you ever seen anything so lovely?"

"I have," I said. "I'm glad you like them, but I'd rather see them free."

"But they love each other!" she cried. "One is male and the other is female. The Colonel has named them Adam and Eve."

One bird was grooming the other, pecking gently at its colorful, useless wing. Meley Jane stuck a finger through the bars and clucked with her tongue, and the birds came to her.

"See my necklace?" she said, and pointed to a leather cord strung with bright green feathers she'd gathered from the cage. "I'm one of them," she said. "The most beautiful bird in the forest."

"You are that," I told her. "Do you take care of them?

"Oh no, that's Mama Peggy, of course!" she said. "Look, here she comes!" Tony's grandmother was descending the back stairs. The neat yard was Mama Peggy's domain. She had planted a bed of hollyhocks and larkspur along the back of the house, and the tall flowers, every shade of purple, were beginning to bloom. She planted these because they attracted hummingbirds, and the tiny, quick birds were already darting in and out of the flowers.

"My rapscallion is back!" she cried as she reached us. "My brave boy!" She grasped my cheeks with hands soft and careworn as my mother's. She was built like my mother, short and round, and whenever I was at the Settlement, she was the closest thing to a mother that I had. All of us kids called her Mama Peggy.

She held a bowl filled with crumbs of last year's pecans. She put some on her fingertips and poked her fingers through the bars of the cage. The birds pecked at her fingers, and she laughed.

"Beautiful birds!" she said. "They're like my children now."

"Can you get them to talk, Mama Peggy?" Alfie asked.

"I'll try, my darlin'," she said. She put her face close up to the cage. "Good boy," she said. "Good boy. Good boy."

The parakeets squawked. Carolina parakeets are not

songbirds. Their cry is harsh as a crow. "Uh-*eye*," one of them let out in a strangled croak, like a man whose tongue has been cut out. "Uh-*eye*."

Mama Peggy smiled, and Alfie and Meley Jane smiled.

"See," Alfie said. "They're happy."

"Chickie, chick, chick," Mama Peggy said, wiggling her finger inside the cage.

"Ick, ick, ick," croaked the flightless birds.

Tony's mother Rachel came down the back stairs, carrying the baby she and Carolina had over the winter. Rachel hadn't had any kids between Tony and this one, and she was so proud and happy.

"Welcome home!" Rachel said. "Look at my baby girl."

"Her name is Hannah," Meley Jane said, putting her finger in the infant's chubby hand. "She looks a bit like me, J.D."

"Naw, she looks like *me*. She's *my* little sister," Tony said.

Carolina's Cherokee heritage was evident in the shape of baby Hannah's face and her ringlets of black hair, which did look a lot like Meley Jane's.

"*Ulihelisdi Agilvgi*," I said. *Welcome, little sister*.

Grandfather's wife Mary opened the back door and called out sharply, "Peggy, Rachel, you're needed in the house."

Mary Bobo was the Colonel's third wife, and not the mother of any of his children. Her face was round as a skillet, and ugly. She was the portliest woman I ever knew and did not like to get out of a chair or lift a finger. She was ill-tempered, too, and no one understood why the Colonel had married her. Her constant demands were wearing on Peggy and Rachel. She sat in her rocking chair and watched and complained, while Peggy and Rachel did all the work.

Granny Mary didn't care for me at all, nor I for her. The Thunder Boys had played more than one trick on her over the years, frogs under her seat cushion and such. She didn't even acknowledge me as she called Peggy and Rachel inside.

"Let's go to the shoals," Jimmy said, and we all ran the half mile down the road to the small waterfall on the creek. My grandfather's gristmill and my father's stillhouse sat above the shoals, where the water rushed over a series of rocky ledges just a few feet high. You could walk right across the low falls and the pool below. We tore off our boots and splashed in. The water was chilly in early spring.

To children, a creek is a world. We went to the shoals every day in summer. The best game was to sit on the slippery rocks and slide from ledge to ledge into the pool. Sometimes we walked up the creek toward the mountain, looking for crawfish. There was an art to turning over the rocks and grabbing them before they scuttled away. The creek's small fish darted around our legs, and Alfie always laughed when they nibbled at her toes. The creekbed was rocky, but our feet were tough back then.

Sometimes we'd find a turtle on a log, and we'd pick it up and watch it hide its snaky head. The snapping turtles would bite, so you had to be careful, and you had to watch out for the copperheads. Laurels and ferns and moss lined the sides, so green and wet it made the creek seem like a secret other world.

All summer long I told Jimmy and Alfie and Meley Jane and Tony stories about the *Nûñnĕ'hĭ*, the Spirit People, and the *Yûñwi Tsundi'*, the Little People. Even though Meley Jane's and Jimmy's mothers were both part Cherokee, they lived in the white world, and Jimmy and Meley Jane didn't know any stories. They didn't even know any Cherokee *words*. I used to talk to them in Cherokee just to scare them, for they found it harsh and strange.

It was Tony who was most curious about the Cherokee world. He knew that his Cherokee grandfather was named Red Fern, and that he belonged to the Wolf Clan. He talked about him a lot. He imagined him as a great warrior, even though none of us knew anything more about him.

I told them how water was a door to the spirit world, and how if you listened to the rush of water over rocks, you could hear the spirits speak. I told them how the *Nûñnĕ'hĭ* were always hiding and watching us, and how I'd heard them drumming on the mountain near my mother's house.

Alfie told us stories her father had told her about the fairies, the fair folk of her people, who made their home beneath a mushroom or a moonflower. You're Irish, Mooney. You know about the fairies. They didn't seem that different from the *Yûñwi Tsundi'*. They'd help you sometimes, but they might also trick you. They'd take you in, but they might not let you go.

Tony told us stories his grandfather Tom told him, stories all the way from Africa. Tom was old enough to remember Africa—being kidnapped from his village, taken to the coast, and loaded on a ship. He remembered seeing real lions and elephants. He could still speak African words. Tom taught stories to Tony, and Tony told them to us. The best ones were the Rabbit stories. Tony could make us laugh so hard telling us about old Brer Rabbit. That Rabbit was so full of himself, always getting into one scrape or another, but he always came out on top. Kind of like me.

Tony's stories were funny, Alfie's stories were pretty, and my stories were all about monsters and heroes, because that's who I wanted to be. The hero always won.

Those summers of our childhood in Wofford's Settlement, we were happy, the Thunder Boys and Alfie and Meley Jane. For just a short while longer, we were children in a fool's paradise.

Chapter 4

The Golden Eagle

Interview Four: James Mooney and James Daugherty Wofford
March 14, 1891; Tahlequah, Cherokee Nation

[Mooney's Notes: Wofford is smoking a chipped, European-style clay pipe. He pulls a plug of tobacco from a tin, tamps it into the bowl, and lights it. He puffs a few times, sending bitter, pungent clouds of smoke into the air. He closes his eyes as he smokes, slumps backwards in his chair, his long legs extending toward me, his head and torso tilting away. Keeping his distance. Then he looks up at me with his strange blue eyes.]

This is my father's pipe. I have kept his things too. They are also a part of me.

You like the things that make us seem most primitive, don't you? If we are cave men, all the things that happened are justified. I know you aren't like that, Mooney. But sometimes, even with you, I feel like a stuffed bird. Yet I will tell you my stories. How else will anyone ever know?

I loved my father, but he didn't pay me too much mind. He was more interested in the stillhouse -- making the whiskey, selling the whiskey, drinking the whiskey. Some of the corn we raised, we ate or fed to our livestock. A lot of it went to the stillhouse. It was a stone building on Nancytown Creek downstream from the shoals and the mill. There were two copper stills in there, great kettles where he brewed corn whiskey and apple and peach brandy. My father's whiskey and brandy were famous, and he travelled and sold it, to whites and to Cherokee.

I spent more time with my grandfather. He taught me to read and write on summer mornings under the great chestnut tree, before the heat of the day grew too strong. Me, my cousins Jimmy and Sarah and Charlotte and Meley Jane, and Alfie and Polly McCracken. He even let Tony sit in sometimes, when there weren't too many chores that needed doing. He called it his school, but really he just wanted an audience. I learned to sign my name like his, imitating the great curlicues surrounding his signature. The giant W in Wofford.

The Colonel would regale us with stories from the Revolutionary War. He was a good storyteller. He paced and waved his hands around as he described his feats. He was always the hero of his own story. He'd served in Colonel Thomas's Spartanburg regiment, him and his brothers James and Joseph, as well as half the men who later came to Wofford's Settlement. He was a true Patriot, a delegate to South Carolina's Second Provincial Congress and first General Assembly in 1776. He told us the story of how he was taken captive by Loyalists near Fair Forest, guarding the Patriots' gunpowder supply with his life, and how another time his Iron Works were destroyed by the Tories. He told us how his brother Benjamin was a Tory, and how he helped get Benjamin released when he was captured by the Patriots. He never spoke to him again. Benjamin was banished from South Carolina for life.

The Colonel didn't brag as much about his battles with the Cherokee under General Williamson, because they were more massacres than battles. He didn't mention the killing of women and children and burning of towns. He told us how he moved to North Carolina and took over Cathey's Fort and fought the Cherokee there and helped the Over-Mountain Men prepare for the Battle of King's Mountain.

Sometimes he'd even take out his brass-hilted sword and show us how to lunge and parry, and he'd let the boys take turns. Sure, I played with the sword just like my cousins. They never made me play the Indian.

Grandfather was a true believer in the Revolution. He'd read to us from Thomas Paine, *The Rights of Man*, and Montesquieu's *Spirit of the Laws*. He knew the Declaration of Independence by heart. He was most fond of Thomas Jefferson's Indian policy, which solved a moral dilemma for him. Jefferson said Indians were in body and mind equal to the whiteman. Civilize and instruct the savages, give them plows and looms and they'd be as good as whitemen. The Colonel even believed in the education of women, which is why he let Alfie and Polly and Sarah and Charlotte and Meley Jane come to his "school." And Tony, because he said he didn't approve of slavery, but like his idol Jefferson, he owned slaves anyway. He treated them well, was what he told himself. He was lifting them up.

His favorite story was how he rode all the way to Washington, D.C. to convince the President to buy the Wofford's Settlement land from the Cherokee and make it part of Georgia. He stormed into the just-built White House and met his hero Thomas Jefferson in person. Jefferson invited him to dinner and showed him all the latest inventions—an indoor privy where your waste was carried down a pipe with a whoosh of water; a call bell that summoned servants from any part of the house; an oil lamp brighter than a dozen candles; a machine that would make a copy of anything you were writing by having your pen connected to a second pen.

And best of all, his wilderness museum, a display of Indian weapons and headdresses, animal skins, rare plants, all collected by Lewis and Clark and Zebulon Pike out west. The Colonel even saw the grizzly bear cubs that Jefferson kept in a cage on the front lawn on the White House.

For the Colonel, the purchase of Wofford's Settlement was a great triumph and the beginning of a dynasty. He saw it as his reward for his Revolutionary War service and his part in conquering the wilderness, civilizing the continent. He would help build the state of Georgia into the greatest state in the Union. Wofford's Settlement cut out a big notch for Georgia into what used to be the Cherokee Nation.

The Colonel taught us that to be a Wofford was special. Woffords were courageous and enlightened, wise and benevolent. A cut above the rest. Even though I was half Cherokee, he taught me to be proud of the Wofford name, and he claimed me as a Wofford.

Not only did Jefferson agree to buy the land for Wofford's Settlement from the Cherokee, he gave the Colonel a set of elk antlers from the Lewis and Clark expedition. Grandfather mounted the antlers on the wall above his cabinet of curiosities, which he'd modelled on Jefferson's wilderness museum. It was a credenza with shelves behind the doors, lined with artifacts he had collected. Children weren't allowed to touch his treasures, but sometimes he would take us in there and bring them out and we would pass them carefully around.

Like Jefferson, the Colonel thought of himself as a naturalist. He was a member of the American Antiquarian Society and the New England Linnaean Society, and he read the pamphlets they published on fossils and plant species and whatnot. He'd take us on long walks to collect plant specimens. He was in his 70s and 80s when I knew him, but he was a tough old bird, wiry and leathery, like a piece of meat cured in the sun. He got around just fine. He always carried a satchel with a leather-bound notebook and a goose quill pen. He'd tell me the Latin name for a plant and I'd tell him the Cherokee name and what medicine it was good for, and he'd write it down in his book, and take flowers and leaves to press. But he wouldn't honor our rule to take only one plant out of four, even though I explained it to him. He wanted them all.

I told him the story of the origin of medicine that my mother had taught me. It was the plants who saved mankind by providing cures to the diseases the animals thought up to punish us for our greed. The animals got tired of the humans spreading their settlements over the whole earth and using their weapons to slaughter them. They held a council at Kuwahi to figure out how they could stop the humans from overcrowding the earth. They invented disease. And if the plants hadn't intervened out of friendship to man, offering themselves as medicine, the humans would have all died out.

That's why my mother taught me that when you gather plants, you should only collect one out of every four that you find. That way, you don't deplete the earth and disturb the *tohi*. You leave plenty to thrive.

The Colonel just thought that my stories were quaint legends. He didn't understand that they were true.

He could draw beautifully, though, sketches of the plants and animals we saw. He collected abandoned bird's nests and stray feathers, different kinds of rocks. Soapstone from Soapstone Mountain, silver from over near Currahee. Quartz, mica, granite, iron, which he knew a lot about from his ironworks. The rocks were the part of his collection I kept. Here, I'll show you.

[Mooney's Notes: Wofford reaches into the leather pouch on the table and draws out a hunk of white crystalline quartz, a smooth soapstone egg, a flaking lump of mica, and cups them in his palm.]

When I touch these, I don't feel connected to my grandfather. I feel connected to the land we lived on. Songs hold the songs of the earth. The stone-songs are silent, but they are real. When you hold them in your hand, your skin is the ear that hears that song.

The Colonel had read about discoveries of bones of ancient animals, mammoth bones. He told us about an elephant he had seen in a traveling menagerie in Pendleton Courthouse, and how some people up north had found the skeleton of an ancient elephant. He was eager to find something like that. He always carried his surveyor's chains so he could measure anything he found.

He picked up the flint and quartz arrowheads that were everywhere in north Georgia, and fragments of old pottery. It was as if, to him, we were already gone. He liked for me to tell him about Cherokee customs, kind of like you, Mooney. He thought it was all a load of superstition, but it was interesting to him in a scientific way. Studying the natives. I would tell him some things, but not the most sacred things. Just like with you, Mooney.

The Colonel also collected words. If he came across a particularly beautiful word, he'd write it down in his book. He read to us from Wordsworth and Coleridge, *Lyrical Ballads*, and Shakespeare's plays. *You taught me language; and my profit on it is, I know how to curse.*

[Mooney's note: Wofford laughs at this and shakes his head ruefully.]

Sometimes he even wrote his own poems. They weren't that good, but he was proud of them. I remember one:

I once had money and I once had friends,
I have lost my money and have lost my friends.
If my life were to live over,
I would keep my money.
Then I would have money and friends both.

One day we were all walking along the Broad River, looking for plants. The Colonel always wore a pocket watch and consulted as he walked, which was so strange to me. If you are walking in the woods, what difference does it make what time it is, or how long the trip takes you? It was another way of measuring and assigning numbers to things, just like he carried his surveyor's chain to measure distances.

He always walked fast, too, faster than me even though he was an old man. That was the settlers' way. Always on to the next thing, and the next thing, and the next thing. Why don't you stay where you are for once? You might learn something.

That day we came across a patch of lady's slipper, that pouchy pink flower that's shaped like a shoe.

"*K'kwĕ' ulasúla*," I told him. "You use the roots to make a tea for stomachaches and fevers."

He scribbled this in his notebook, then knelt and began to yank the flowers out by the roots. So different from how my mother taught me to gather plants.

Suddenly Jimmy, who had walked ahead a bit, called out

"Grandfather! An eagle!"

We ran to where he stood and looked down at the carcass of a golden eagle. I don't know what could have killed it, old age maybe, because there was no blood, just the gold feathers gleaming, the great white tail feathers tipped with black, and the powerful beak and talons. His dead eyes open and staring.

I was frightened. Among us, the eagle, *awâhïlï*, is very sacred. Only certain specially trained hunters are allowed to kill eagles, and there are prayers that must be said. Eagle feathers can only be worn by a great warrior. A normal person is not allowed to touch an eagle, or even an eagle feather. The eagles in the Above World would not be happy. Even if you find a dead eagle, you should not touch the feathers. If you do, someone in your family will die. Just finding a dead eagle seemed like a terrible omen.

"Don't touch it," I cried. "Leave it be."

"Nonsense," my grandfather said, and knelt down to touch the feathers. "See, children," he said in his schoolteacher's voice, "the eagle is the most powerful bird of prey. Look at these talons, look at this beak. Look at how strong and muscled his legs are."

And to my everlasting horror, he pulled a hunting knife from his satchel and sawed off the talons and the beak and pulled out the beautiful tail feathers. "For my collection," he said, and wrapped them in a piece of hide and stowed them in his bag.

I ran away, everyone shouting after me.

I ran all the way to Stone Grave Ridge, on the other side of Leatherwood Mountain. There was a rock wall there, built by the ancient ones. I built myself an *âsĭ*, a little hut, out of branches and saplings and vines. I stayed there for days, dreaming and praying, fighting off the Great Black Loneliness. A white boy who is ten years old couldn't stay in the woods alone for days, but I could. I had my blowgun with me. I could feed myself.

While I was staying there, I dreamt that my grandfather had cut off the hands and feet of a human corpse and put them in his cabinet. I saw the fingers and toes, the exposed bones. I dreamt of eagles for months. I knew they were angry. But there was no one to do the eagle dance, no one to free me from the nightmares. I knew that it would bring a death or some other disaster.

You are the first person I have told this story to, Mooney, because it would hurt my Cherokee family too much to hear it. When my grandfather died, about ten years later, I went into his cabinet of curiosities and fetched the feathers and talon and beak, trembling all the while. I made a fire out in the woods and prayed over them and burned them.

But other curiosities, I kept. No one else wanted them.

How do you love someone who has committed a desecration? How do you love the part of yourself that comes from him? And yet I did.

Did the eagle bring disaster, you ask. Not for my grandfather. He lived to be 95 years old, in perfect health 'til the day he died. But upon the Woffords, yes, the disasters would come. Of all of my grandfather's descendants, only one, my cousin Benton, stayed in Wofford's Settlement. And his children, too, would later leave. The land the Woffords took, they did not keep.

Exiles, every one.

Chapter 5

The Leatherwood

Interview Five: James Mooney and James Daugherty Wofford
March 15, 1891; Tahlequah, Cherokee Nation

[Mooney's Notes: Wofford holds up his left hand and wiggles his fingers, and I notice for the first time that he has only four fingers on that hand. He is missing his left pinky finger.]

Now I'll tell you the story of how I lost my finger.

We called it the Leatherwoodthe stretch of thick forest across the dozen or so small mountains between the Wofford homestead and Currahee. These mountains weren't half the size of Pisgah and Kuwahi, but they were steep and rocky enough to make them hard to farm. The Middle Fork of the Broad River threaded through the Leatherwood. There were a few settlers in the bottomlands along the water, but for the most part that forest was as thick as any in the Nation.

The Leatherwood was our own secret kingdom. I say "our" because it was always the Thunder Boys plus Alfie and Meley Jane.

I was the leader because I had the best woods skills. It was easy to get lost in the Leatherwood. There were ravines and summits, saddles and steeps, springs and creeks and swamps, thickets of laurel and rhododendron that forced you to go a different way.

There were still wolves in those mountains, and panthers and bears and bobcats and mountain lions. It gave us a thrill of danger just to enter it. I always carried my blowgun and my dagger, and the Colonel let us bring one musket, which the boys took turns carrying.

We never used the musket, but we used the blowgun a lot. I taught Jimmy and Tony, and even Alfie and Meley Jane, to shoot targets and game with the blowgun. Sometimes we'd bring a rabbit or squirrel back to the Settlement for dinner.

We always brought the conch, and we had a code with the Colonel and my father and uncle that if something bad happened, we would blow five times in a row.

There were not just natural creatures in the mountains. There were magical creatures as well. Monsters.

My world, the world I told my friends about, was filled with Spirit People, good and bad. There are Yûñwi Tsundi', the Little People. The Nûñnĕ'hĭ, the Spirit People who live in caves. There are witches and wizards, like the *Ka'lanu Ahkyeliski,* the Raven Mocker, or *U'tlun'ta*, Spearfinger. Water monsters, like the Leech of *Tlanusi'yi.* Giants, like the Stoneclads.

Spearfinger, was the one that scared me the most. She was made of stone but she could change her shape. The index finger of her right hand was a knife. She stabbed her victims in the back of the neck or through their heart, and she ate their livers. She would sing a song: *Uwe la na tsiku. Su sa sai. Liver, I eat it. Su sa sai. Uwe la na tsiku. Su sa sai.* Her mouth was stained with blood from all the livers she ate. Her only weak spot was the palm of her right hand, which contained her hidden heart.

I told my friends how Spearfinger would disguise herself as an old woman and follow children as they walked the trails. Spearfinger liked little girls best of all. She would comb their hair with her deadly finger, lulling them to sleep, then stab them and cut out their liver and eat it.

Alfie and Meley Jane would scream in horror at my stories, and sometimes I even scared myself. I told them about the Raven Mocker eating the hearts of dying men, and how you know it's a Raven Mocker when you hear the cry of the raven diving through the air, and a rushing sound like the noise of a strong wind.

I told them that there was an old medicine man on Leatherwood Mountain who would put a curse on them if they ever stumbled across his hiding place. This was possibly true. Before the Woffords and the other settlers got there, there were three Cherokee villages in those mountains -- Nancytown, Leatherwood and Dick's Town. Nancytown was named after Nancy Ward, the woman warrior from the Battle of Taliwa. She was married for a time to a white settler, Bryant Ward, and they lived along Nancytown Creek, above the shoals. There were still some Cherokee living over near Currahee.

I also told them that the Tsul'Kalu lived in the Leatherwood. Of course, Tsul'Kalu didn't live there, he lives near Jutaculla Old Fields and Jutaculla Rock. But they didn't know that. The Tsul'Kalu is a giant with slanting eyes. I told them that Tsul'Kalu was the same as the Christian devil, and that he roamed the earth looking for souls to devour. There was a creek on Leatherwood Mountain called Devil's Den Branch, after the cave on the ridge where it started. I told them that's where the Tsul'Kalu livedin the Devil's Den.

One day that summer, we decided to find him. We were going to kill the devil! Only kids could think this was possible. Only kids could think there was only one devil. Later, I learned you don't need to go looking for no devil. The devil's gonna come to you.

I told them that we could be like Aganunitsi, who killed the Uktena, the great underground serpent. Aganunitsi was a Shawano medicine man captured by the Cherokee in battle. They were about to put him to death but he begged for his life by promising he could get them the Ulûñsûtĭ, the crystal from the head of the Uktena. The Ulûñsûtĭ would give great power to whoever possessed it. Aganunitsi found the Uktena sleeping on a mountain top and shot him through the heart. The Uktena spit poison all over the mountain and rolled down the mountainside, crushing every tree in his path. After seven days Aganunitsi returned and found that the Uktena's body and bones were eaten by birds, but the crystal was resting in a tree branch where a raven had dropped it. Aganunitsi wrapped the crystal and took it with him and became the greatest medicine man ever known.

That will be me, I bragged, only I'll steal the power of the Tsul'Kalu.

I told them the Tsul'Kalu looked like a combination of a bear and a human. Tall and hairy with filthy matted fur and blood-red slanted eyes. Horns on his head, a long pointy tail and a pitchfork. That last part came from a picture of the devil I'd seen in one of my grandfather's books.

I had my friends convinced I had some kind of special powers. I told them about saving the boy from drowning and about seeing the Leech in the river. I told them I was a slayer of monsters. I told them I could protect them.

We decided to follow Devil's Den Branch up from where it came into the river. I was always trying to find the origin of creeks. It seemed like it would answer so many questions, to find where the water started. But every time I tried, the creek ended up splitting into smaller branches and finally marshy puddles. There was never one place you could say it started.

"Here come the Thunder Boys. Get out the way, you old Devil," Tony shouted. We entered the woods and started up the mountain, following the creek. The water flowed down and we walked up, almost like walking back in time. The rhododendron were in bloom along the creek, hillsides white with flowers, like something from an earlier time, before the world got old. More Eden than Devil's Den.

Then again, Eden *was* the Devil's Den, wasn't it? Every garden has its snake.

We followed that creek for hours that summer day, trudging upward and upward, sweating in the rising heat of the day. Alfie and Meley Jane tucked their dresses up into their pantaloons. They were both tomboys at that age. Whatever the Thunder Boys did, they wanted to do too.

Everywhere we went, we dared each other and raced each other. Who could run the fastest, who could throw the farthest, who could climb higher up a tree or higher up a cliff, who could hit a target with the blowgun.

We ended up mostly walking in the creek because the rhododendrons were so dense. It was shadier too, and the water cooled our feet. We slipped our way over mossy rocks, boots on because of snakes. Splashing each other and horsing around.

Along the creek, Alfie found the biggest spider web we'd ever seen, with a fat yellow spider in the middle, the kind with the long black and yellow legs. The web glistened in the morning sun like a little piece of heaven. Alfie sang a song to the spider. She just made it up right there. She found beauty everywhere. It could be a spider or a butterfly or a dragonfly or a pretty rock, it didn't matter. That was what we had in common. A way of seeing the world. Noticing things.

Then Jimmy came and broke the web with a stick. He wasn't being mean. That's just what boys do. Alfie was mad and she smacked him. She and Meley Jane yelled at him for ruining the spider's house.

He ran off laughing through the woods, and we followed. All the way up, it was *I bet you can't climb that tree. I bet you can't lift that rock. I bet I can throw it farther than you.*

And Tony would imitate the song of every bird we heard. He was such a good whistler. And he could do the chatter of a squirrel, a bear's grunt, a wolf's howl, a panther's cry.

He could do silly voices too, especially the Colonel's and Granny Mary's. "Now Peggy, I done told you how I like my tea. And now look, you've gone and spoiled it again," he would whine in Granny's quavery voice. And we would laugh and laugh.

I remember that day he was telling one of his Brer Rabbit stories.

"Did I ever tell you," he said, "about Brer Rabbit and Brer Bear and the bee-tree? Brer Rabbit was always wanting to play a trick on Brer Bear. So, one day Brer Rabbit tells Brer Bear he found this big hollow bee-tree with a honeycomb just oozing with honey. 'You get that honey, he told Bear, it'll feed you and your family for a month.'" And Tony did Brer Rabbit's voice so it sounded a bit like mine.

"I do love me some honey," said Brer Bear. And Tony made the voice sound like Jimmy.

Tony went on: "When they got to the tree with the bees flying all around, Rabbit said, 'You climb up to the hole, Bear, and I'll push the honeycomb up from the bottom with this here pine pole.' So, Bear shimmied up that tree and stuck his head inside the tree. And Rabbit poked the bottom of that bee's nest as hard as he could, til that whole hive of bees flew up at Bear's face. And they stung him and stung him til his face swelled up bigger than a dinner pot. And down below Rabbit was laughing so hard he was rolling on the ground laughing. And he was yelling, 'You gotta watch them bees, Brer Bear. You gotta watch them bees!'"

"The Rabbit always wins!" I shouted.

"Only in stories," Jimmy said. "In real life, the Bear is a fearsome creature, and the Rabbit is dinner."

"Only if you can catch him," I said, "And you never will!"

And we chased and laughed our way up the creek, forgetting our serious mission.

When we finally reached the top of the ridge, the creek disappeared beneath a spill of boulders, like a broken stairway for giants. There was a steep cliff at the top with what looked like a small opening. None of us had ever been on this part of Leatherwood Mountain before.

We looked up and remembered why we had come. If the Devil was going to live somewhere, this seemed like the right place.

Tony did a whistle that sounded like the cry of a raven, maybe a Raven Mocker, and it gave me a chill, but I acted like I wasn't scared at all.

"I don't know about this," Jimmy said. "I don't believe in Tsul'Kalu or the devil, but I do believe in snakes, and this looks like a good place to get snakebit."

"The devil's real and so is Tsul'Kalu," I told him. "You're a fool if you think he ain't."

"You're a fool if you go up there," Jimmy said. "I'm not going."

"Then you're a chicken," I said. "I'll go first. Y'all can

follow after I make sure there's no monster, or else I kill it."

"Why don't you take the musket?" Alfie said.

"I'm Cherokee," I bragged. "I don't need no musket to kill a monster."

And with that I started up the boulders, clambering over the bigger ones on my hands and knees. When I reached the cliff, it was awfully steep but I could see the opening. I was a little scared to find out what was in there, but I was curious too. I thought about the story of the Thunder Boys, when they followed Kanati to his cave and let all the animals out. Who could see a cave and not want to look inside?

The cliff went straight up but it wasn't too high, maybe about three times my own height, and there were enough ridges in the rock that I thought I could climb it. I got a handhold, then a foothold, and started pulling myself up. The sun was beating down hard and I was sweating and my hands were getting slippery from the sweat, but I kept on.

I reached the opening and put my left hand on the edge. I didn't hear the rattle until it was too late. I never saw the snake. So fast it was like it was invisible. Two bites, one on my pinky finger and one on my arm. The pain was terrible. I lost my grip and fell to the boulders below. It knocked the wind right out of me and I was lucky I didn't break any bones.

It was Jimmy who got there first and Jimmy who took out his knife and cut the deep x across each wound and sucked out the poison. Sucked and spit, sucked and spit. He tore strips from his shirt and Meley Jane tied them as tight as she could below my elbow and around the top of my pinky finger. Alfie was crying but Meley Jane stayed as calm as you please.

Jimmy and Tony dragged me stumbling down the

mountainside, one on each side of me, back to the homestead. My lips and tongue went numb, my hand and arm swelled up, and I wasn't breathing too good. The pain drove me nearly out of my mind.

I remember Alfie saying, "Hold on J.D., just hold on," over and over. Putting a canteen to my lips, but the water just dribbled down my chin.

When we were within a mile or so of the Settlement, Meley Jane pulled the conch shell from my pack and blew as hard as she could, five times. Boom, boom, boom, boom, boom. In a few minutes, the Colonel and Uncle Nathaniel rode up on us. The Colonel snatched me up on his horse and rode like hell for the homestead.

They sent for Aunt Lydia, who was the best healer in the Settlement. She knew some Cherokee plant medicine from her mother. My grandfather put me in his own bed. I was thrashing and sweating and throwing up and moaning. I remember Aunt Lydia putting a poultice on the bites, probably tobacco and snakeroot but I'm not sure. I remember she had a madstone, that was a stone from the stomach of an albino deer. They called a madstone because it was good for a bite from a mad dog or a snake. You would boil it in milk and put it on the bite, and it would draw out the poison. I remember Aunt Lydia pressing the smooth white stone to my arm.

That's about the last thing I remember before I passed out.

Later, they told me this went on for five days. Jimmie and Alfie told me that the bites turned black, and red streaks climbed up my arms. They despaired of my life.

Here's the part where I'm not sure what's true and what's not true. Through the fog in my mind I saw a very old Cherokee man. His face was as wrinkled as an old apple and there were circles of white paint around his eyes. His hair hung down in two long white braids. He was standing over me and shaking a rattlesnake rattle. It whirred and clicked like there was still a snake on the other end. Then he drew from his bag the jaw and fangs of a rattlesnake and raked the fangs deep into my arm and hand. He was singing a song, probably the snake bite prayer I later learned from Yonaguska.

[Mooney's note: Here Wofford chanted a prayer in Cherokee in a low plaintive tone, resembling a lullaby.]

> Dûnu´wa, dûnu´wa, dûnu´wa, dûnu´wa, dûnu´wa, dûnu´wa.
> Dayuha, dayuha, dayuha, dayuha, dayuha.

This means,

> Listen! Ha! It is only a common frog which has passed by and put it into you.
> Listen! Ha! It is only an Usu´'gĭ which has passed by and put it into you.

It is the custom to never name the snake, but instead you call it a frog or a rabbit, to show that it is not so powerful and to avoid the attention of the rattlesnake spirits in the Above World.

The old man sang this and traced circles around the bites, and then blew on the bites.

What happened next shows that it didn't work. Because I was not in that room anymore, I was inside the Devil's Den. And inside the cave I saw a pile of rattlesnakes slithering over each other, hissing and rattling and baring their fangs at me.

And behind them, at the back of the cave, I saw the Uktena. It was a snake as thick as a tree trunk, with horns on its head, and a bright blazing crest like a diamond on its forehead. Its scales glowed like sparks of fire. It had rings of red and gold along its whole length. That blazing crest is the Ulun'suti, the jewel that Agan-uni'tsi captured. I wanted to run, but I was so dazed by the Ulun'suti's light that I kept moving toward it, stepping through the rattlesnakes coiling and wrapping around my legs. The breath of the Uktena was foul and I gasped for air but I kept on until I touched its blazing scales and its mouth opened wide.

At that moment my eyes flew open and I saw my hand gushing blood and my pinky finger lying on the wooden planks of the floor in my grandfather's house. The old man stood above me with a bloody hatchet, grinning. And I blacked out again.

When I awoke, maybe the next day, I don't know, my hand and arm were wrapped in bandages.

My father was sitting in a chair by the bed, and I was very surprised to see my mother sitting next to him. I hadn't seen those two in the same place in years. I found out later that he had sent Meley Jane's mother Betsy to the Valley Towns to fetch her, thinking I might die. Betsy and my mother had both lived near the Woffords during the years they lived in North Carolina, before they moved to Georgia. That's where my father met my mother, where Nathaniel met Lydia, and where Nathaniel met Betsy too.

As soon as I opened my eyes, my mother rushed to embrace me. "*Tsisdu*," she said. "We thought we lost you." This time when she hugged me, I didn't push her away. "*Etsi,*" I said, and clung to her for a moment. There might have been a tear or two sneaking down my face. She rode for two days to come to me, thinking I might die. I was her only child. I'd never thought before about what it would be like for her to lose me.

"You foolish, foolish boy," my father scolded. "We sent for Doctor Hopkins from Tugaloo, and he said taking the finger off was the only hope." I could tell that my father had been drinking, because he slurred his words and his body swayed as he spoke. But he was there. I later learned he hadn't left my side.

"Doctor Hopkins?" I said. "That's not who took my finger. It was the old man, the medicine man."

My father laughed. "You must have seen that in your raving. You had us so worried." He was laughing, but I saw the pain in his watery eyes. I saw that he'd kept vigil over me, even if he had softened it with whiskey.

"What did the medicine man look like?" my mother asked.

I told her the whole vision—the old man, the rattlesnake rattle, the song, the Devil's Den, the Uktena. She carefully unwrapped the bandage and we looked together at my mutilated hand. There was wound where my little finger used to be, and a deep trench in my arm where someone had cut out a layer of flesh.

"You've been marked by Grandfather Rattlesnake," she said. "This is a grandfather who can love you or hate you, kill you or save you. From now on, you will have *inadö danskitsöi*, 'when they dream of snakes.' These nightmares will cause you much darkness." And she was right, because I've had these dreams my whole life.

"I'll gather you some medicine," she said. She went out and came back a couple of hours later with a bundle of rattlesnake's master and sedge. She tied it in a bundle and put it in a pouch for me. "Carry this always," she said. "It won't stop the dreams, but no snake will ever bite you again."

Later, I put that bundle in my medicine pouch, but I can't show you that. It has stayed with me my whole life, and I've never been bitten by a snake again.

It dawned on me then, for the first time but not the last time, that there was more to my mother than I thought. She was Red Paint Clan too. She knew about plants and medicine, and I learned the most important stories, like Kanati and Selu, from her. I was seeing her through white eyes, to think that she didn't matter. It still makes me sad to think about how she threw herself away on Ebenezer. She was worth so much more, and even I didn't see it.

Jimmy and Tony and Alfie and Meley Jane came in while my mother was there. They had known her years ago, when we were small, but they didn't really remember her. She spoke very little English, and they spoke no Cherokee. But she held out her arms and they all hugged her, and then stood fussing over me.

Alfie and Meley Jane shed some tears, and I was embarrassed, but secretly I enjoyed the attention.

I saw Alfie throwing secret glances back at my mother. I was worried that she was judging her somehow. My mother was dark-skinned, and she dressed like a Cherokee in buckskin leggings and moccasins. With her jutting teeth and her pockmarked face, she wasn't beautiful. She darn sure wasn't white. I moved so easily among whites and Cherokee. My mother did not.

"I made you something," Jimmy said. He pulled a sling out of his pocket. And here it is, right here. I've never let it go."

[*Mooney's Note: Wofford rummages in his trunk and pulls out an old leather sling.]*

Jimmy braided the leather himself. See, here's the pouch where you put the stone. Now they have slingshots with rubber strips, but this is the old-fashioned way. You fling this thing hard and you can take down a giant with a rock, just like David in the Bible.

Jimmy told me, "If you ever find another monster, you can kill it before it kills you. I don't know if there's a devil or Uktena, I just don't want nothing getting you again." Jimmy's eyes were wet, and that was about as many words as Jimmy was going to say about anything.

"You old Rabbit," Tony said, and punched me in my good arm. "Who's gonna lead us through the woods if you go on and get yourself killed?"

My missing finger and the part of my arm that's missing, it feels like the mark of the one who got it wrong, the one who went astray.

[*Mooney's note: Here Wofford held up his left hand again and showed me the gouged scar on his arm.*]

I wanted to be Abel, whose sacrifice was pleasing to God. Sometimes I think I'm more like Cain. The one who killed his own brother.

Someone told me once that if you're having a bad dream, the way you can know if it's a dream is to look at your hands. If there is something wrong with your hands, like a missing finger or an extra finger or no lines on your palms, that means you're dreaming. Does that mean that everything since the rattlesnake bite, the Trail and all the deaths, were just a dream? Maybe the real J.D. is back in the Currahee hills, reaping the fruit of the land.

Chapter 6

The Line Baptist Church

Interview Six: James Mooney and James Daugherty Wofford
March 15, 1891; Tahlequah, Cherokee Nation

[Mooney's Note: On Wofford's table sits a tattered old Bible. Torn strips of paper poke out of the top newspaper, envelopes, receipts.]

All the members of the Settlement went to church at The Line Baptist Church, which had that name because it sat on the line between the state of Georgia and the Cherokee Nation. Sitting in the pews, you could look out the window at the boundary. The church itself was made of logs, maybe the very logs cut down to make that treeless stretch. And inside were hard wooden pews, maybe cut from the same wood too.

The pastor at The Line Baptist Church was Littleton Meeks, and he was the reason I became a Baptist. Meeks was still young at that time, but already stooped and skinny with a long neck like a goose and bright goose eyes.

He liked to preach to the Cherokee, and he had his eye on me from the time I was a little boy. He was always asking me to do things, like help with the service or sing. His congregation was mostly white, but he would ride out into the Nation for days at a time, preaching in Cherokee villages, and as I grew older he started taking me with him to translate. He even gave me my first Bible, this Bible, and I have it still. I don't believe in throwing away a Bible that's been soaked in somebody's tears and sweat and blood. This book has seen it all, the births and deaths, the thousand-mile walk. I was tempted to throw it away a few times, at my lowest moments. But I never did.

[Mooney's Note: Wofford flips the Bible open to the front page, where a list of names and dates in different inks, different sizes. I recognize the names of his children, his first wife, his second wife, his cousins Jimmy and Alfie and Charles. The names at the top are scrawled in Wofford's big loopy handwriting. The writing becomes smaller and cramped as he tried to fit them all in. So many Woffords, they run onto the title page. I see "Born," "Married" and "Left this world" many times over.]

Actually, Meeks' congregation wasn't as white as you might think. There was me and Aunt Lydia, and Nathaniel and Lydia's children in varying shades from Benton's pale skin to Charles' nut brown. Since my father never came, I always sat with them, next to Jimmy. They took up two whole pews. From oldest to youngest, my cousins were Benton, Charles, Sarah, Jimmy, Charlotte, John Thomas, and T.J., just a baby that year. Lydia had been having babies for twenty years. And sometimes Meley Jane was there, and Lydia treated her like another daughter.

There was bad blood between my two oldest cousins, Benton and Charles, the whitest and the darkest. They had opposite temperaments, too. Benton was very prim and proper. He was an old man even when he was young. Later he was a politician in the Georgia House of Representatives, and a Baptist minister. He never acknowledged that he had any

Cherokee blood. But Charles was never at home in the white world, even though that was all he knew for a long time. He liked to hunt, he liked to fight, he liked to farm. He was tall and strong and pretty ornery, too. You didn't mess with Charles. And Lord have mercy, those two hated each other.

Benton was best friends with my half-brother Will, who sat with his wife Mary Tatum and their new baby, Mattie Ann. They all sat with my father's supposed wife Mary Hollingsworth, and her father and mother and brothers. Mary hadn't lived with my father since before I was born. No one ever talked about it. That whole family hated Indians, especially me, the symbol of Mary's humiliation. At church, they just pretended I wasn't there, wouldn't even look at me.

But Will was always good to me. When he was at our father's or grandfather's house he took pains to play the role of an older brother. In his friendship with Benton, Benton was the leader and Will was the follower. Like me and Jimmy, they were born the same year, and like me and Jimmy, they had the same name. Benton was William Benton Wofford, and Will was William Hollingsworth Wofford. They were the Colonel's namesakes and firstborn grandchildren. Will was tall and blonde. The only feature we shared was our blue eyes.

And of course, the Colonel was always at church, although I don't think he believed a word of it, and Granny Mary, and my two aunts Charlotte and Ann, and their husbands and kids. There were a lot of Woffords.

One Sunday morning at the Line Baptist Church, the first crack in the solidarity of the Wofford clan appeared. All the families in the Settlement were seated in their regular pews—the Woffords, the Hollingsworths, the McCrackens, the LeCroys, the Brights, the Grants, the Vaughans. The kids hated it that we had to sit with our families instead of each other. Especially in the summer, it was hot and stuffy, even with the shuttered windows open to the air. The ladies fanned themselves, and we all squirmed and sweated through Reverend Meeks' long sermons.

In the McCracken pew, Alfie's mother presided over a row of six redheaded girls and one boy, with another on the way. At the back of the church sat the Colonel's slaves—Peggy, Tom, Carolina, Tony, and Rachel holding baby Hannah.

Every week, the Reverend exhorted the faithful to confess they were sinners and to kneel at the altar. This particular Sunday, he announced that he'd be preaching on the Heirs of the Kingdom. Revered Meeks liked a little response, so a couple people cried out "Yes Lord" and "Bless him Lord."

"The earth is the Lord's and He made it," he began. "And the fullness thereof, and all that dwell within it."

"Yes Lord," came the response. "Amen, Brother Meeks."

"Where does the Lord dwell? He dwells among us. The wolf shall dwell with the lamb, the leopard shall lie down with the kid. They shall not hurt nor destroy in all God's holy mountain."

"Bless him Lord," someone shouted.

"And where is this high and holy mountain? Is it Mount Zion, where Jerusalem's walled city stands? Oh, yay! Is it Mount Calvary, where our Lord was crucified? Oh, yay! Is it Mount Currahee, Mount Yonah, Mount Chenocetah? Oh yay, for the Kingdom is among us!"

That woke people up a bit, to hear our own mountains named. They weren't in the Bible. There was a stirring and crossing and uncrossing of legs in the hard pews. I liked it, though. I'd already thought about how there are sacred mountains in the Bible just like there are for us.

"And where is the river of the water of life?" the Reverend continued. "Is it the Jordan River, where our Lord himself was baptized? Oh, yay! Is it the Red Sea, that the Lord parted for the Israelites to escape? Oh yay! Is it Nails Creek out yonder, where we baptize? Yes, it is! Is it the Broad River, the Oconee, the Tugaloo? Yes, and amen! Is it in villages where heathen men and heathen women hear the word of God proclaimed? Oh, yay!"

I could see that Jimmy's brother Benton, down the pew from me, was getting restless. His feet were scuffling around like there were ants in his boots. Everyone knew that Revered Meeks preached to the Cherokee, but Benton didn't want to hear about it in his church.

"And who are the heirs of the Kingdom?" Reverend Meeks continued. "St. Paul tells us who. For there is neither Jew nor Greek, neither bond nor free, neither male nor female: for if ye be Christ's, then ye are Abraham's seed, and heirs of the promise."

Benton was rigid now. It was bad enough to suggest that God might actually care about the heathen. But the "neither bond nor free," that was the verse anti-slavery preachers used. I could see the Colonel trying to catch Reverend Meeks' eye and head him off before he went any further, before he crossed that line.

But this was the Reverend's Red Sea moment, and he was bound and determined to cross.

"This right here is the new Jerusalem!" he cried. "And all are welcome at this table. The redman as sure as the whiteman, the slave as sure as the master. In the eyes of the Lord, there is no difference! All who call on the name of the Lord are heirs of the promise!" he shouted triumphantly. "Take off your shoes!" He bent down, pulled off his boots, and flung them across the front of the church. "For you stand on holy ground!"

"Praise the Lord!" came a quiet but firm voice in the back row. I recognized it as Mama Peggy's voice. Benton turned around. Peggy was cradling her new granddaughter Hannah in her arms and rocking her back and forth.

"What did you say?" Benton roared. He had also recognized her voice.

"She says, praise the Lord," came another voice from the pew right in front of Benton. It was his own mother, Lydia. Lydia was usually very quiet. She was a plain woman, practical, motherly. She was the kind of woman who doesn't get noticed much but who takes care of everyone and everything. She put up with a lot from Nathaniel and never complained. This was the first time I ever remember her speaking up. Nathaniel gaped at her in wonder, and all of her children looked at her like she'd grown a second head.

Benton stood up and bolted from the church. He never set foot in that church again. He started attending Leatherwood Baptist Church, and so did Will and the Hollingsworths. In fact, Benton later became a pastor there. He became one of those the-slaves-are-the-sons-of-Ham pastors. And I became a preacher too. On the other side of the Line.

Revered Meeks picked the wrong word for Benton, talking about heirs. Benton was sensitive on the topic of inheritance. His father had a lot of children, and our grandfather had a lot of grandchildren. Grandfather owned ten thousand acres. Benton saw himself as the true heir. Him and Will. Both William Woffords, both whiter than snow.

That fateful Sunday, the Reverend ended the service by calling on me, Alfie, and Tony to sing. Tony's face looked closed off and strained. I knew he was worried that his grandmother would get in trouble. The Colonel might have said that slaves were family, but all slaves, no matter how young, knew that when a master got mad, anything could happen. Reverend Meeks chose me and Alfie and Tony because we had the best voices in the congregation. But the symbolism of the three of us was lost on no one. This is what he had us sing:

[Mooney's note: Wofford sings the verses in a quavering but tuneful tenor.]

> Jesus, thy blessings are not few,
> Nor is thy Gospel weak.
> Thy grace can save the heathen too,
> And heal the dying Greek.
> Beyond the reach of Satan's rage,
> Does thy salvation flow,
> Tis not confined to sex or age,
> The lofty or the low.

Part III

Kituwah, Cherokee Nation East

January 1813

Chapter 7

The Great Booger Dance

Interview Seven: James Mooney and James Daugherty Wofford March 16, 1891; Tahlequah, Cherokee Nation

I will show you this.

[Mooney's Notes: Wofford reaches into his trunk and pulls out the most splendid specimen of a booger mask I have ever seen. Time has not faded the vibrant red of the big square teeth or the snaky lines of hair. I think of the Medusa in Greek mythology, and how the Greek hero Perseus had made Medusa's severed head into a weapon. And Athena wore the image on her shield. I wonder briefly if I might turn to stone.

Wofford runs a finger along the snaky lines of the mask, then puts it in front of his face.]

Now who am I? I have worn so many masks, so many different faces.

My grandfather Alickee, my mother's father, made this mask. I saw it for the first time at the Great Booger Mask Dance. But I didn't own it until after Alickee died.

There were many Booger Dances, but this one is most remembered. It happened at Kituwah, the mother-town of mother-towns.

The year I turned eleven, I was apprenticed to Kituwah's White Chief Yonaguska as his *tsila*, learning the medicine ways. Yonaguska heard how I rescued the boy in the river and how I saw the leech of *Tlanusi'yi*. And how I had danced in the Ghost Dance with Tsali. My mother agreed to let me start the training. She knew I had it in me, but it was hard for her to let me go. It meant I would spend most of the winter with Yonaguska and not with her.

Yonaguska had a son around my age, Bigwitch, but Bigwitch was never going to be a medicine man. Bigwitch liked to hunt and fish. He was rowdy and strong and just a little slow-witted. He didn't have any interest in the Spirit World. But he was a wonderful horseman. He had a big fluffy gray dog named Gola, half-wolf probably, who followed him everywhere.

When I think of the East, it's Kituwah I long for. The great mound by the Tuckaseegee River, in the shadow of Kuwahi Mountain. Our ancestors received our laws and the first fire on Kuwahi, and brought it down to Kituwah, where it was never allowed to go out. To us, Kituwah was the holy of holies. That's why Tsali took his people to Kuwahi to hear from Yowah.

The ancestors built the mound there, fifteen feet high, with a seven-sided council house on top, and steep stairs you had to climb to get up there. Every big Cherokee town had a mound. They were the spiritual center, the place for ceremonies and dances. Ancestors were buried inside of them. When the Kituwah mound was built, the ancestors placed the sacred fire inside of it, and it still burns there. You ask, how can a fire burn beneath a pile of dirt? You ask that because you still think that the Seen is more real than the Unseen. That's where you're wrong.

The Americans destroyed the entire town during the Revolution. Yonaguska was a young man at that time and watched it burn. Most of the people left, but he stayed and rebuilt the council house and tended the fire. He had a vision when he was twelve, a lot like Tsali's vision. He saw that the white ways would destroy the Cherokee people. He vowed that he would never leave Kituwah, and he didn't. When most of us left on the Trail, he stayed. He was the guardian of the mound.

I was shy with him that first winter. He was a Firekeeper and a White Chief, and I was a half-white Intruder's son. He was very tall, about six foot five, and I was always short for my age. All of my boasting and bravado at the Settlement meant nothing at Kituwah. But he was a kind man, with the heart of a healer and a father. He had two daughters, Sally and Jenny, plus his son Bigwitch. I was jealous when he'd roll around with his children in the grass and carry them around piggyback. They'd throw sticks for Gola and chase him around and all end up rolling around in the grass together. My father and grandfather had never played with me like that. No one had ever rolled around in the grass with me, except maybe Jimmy and Tony.

Bigwitch, for his part, was a little jealous of me. He had no desire to be a medicine man, but he resented the attention his father paid to me. And I resented the fact that I was just an apprentice, not a son.

I was excited about the Booger Dance that year because I would get to see all of my uncles and cousins and my mother's father Alickee. There was talk of a big hunt afterwards, and I was hoping I would be allowed to go.

But I was worried, too. There was one problem with Yonaguskahe liked the Black Drink, the rum. And he couldn't hold his liquor. If he drank even a little, he couldn't stop. You never knew which Yonaguska you were going to get. I was already all too familiar with this problem, from Ebenezer and my mother and sometimes my father.

So that morning I looked for the signs a stumbling gait, a slurring of words. But Yonaguska seemed hearty and hale. He woke me and Bigwitch just before sunrise and dragged us out of our warm furs and the snug winter house, down to the river to go to water. Bigwitch complained the whole time. It was mid-winter and the water was freezing cold. The Tuckaseegee River comes down off the high mountains, and you could see the snow on the mountaintops.

Yonaguska walked into the water without flinching. He was tall and broad-shouldered, with a high forehead and handsome features. He kept his head shaved except for a topknot and had the traditional tattoos of a medicine man, a ring of blue crescents and stars encircling both arms.

Bigwitch was a head taller than me, but he thrashed around in the river like a big puppy. He couldn't stay either still or quiet. And his faithful Gola waited on the shore, barking. He didn't really like to swim, but he wanted to play.

But I willed myself into stillness as Yonaguska chanted the prayers. When he prayed, he had a voice that seemed to come from under the earth.

"Time isn't real," Yonaguska would tell me. "Time is a story we tell ourselves." And it's true. If you close your eyes and feel the earth beneath you or the water flowing all around you, time slows down and then it stops. You catch a glimpse around the corner of the universe, like seeing the Nûñnĕ'hĭ, before they disappear.

We came out of the river shivering and numb, stumbling because we couldn't feel our feet. Eager to get close to a fire and thaw out. Lucky for me, the next thing was to build the fire. The sacred fire inside the townhouse always burned, but since this was a celebration, we would light a bonfire on the mound.

Bigwitch, on the other hand, was assigned to take care of the visitors' horses. He was mad that I had a more important role.

The day before, I'd gathered the wood from the eastern side of seven trees: white oak, black oak, water oak, blackjack, basswood, chestnut, and white pine, and carried it up to the top of the mound. That morning, Yonaguska and I added long stalks of *ihyâ'ga* weed, also called *atsil'-sûñ'tĭ*, fire-maker. We lit a torch from the sacred fire inside the Council House and carried it to the wood outside. We prayed over it, special prayers I cannot tell you. The fire climbed the stalks and caught the tinder. And the smoke carried our prayers to God.

Then I helped Yonaguska get the masks ready. His masks were very famous, funny and scary, crazy characters made out of gourds and hornet's nests. In the weeks before the dance, I helped him glue on possum hair and horns and snippets of fur. We painted snakes on the masks, and the great sharp teeth of wolves and bears.

You would think a medicine man would be serious all the time. You would also think that the White Chief of a dead town might be sad. But back then Yonaguska could act like a clown. As he made the masks, he created voices for them and made them talk to each other, like little plays. He made me laugh so hard. We would sit in the winter house, him making masks or grinding dried plants to powder, mixing medicines, teaching me which plant is good to heal which illness. He gave me a medicine pouch, *this* medicine pouch.

[*Mooney's Note: Wofford pulls a small pouch out of pocket in his trousers.*]

This pouch has not left my side, all of these years. I still carry certain plants for healing, and certain other things I cannot tell you. I cannot show you what's inside.

And Yonaguska taught me the stories and the prayers. My mother taught me many stories when I was small, but the rest I learned from Yonaguska. Most of the prayers I know, I learned from him. You're a Catholic, Mooney. You must understand this. Certain prayers hold great power, and a priest knows these prayers. The words are sacred, and when they are spoken, it creates a doorway between the Spirit World and our world.

That morning, I helped Yonaguska arrange the masks along one side of the Council House. And then he said to me, "I must have some time alone to pray. Keep guard at the door and let no one in, no matter who they are."

This had never happened before. He often took time alone to pray, but whenever we had visitors, he greeted them and welcomed them. And that day, we were expecting dozens of visitors, important people. I was nervous about turning them away. And also, at the back of my mind, I was worried about what he was doing in there. What if he had hidden some rum in there? What if he came out later stumbling and sloppy drunk, on such an important occasion?

But I kept my vigil at the door to the Council House. By mid-day, visitors began to arrive, climbing the steep steps, carrying food for the feast, which Yonaguska's two wives, Nigudayi and Coluchee, arranged on long tables on the top of the mound. My mother came, shyly presenting her kettle of hominy to Nigudayi. Thank God she'd left Ebenezer at home. I shrugged off her smothering hug. I thought I was so important, now that I was a *tsila*. I wasn't her little boy anymore. I could see the hurt on her face as she went to help the other women with the feast.

I was most eager to see my uncles George Lowery, we called him Agili. Junaluska, who would later become the hero of Horseshoe Bend. Sequoyah, and the third John Watts. My mother and my uncles were all grandchildren of the Trader John Watts and Wurteh, the sister of Doublehead. John Watts was also known as Forked Tail Watts and Forked Tongue Watts. He himself was mixed blood and spoke Cherokee and English. He could talk anyone into anything, in either language.

But most of his sons and their sons spoke no English. Cherokee men belong to their mother's family, and my uncles grew up in the Valley and Out Towns where most people were full-bloods and English was not spoken. They were famous men. Doublehead, though he later sold out to the whites, was a great warrior. John Young Tassel Watts, my grandmother's brother, led the Chickamaugan rebels fighting the whites after the Revolutionary War.

You might think the Wofford name would be enough to make them hate me, but it wasn't that way, at least for most of them. I was my mother's son, that was enough. She was Cherokee, so I am Cherokee. She was *Ani'-Wâ'di*, Red Paint Clan, so I am Red Paint Clan.

George Lowery, Agili, was the first of my uncles to arrive. I had only met him a few times, because he lived in Tennessee. His father was a Scotsman, and he inherited a great jutting chin from his white father. He was the only one of my uncles who spoke fluent English. He strode up to the Council House and asked me where Yonaguska was. He didn't recognize me at first, but I knew who he was.

"He's in the Council House," I squeaked out. "He doesn't want to be disturbed."

"And who might you be?" he asked. He was an imposing figure. He wore a turban and a sash and what I later learned was a medal from the President of the United States. I knew he was part of the Light Horse Brigade, the newly formed Cherokee police force. He wore a silver nose ring, a silver gorget, and heavy silver earrings that tinkled like wind chimes when he walked.

"The son of Nancy Watts, I mean Nancy Natchez. Your cousin." I couldn't have been more awkward, but he smiled down at me.

"Oh yes, I remember," he said, in English. "You and I, we are the half-breeds." And he winked at me.

Then, switching back to Cherokee, he asked, "How *is* Yonaguska today?" I caught the emphasis on the word "is." He was asking the same thing I was worrying about.

"He seemed good this morning," I said, trying not to betray my own concern.

Just then, a voice cried out a greeting, and we turned to see Seqouyah limping toward us. The two men embraced. They were brothers-in-law. Agili was married to Sequoyah's half-sister Lucy. While Agili lived in Tennessee, Sequoyah lived two days' ride to the south, in what would later be Georgia.

Sequoyah was wearing a turban and rich robes in brilliant colors. He wore silver earrings and an intricate necklace he had made himself. He often visited my mother in the Valley Towns and knew me well.

"J.D., my boy, I'd heard you'd become Yonaguska's *tsila*. Well done. And how is your good mother?"

"She's just over there," I said, "helping with the food."

"And where is Yonaguska?"

"He's in the Council House," Agili told him. "He's asked

not to be disturbed." Agili raised his eyebrows and exchanged a look with his brother-in-law. "Let's hope he joins us soon."

Our attention was caught by shouting at the foot of the mound. John Watts was yelling at Bigwitch, who was leading the visitors' horses to a small corral where he watered and fed them.

"How do I know you won't steal it?" Watts shouted. Poor Bigwitch was trying to explain to him that he was taking care of everyone's horses.

Gola was yapping at Watts because he was yelling at Bigwitch. and Watts kicked at him and shouted, "Get that damn wolf away from me."

"Our most esteemed cousin," Agili said sarcastically, as Watts finally thrust the reins at Bigwitch and climbed the steps of the mound.

"Where's Yonaguska?" he shouted irritably at Agili and Sequoyah. And when he saw me, "What's the *tsisdu* doing here?"

He liked to call me *tsisdu*, Rabbit, and mock me for being small and part white. He was the only one of my uncles who didn't like me. His father was a hero and a Principal Chief, but he himself was arrogant and boastful. He was married to the daughter of Hanging Maw, and everyone knew that he was fed by his wife and his mother-in-law. He was a lout with a big belly, too lazy to hunt. There was a rumor that he was also a horse thief, but no one knew for sure.

"J.D. is Yonaguska's *tsila*," Sequoyah explained, and Watts spit on the ground.

"I'm going in the Council House," he said. "Get out of my way."

"No, you're not," Agili said, and blocked the door. "Yonaguska will come out when he has finished his prayers."

"Prayers? Is that what he calls it?" he sneered. He had oddly sharp teeth in his fat face, and when he sneered, he looked like a cowardly dog who bares his teeth over a bone but would really run away with his tail between his legs. "Doesn't seem like they do him much good. He calls himself a holy man, and look at him."

"Say one more word," Agili said, "and I'll tan your sorry hide."

"But Kituwah is a Peace Town," Watts mocked. "No fighting allowed."

"It wouldn't even be a fight," Agili said. "Just a whipping."

We realized suddenly that the crowd on the mound had gone silent, and we turned to see my grandfather Alickee striding toward the Council House. Everyone was looking at him. He wore a coat made of many feathers, every color of the rainbow, a Natchez garment few of us had ever seen. Later, when I read about Joseph and his coat of many colors, I thought of Alickee. He wore a turban with the plume of a swan sticking out, and earrings made from the tiny skulls of birds.

"Now the dance can begin," Sequoyah cried. "*Ulihelisdi,*" he said, grasping Alickee's arm. *Welcome.*

"Where is that grandson of mine?" Alickee asked, and I stepped forward, eyes fixed on the ground because I was too scared to look at him.

I was pretty sure Alickee was a wizard. He was *Ani-Natsi,* one of the Pine People. They were Natchez who took refuge with the Cherokee after escaping from slavery with the French. Alickee's father slit the throats of his French masters in their sleep. He and other fugitive Natchez settled in a Cherokee village called Notchee Town, where the Valley River meets the Hiwassee River. They were helped by a white trader named Cornelius Daugherty, and my-great-grandfather married one of Cornelius Daugherty's daughters. That's why my middle name is Daugherty.

Alickee was a Chickamaugan, the group that fought against the whites under Dragging Canoe and John Young Tassel Watts. That's how he must have met my grandmother, who was Young Tassel's sister. My grandparents' romance must have been short, since my mother was their only child together.

Notchee Town was only an hour's ride from where my mother and Ebenezer lived, but we didn't see Alickee that often. The Natchez were a fierce and mad people who worshipped the sun. Alickee made beautiful bowls and pots, but he frightened me, with his odd tattoos and the skulls in his ears and the strange accent when he spoke. I didn't know how to talk to him.

But he took me by the shoulders and crooned something in a language I didn't understand. "I heard what you did at the river, how you saved the boy. I am proud you are my grandson," he said in Cherokee, and I blushed.

Alickee had come because Yonaguska sent him a message that there was to be a long hunt and that the hunters would go all the way to our old hunting grounds in *Gan-da Giga-i,* Kentucky, seeking buffalo. The Cherokee had not hunted buffalo for many years. Buffalo had not been seen near the Valley Towns and Out Towns since my mother and Yonaguska were children. But the Natchez had been great buffalo hunters, coming from further west where there were still many herds. And Alickee and Yonaguska were cousins, both grandsons of Cornelius Daugherty.

"Will you go on the hunt with us?" Agili asked him.

"Yes, yes," he said. "We will go on one last hunt. But where is Yonaguska?"

"Praying," chimed three voices.

Alickee didn't even blink. He nodded. "As it should be."

I watched as he went to where the women were preparing the feast and embraced my mother. I think she might have been a little scared of him too. She was plain, dressed in a simple wool dress, while he was so fancy and strange. But I heard him call her *usdi Doya*, little Beaver, as he wrapped her in his arms.

A shrill whoop came from below the mound, and we all turned to see Junaluska riding toward the mound, leading a second horse with the carcass of a bear slung across it. Junaluska was Yonaguska's best friend. He lived not far from Kituwah, in Soco Gap, and often visited us. Those two were opposites. Yonaguska was quiet and thoughtful, while Junaluska was loud and boisterous. He was a warrior, a Red Chief. You would think that Junaluska and Yonaguska would be at odds, a White Chief and a Red Chief, but they were close all their lives.

Junaluska presented a fierce appearance. Instead of one topknot, he shaved his head except for two sprigs of hair that he braided so that they stood straight up, like the horns of a bull. That day he was wearing his red face paint in honor of the occasion.

He liked to make an entrance. He jumped off his horse and got Bigwitch and a few other men to help him push and pull the entire bear carcass up the steep steps of the mound, Gola following and barking at the carcass. It was a difficult and odd thing to do, dragging the whole bear up there, but that was Junaluska. He did nothing by half-measure.

He left the reeking bear carcass next to the bonfire and

walked over to our small group at the Council House door. Bigwitch, trailing behind him, glared at me.

"My friends!" Junaluska shouted, and embraced each of us. "I've brought the meat for the feast!" He looked around. "But where's our Yonaguska?"

Agili pointed to the door.

"Ah, well," he said. "Let's hope the spirits are speaking to him. The *real* spirits."

"In any case, we need to dress the bear. J.D., will you help me?" Junaluska peered down at me.

"Yonaguska told me not to leave the door," I said. I was worried he would be angry.

"Bigwitch, then?"

Bigwitch smirked as he followed Junaluska back to the bear. Gola followed eagerly, hoping to get a big bite of bear.

The first thing Junaluska did was cut out the bear's tongue, say a prayer over it, and offer it to the fire. You could smell the stench of the bear all across the mound, as they slit the belly open, gutted it and skinned it and cut it into hunks. Gola got his share. But when they wrapped the chunks of meat and lay them in the coals of the bonfire, the delicious smell of roasting meat filled the air.

The drumming had begun, a light thrum, a warming up.

And Yonaguska still had not come out.

There was close to a hundred people on the mound, eating and laughing. But as the sun began to set, the tension rose. Would Yonaguska come out? And how would he be? He was much beloved, but everyone knew his weakness.

Suddenly, from within the Council House, we heard the deep boom of a horn being blown. I had seen Yonaguska's buffalo horn, used by the White Chief for special ceremonies. But I had never heard it before. The sound sent a shiver down my spine.

The door opened, and there Yonaguska stood, in his ceremonial white buckskin shirt and breeches, a cape of white feathers, and a swan's feather tied to his topknot. Around his neck hung a pouch with his divining crystal, but he kept it hidden. I myself did not see it until many years later. He held the buffalo horn to his lips and blew one more time. And then there was complete silence. He swayed slightly as he stood, like a tall tree in a strong wind, and I was closest to him and could see that his eyes were strangely bright. *Oh no*, I thought.

But then I caught the scent of his breath. It smelled of the White Drink, not the Black Drink. The White Drink is actually black in color, but it's called "White" because the White Chief drinks it when he wants to have visions. It's made from holly and it has a dreadful smell and taste, like turpentine. But it opens the door to the Other World.

Yonaguska stepped toward the bonfire, the flames flickering in his strange eyes. There was no mistaking his power as he prayed:

"Yowah, we praise you,[;] we keep your fire.
Yowah, Giver of All Things.
Yowah, you are made of three beings,
the Elder Fires Above.
You created the sun, the moon, the stars.
You live in the seventh heaven.
Yowah, we are the Ani-Kitu-hwagi, the people of God.
We are a holy people, a chosen people.
A people set apart."

Yonaguska always called God *Yowah*. Many Cherokee call God *Unetlanvhi*, the Creator. But for the Kituwah people, God is *Yowah*. No one knows what this means, but I think it is an older name for God. The Kituwah people knew many secrets going back to the time of the *Ani'Kuta'ni*, the ancient priests who became so corrupt they had to be killed off. This is why the Kituwah people and the Natchez refugees were drawn to one another. They remembered things that everyone else had forgotten.

Then Yonaguska addressed the crowd:

"Last year, the prophet Tsali went up to Kuwahi, just like in the old days, to speak to Yowah. Yowah spoke to him on the mountain. Yowah told him that he is angry with us. We have strayed from the right path, the path of our fathers and mothers.

I, too, have seen this. The march of the whiteman is ever toward the setting sun. They will spread and spread and never stop. The whiteman's nature and the Cherokee's nature tell a different story. The whiteman's promises are always broken, like the reeds of the river. They are all lies.

Tsali told me what Yowah told him. We must go to *Gan-da Giga-i*, the bloody ground, and find the buffalo. We must find the Great Cave. We must kill a buffalo and make shields from its hide, and a headdress from its horns. With these shields we will be protected."

The people murmured in wonder. It had been many years since a prophet had gone up to Kuwahi and brought a word from Yowah down to the people.

But when Yonaguska said all of this, I remembered what Tsali had told me about a vision of an Unspeakable Road and me on that road. I thought this trip to Kentucky must be what he was talking about, and I wondered if I would be allowed to go, and whether it would be me that killed that buffalo. But why would the journey be unspeakable?

I also thought about what Yonaguska said about the

whiteman, and how all his promises are lies. And I knew in my heart that I was a part of this. It wasn't just that my grandfather and my father were liars. I was a liar, too. Because I was trying to be two things, two people.

The dance started that night with the Cold Moon Dance. If you have never danced on a mound beneath the moon in the dead of winter, you cannot understand the otherworldliness of this. I was dancing, everyone was dancing, from the oldest grandmothers to the young children. I was trying to forget the things that troubled me. The women had the tortoiseshell rattles tied to their legs, even my mother, and I took her hand and danced beside her, the swish-swish of the rattles lulling me into peace.

When suddenly a man in a mask pushed his way into the center. This was a mask I'd never seen before. It was a mask with two heads and sticking out from each head was a long, forked tongue. The mask wearer danced clownishly, as if he were drunk, running at different people in the crowd, who laughed as they backed up.

"Give me your coins," he said. "I'll sell you the whole world for some coins."

It took me a minute to realize the man was pretending to be Doublehead. Most of the people at the gathering were related in some way to Doublehead, But the bitterness about his betrayal ran deep. It made me feel a little sick, because the Wofford Settlement was part of what he'd sold to the whites.

I felt even sicker when the next mask-wearer broke through the crowd. This one was painted white, with big bushy eyebrows, a crown of floppy white hair, a thick white beard, and a pipe sticking out of his mouth. I knew who this was supposed to be. This was Benjamin Wofford. My father.

This one was mincing around, doing little European

dance steps, like a jig. He put one hand on his hip and hopped on one leg, swinging the other leg out, singing Hey Ho, Hey Ho. "I need a woman," he shouted. "Where's my Indian woman?" And he chased a few women in the crowd. He opened his cloak and pulled out a long fake phallus, a thick vine painted pink. He grabbed it and shook it at the women.

The men in the crowd were laughing so hard that some of them fell down on the ground. They were laughing so hard they were crying.

The dancer pretending to be my father lifted the white mask for a moment. It was John Watts. He was looking for me, and when he caught my eye, he leered at me and shook the fake phallus lewdly.

I ran toward him and pounded him with my fists. I was eleven, so I can't say I got much force into it. I wasn't even tall enough to hit his face, so I ended up hitting him in the chest. He shoved me and I fell backwards onto the ground.

"How do you like knowing where you came from?" he mocked. "Where's that Intruder-loving slut you call mother? The *Doya,* with her ugly teeth. Probably stumbling around drunk somewhere."

"I'll kill you," I yelled, climbing to my feet.

"The *tsisdu* isn't a fighter," he said. "Run away, little *tsisdu*. Run away to your mama."

I wanted to hit him again, but the crowd had gone silent and both of us turned to see another masked figure push through. This one was wearing a buffalo face, and buffalo fur and a tail. But it was limping, and I knew it was Sequoyah. The mask had long curved horns and a snout with big nostrils and a long furry beard. The buffalo figure lowered its head and pawed at the dirt.

Then another masked figure entered. The grace and intricacy of his steps made him instantly recognizable. It was Alickee. He was wearing a deerskin shirt and breeches dyed white. Emblazoned on the shirt was a yellow sun made of tiny beads. I knew at once that he had made the mask he wore, because it looked like his pottery designs. It was carved from buckeye wood, not like the gourds that Yonaguska used. It was a scary face with big nostrils, giant red teeth, and squiggly lines for its hair and beard. The squiggly lines looked like the hair and beard were made of snakes. I'd seen these same kind of lines on his pots. It was *this* mask.

[*Mooney's note: Wofford brings the mask to his face again.*]

Alickee was carrying a long knife. At first he did not seem to see the buffalo and was turning in tight circles, looking inward, dancing a dance that was all his own.

Then he looked up and saw the buffalo figure pawing the ground. Alickee stepped so lightly, it was like he was walking on air, tiptoeing toward the buffalo. Even the drums grew hushed. He began to circle the buffalo, spiraling closer and closer in, the buffalo turning in one place until it grew dizzy and dropped to its knees, as though under a spell. Alickee stood above it and held up the knife, then reached down and it seemed as though he were slashing its neck. I don't know how he did it, but a red liquid gushed out and soaked the buffalo fur and the ground around it. I thought for a horrible second that Sequoyah was dead.

But Alickee leaned down and extended his hand, and Sequoyah stood and embraced his friend. The crowd cheered, and everyone went back to dancing.

But not me. The evening was spoiled for me. I looked

around for John Watts, to finish my business with him. And I looked around for my mother. I couldn't find either of them. I felt a sting behind my eyes and a lump in my throat, and it was shame. For my name and my blood.

Chapter 8

White Drink, White Bear

Interview Eight: James Mooney and James Daugherty Wofford
March 16, 1891; Tahlequah, Cherokee Nation

[Mooney's Notes: Wofford is waiting for me, a bow and a musket arranged on his table. The bow looks freshly oiled. The musket is of the old-fashioned muzzle-loading variety, what they used to call a Brown Bess, with a long iron barrel, a wooden stock, and a flintlock mechanism. It appears recently polished.]

I never was a warrior, but I could shoot. In those days, it wasn't a choice. If you didn't shoot, you didn't eat. Sometimes, if you didn't shoot, you died. The only choice was which weapon. By the time I came along, most of us had guns. But we still had bows, too. When it came time to hunt the buffalo, the bow was more use than the gun.

Winter was the season to hunt. Yonaguska, Bigwitch, and I would ride up into the mountains, where there was still some game, although not as plentiful as it used to be. Yonaguska kept a small herd of horses, tough little mustangs descended from Spanish horses. They were bred to be hunting horses, able to scramble up rocky mountain sides. I learned about horses and became a good rider during my winters with Yonaguska, but Bigwitch had an almost magical way with horses. Maybe that's why they called him Bigwitch, because he wasn't any other kind of witch.

We started to prepare for the journey to Kentucky the morning after the Booger Dance. Yonaguska, Alickee, Agili, Sequoyah, Junaluska, and John Watts gathered around the embers of the bonfire to talk about the journey. Bigwitch and I were allowed to tag along. I was still fuming about Watts. I told Alickee about it that morning. He didn't let it show, but I knew he was angry. Alickee didn't like whites either, but I was his grandson.

Yonaguska and Junaluska talked first about a visit they'd had from the Shawnee prophet Tecumseh. Tecumseh visited them in Soco Gap to convince them to join together with other tribes against the whites. The Redstick Creeks, the most traditional and warlike Creeks, were getting ready to fight the Americans.

In a way, Tecumseh and the Redsticks were saying the same things that Tsali and Yonaguska were saying. There was no compromise with the whites. They weren't going to stop taking our land, and we had to resist. But even Junaluska, as fierce as he was, was wary of starting another cycle of killing, with more villages burned and more people slaughtered. Also, the Creeks had long been our worst enemy. It didn't seem right to fight alongside them.

There was no easy answer, and my uncles debated, the same debate we'd been having for a century and would keep on having. Was it better to be friendly and peaceable with the whites, hoping they would let us keep enough land to survive on? Or was it better to fight?

Yonaguska was back to his normal self that morning. He told us more about what Tsali had said. Inside the Great Cave, Tsali had told him, we would find a woman with a necklace of fawn hoofs and another necklace made from the claw of an eagle. This woman would give Yonaguska a vision. And near the Great Cave we would find a one-eyed buffalo. This was the buffalo we had to kill.

"Bigwitch will go," Yonaguska said. "It's time to make him a man. And J.D. will go. It's early to make him a man, but time is running out for us."

John Watts jumped to his feet. "This boy is an Intruder dog," he shouted. "If he goes, I do not go." He spat on the ground.

I jumped up, ready to go at him again, but Alickee rose and got to him first. Alickee was not a tall man, but even in his sixties his body was hard and agile and tightly wound. "Your father was my friend, but you insult my grandson," he said, "and you insult me." He fingered the knife he always kept tucked in his belt.

"Peace," Yonaguska said. "The boy goes. I have seen this. He rescued the child from the river, and he will rescue more. John Watts, you are too hot-headed. Listen or your tongue will keep you deaf. Go dunk yourself in the cold river."

Watts glared at Alickee and me but walked away. Agili reached over and patted my shoulder. "He does not speak for us. He's always been like the possum who is proud of his big bushy tail, when everyone else knows it is bare."

"*U-tse-tsdi ga-do-ga*," Sequoyah joked. "Possum Tail Watts!"

Alickee grinned his wolfish grin. "Possums make good meat, if you stew it long enough."

"Let us talk of *Gan-da Giga-i*," Yonaguska reminded them. "We'll follow the Warrior's Path. I've always longed to see a buffalo."

"I know the road well," Agili said. Everyone knew that as

a young man Agili was part of the Cherokee delegation that had traveled the Warrior's Path to Virginia to meet with George Washington and demand the money he had promised us. And George Washington was so impressed with Agili that he sent him on a mission all the way to Canada to give a secret message to the French. That was why Agili wore the medal from the President.

Just the name Warrior's Path filled me with excitement. I'd never been farther than Kituwah and Wofford's Settlement. The Warrior's Path led beyond the mountains, to places where Cherokee fought with other tribes like the Shawnee and the Chickasaw. And for my uncles to think I was worthy to make this journey, that was something.

Right away, I had visions of being the one to kill the buffalo. All my life I had heard tales of heroes, like Aganunitsi who killed the Uktena or the warriors who killed Spearfinger. Or real-life heroes like Dragging Canoe and Young Tassel Watts. I wanted to be the one to save my people. Yonaguska had even said that he had seen that I would rescue more than just the boy in the river.

The night before we left, we camped on the summit of Kuwahi. Yonaguska said we should go there to hear directly from Yowah before we left. It was snowing on the mountain and bitterly cold. The moon was a thin sliver and the stars blazed in the black sky. We sat around the fire drinking the White Drink.

That was the first time I drank it, and it made my head spin and made me sick to my stomach. I walked out into the field, away from the fire, to retch. I fell on my knees in the snow. And it seemed suddenly that the snow was a sheet of purple water, purple, pink, and orange like a sunset, and beneath the surface of the water I could see many fish swimming. I looked up at the stars and they had grown larger and brighter, and above my head flocks of ducks and pigeons swooped and wheeled in the swirling snow. I was seeing the medicine lake, Atagahi. I plunged in, I was swimming in it, but the water was warm, not cold, and a strength came into my body.

And at the edge of the lake I saw the White Bear, the Chief of all Bears. The one who bathes the wounded animals in the lake and heals all their sorrows. His white fur glowed like the strange new stars.

And I swear to you, that Bear was weeping. Tears flowed down his fierce and gentle face, for he knew everything that would happen. He knew the Trail we would walk.

And then I heard a voice as loud and sudden as a crack of thunder. That was the first time I heard the God-voice. I was drowning in the purple water, and the voice called out, *I:gagadi. Radiant Light,* is the best I can translate it. *Holy Light. The Light that defeats the Darkness.*

I saw for a moment this blinding holy light, and I did not avert my eyes.

The flash burned through me like lightning, like my head was on fire, and I cried out, "Holy! Holy!" And then it was gone, and the lake was gone, and I was lying in a snowy field. Splintered and blessed, like a lightning-struck tree.

I did not tell Yonaguska about my vision until many years later. I turned it over in my mind so many times. What was *I:gagadi*? And why did the Great Bear weep? Was this a vision of Tsali's Unspeakable Road? Was our journey to Kentucky cursed or blessed?

Many years later, I would travel through Kentucky again, on the thousand-mile walk to Oklahoma, with a thousand people in my care. Also in midwinter, in the coldest winter anyone had ever known. And I would fail them. I would find out then what Tsali meant by the Unspeakable Road. Whatever struggles we faced in that first trip to Kentucky, they were nothing compared to the trials that awaited us on the Trail Where They Cried.

It was mid-January when we set out. John Watts decided to go. He did not want to be left out of the great hunt. But he refused to look at me or acknowledge me, and Alickee's eyes followed him like a hunter tracking prey.

Alickee said the journey to Kentucky would take us two weeks. Yonaguska rode his favorite horse, a brindle stallion named Tooantuh, Spring Frog, and he let me ride a young chestnut stallion named Gata, Fire. Alickee's horse, Ayita, First to Dance, was a high-strung stallion, fast as the wind.

And Bigwitch rode his favorite horse, Ooneley, Wind. I was glad that Bigwitch was going, so there would be someone else my age. But our friendship was uneasy. We were rivals more than friends.

We tied our bundles of furs, tents, food, and weapons to the hide and bearskin saddles we used for long journeys. Even Bigwitch's dog Gola carried a pack. Everyone carried a gun except Alickee, who was like Tsali, rejecting anything from the whites.

That morning, Alickee gave me this bow. I was getting ready to mount Gata when he pulled it from his pack and handed it to me. "For you, grandson," he said.

He had carved it just like he carved the mask, only the bow is made from Black Locust. Black Locust wood will not let you lie. If you carve it wrong, it will crack across the belly. You have to cut to the heartwood and bend it so carefully. And use your fingers to find the stiff spots and shave them down. The wood talks to the carver, if the carver will listen. A tree can teach you how to bend without breaking, if you close your eyes and listen with your hands.

Alickee told me all of this that morning, and he told me that it was better to hunt buffalo with a bow than a gun, because it takes too long to reload a gun. But a good hunter can notch another arrow more quickly than even a buffalo can run, and buffalo are faster than you think.

He himself brought a long lance with a flint tip he had honed so sharp it would make your finger bleed just to touch it. He had hunted buffalo with his people as a young man. He told us he would show us how it was done.

We all carried a small hatchet and a long hunting knife on our belts, and a pouch with bullets, flints, and brass powder flasks for the muskets. I'd been around guns my whole life, with both my father's and my mother's people. I'd practiced shooting many times. But this was the first time I had a gun of my own, and it made me feel like a man. I'm ashamed now to say that at that time, I was more excited about the gun than the bow that my grandfather gave me, the bow he made with his own hands. That's how foolish I was.

Our plan was to cut through the Catawba Gap to the Warrior's Path and follow it north to Cumberland Gap. From there, we would head west into what they called the Kentucky Barrens, where the grasslands began.

We rode hard every day, stopping only to eat and sleep. East for the first two days, to *Untakiyasti-yi*, what the whites call Asheville. There we intersected with the Catawba Trail, which took us north. It was a sad journey through dead Cherokee towns and lost Cherokee land, abandoned townhouses and cabins and fish weirs in the river.

During the Revolution, the Americans had destroyed all of the Cherokee towns east of the Tuckaseegee River. What was once the Cherokee Nation was now North Carolina, inhabited by Intruders. My father lived near here at one time, on the North Fork of the Catawba River. My grandfather, after fighting the British and the Cherokee in South Carolina, settled in North Carolina for about ten years before moving to Georgia. He built a fort and fought off the remaining Cherokee. Somehow my father met my mother there. Neither one of them ever told me that story.

We rode through a landscape, brown and gray except for stands of fir and rhododendron, and the beech trees, which hold their gold leaves all winter. We avoided the white settlements. Because it was winter, there were few travelers, no cattle or swine drives. Whenever we spotted a traveler or a white settlement, we left the road and made our way through the woods.

Each night we found an overhanging rock and pitched our deerskin tents beneath it. We kept a fire burning all night to ward off wolves and panthers. As we ate the plain food we carried bear's fat, dried venison, hickory nuts Yonaguska told us stories. There was no place, no river or mountain, that did not have its story. Every rock, every tree, every creek, was peopled with creatures and spirits. They weren't all good, but they were all alive.

Yonaguska loved to play it up and act out the voices and the actions of the characters. He could be funny or scary. His voice would get louder or softer, higher or lower. He could do men's voices and women's voices. He would start out sitting but end up standing, like a play where he played all of the characters. Sometimes he would get me or Bigwitch or Alickee to play a role. Alickee loved to become characters and use his body to tell a story. He could become any animal or a Nûñnĕ'hĭ or an old woman.

The first night, we camped near Shining Rock, the mountain where the story of Selu and Kanati happened, and Yonaguska told us that story.

A long, long time ago, Yonaguska said, *soon after the world was made, a hunter named Kanati lived with his wife Selu right here, near Shining Rock. They had a son*—here he gestured for Bigwitch to stand up—*who played every day with a boy who lived beneath the river*—he gestured for me to play the role. *One day, the son wrestled with the boy*—at this I grabbed Bigwitch and we fell to the ground and rolled a few times, Bigwitch taking the opportunity to pin me down and show off his strength—*and took him home to live with Kanati and Selu. They tried to tame the boy, but he was wild and had magic powers*—I rubbed my hands together as if working the conjuring beads—*so they called him Wild Boy*. I grinned at that. I liked being Wild Boy. *He led his brother into all kinds of mischief.*

The boys grew curious about the game that their father Kanati brought home every day for their food. One day, the two boys followed Kanati—Bigwitch and I tiptoed around the campfire—*up Shining Rock to see where the animals came from. They watched as Kanati went to a cave at the top of the mountain*—Yonaguska stood and used his hands in a pushing motion—*and rolled a stone away from the entrance. Out ran a buck which Kanati shot and carried home.*

The next day, the boys went back and rolled the stone away themselves. (Bigwitch and I rolled the stone.) *They had fun shooting the deer* (we drew our bows and shot) *as they ran out. But soon all of the deer in the cave were gone, and the other animals began to run out as well—raccoons, turkeys, pigeons, partridges.*

The birds made such a ruckus with their wings that Kanati heard it (Yonaguska put his hand to his ear and came to where we were standing) *and went to the cave. He was so angry at what the boys had done that he went into the cave and kicked over the jars* (Yonaguska kicked) *that held all the insects, and bedbugs, fleas, lice, and gnats swarmed all over the boys* (Bigwitch and I swatted at the bugs).

"You rascals," Kanati told them. "You always had something to eat because I brought it home from the cave. Now you will have to go out and hunt for your food. Go home and ask your mother for something to eat."

The boys went home and told Selu (Yonaguska gestured for Alickee to play Selu) *they were hungry. Every day Selu would go out to her storehouse with a basket and bring back corn and beans. The boys decided to follow her into the storehouse* (we followed) *and see where she got the food. They watched as Selu* (Alickee) *leaned over the basket and rubbed her belly, and the basket was half full of corn. She rubbed her armpits, and the basket was filled to the top with beans.*

"Our mother is a witch," the boys told each other (we pointed). *"We must kill her."*

Selu knew what they were planning. "If you must kill me," she said (Alickee used a high-pitched voice), *"clear a piece of ground in front of our house. Drag my body seven times around in a circle. Then drag my body seven times around inside the circle. Stay up all night and watch. In the morning, you will have corn."*

The boys killed her, cut off her head, and put it on the roof, facing west (we threw Alickee to the ground and pretended to slit his throat). *They dragged her body around the circle, and wherever her blood fell, corn grew.* (The dragging took some work.)

When Kanati came home and saw that his wife was dead, he was very angry. He told the boys he was going to live with the

Wolf People. Wild Boy changed himself into a tuft of feather and went with him, sitting on his shoulder. Wild Boy listened as Kanati asked the wolves to kill the boys. (Yonaguska gestured for John Watts to play the wolves, but Watts looked behind him and scowled.)

Wild Boy went home and told his brother, and when the wolves came (John Watts did *not* get up and pretend to be a wolf), *the boys trapped them in a circle of fire, and shot at them with their bows and let the others burn.*

I drew back my imaginary bow and pointed it at Watts' head, to hoots of laughter from the other men. Watts jumped to his feet and lunged at me, but I dodged him and made a silly face.

Oh, Watts was angry! But there was nothing he could do about it. He sat back down with his back turned, but even his back was tense like a dog that is one step from biting. Yonaguska finished the story.

Later, the two boys traveled to the end of the world, where they found their parents. Kanati and Selu welcomed them but told them they must journey to the Darkening Land and stay there, where the sun goes down. They became the Thunder Boys, and when they talk to each other we hear thunder in the west. Before they left, the Thunder Boys taught the people seven songs to help them hunt. And these are the songs the hunters still sing.

So you see, this story is where I got the name Thunder Boys for me and Jimmy and Tony. The Thunder Boys were curious and adventurous and wild. That's who I wanted to be. But I always wondered, why did they have to cut off their mother's head? Why does everything come down to blood?

The next morning, the ground was covered with snow. It would be hard going for the horses, especially when we had to leave the road. But it was glorious, mountains as far as the eye could see, blanketed in white, and the boughs of trees heavy with snow. The tickly smell of snow in my nose.

The sunlight flashed on the white peaks, and the world seemed clean and pure. But I knew we were heading toward the place where the Woffords had built their fort on the north fork of the Catawba.

"Want to stop by Turkey Cove, *tsisdu*, little Rabbit,?" John Watts jeered. "We could stop by Fort Wofford. Look for the bones of dead Cherokee."

I just looked straight ahead, ignored his taunts. But he wasn't saying anything I hadn't said to myself a thousand times.

Chapter 9

The Wampum Belt

Interview Nine James Mooney and James Daugherty Wofford
March 15, 1891; Tahlequah, Cherokee Nation

[Mooney's Notes: Wofford holds in his hands a wampum belt made with tiny purple and white shells. There is a strip of white beads down the center, and the edges are zig zags of white and purple. I have heard of this wampum belt but never seen it. I find it difficult to contain my excitement upon seeing this rare specimen.]

Yonaguska gave me this belt. It belongs to the Keetowah Society now. But he showed it to me for the first time on the trip to Kentucky. It is a very famous belt, given to us by the Iroquois as a symbol of the end to war between our two nations, in the time before I was born. For many years, the Iroquois and Cherokee had fought one another, Iroquois warriors making raids into Cherokee territory, taking captives and plunder and destroying villages, Cherokee warriors doing the same. Finally, they agreed that the Tennessee River would be their boundary, and they would cease to fight.

Sometimes I look at this belt as the story of my life and the story of my people's life. At the center is the white path, the path we all want to walk. But my life is more like the zig zags, up and down, forward and back. A crooked road. Never the road I wanted.

We reached the Catawba Trail on the second night of

our trip and stayed at a hunting camp that we still secretly used sometimes, where Bent Creek meets the French Broad River. We had long ago ceded the land, but there were few deer left in mountains near the Valley Towns, and by necessity the hunters went farther up into the mountains. We could see Black Mountain, the highest mountain in the old Cherokee Nation.

We stopped before dusk so that we could hunt. We found an overhanging rock where the snow was scant and we could build a fire. Junaluska, Agili, Watts, and Bigwitch set off into the woods. But Yonaguska told me to stay back with him for some *tsila* training, and Sequoyah and Alickee didn't want to go. Alickee avoided Watts as much as possible. But Bigwitch had taken to following Watts around and imitating his loud, crude ways. I could tell that Yonaguska didn't like it.

When Yonaguska told me to stay, I could read Bigwitch's jealousy in the tension in his shoulders and the way he loudly bantered with Watts as they mounted their horses and rode off, Gola trotting behind them.

We sat around the fire and warmed ourselves as Yonaguska told stories. He took out his ceremonial pipe, the one with the carved bear, and filled it with tobacco. He took a puff, then passed it to Alickee and Sequoyah. When Sequoyah handed it to me, Yonaguska nodded, and I smoked the pipe for the first time. My heart swelled with pride, though I coughed a few times and the others smiled. The tobacco made me feel both a little sick and more alive than I had ever felt before.

Sequoyah was carving designs into a piece of wood. His hands were never still. He scratched and carved while Yonaguska told us the story of the famous race between the deer and the terrapin, which had happened on Black Mountain.

"Once in the olden times, when the animals had the power of speech," he said, "the deer was filled with pride and bragged of his great speed. He ridiculed the turtle for his slowness and challenged him to a race across the seven high hills of the Black Mountains. On the appointed day, the deer started away at breakneck speed.

But the turtle was smarter. He tricked the deer by getting his fellow turtles to station themselves on each peak in the mountain range, so that the deer would see the turtle ahead of him each time he climbed a ridge. The deer finally gave up and went back to the starting line, where the original turtle had never left. The mind is more powerful than the legs, the turtle told the deer. Next time, you won't underestimate me."

Sequoyah slapped his leg in agreement. "This is my saying—the mind is more powerful than the legs. I am the turtle!"

"Maybe this is a story about who is stronger, the medicine man or the warrior," Alickee said. "I think I'd rather be the deer. The turtle only beats the deer in stories."

"Which is the better path?" I asked. I wanted to be the deer, but I knew I was the turtle. The turtle was like the *tsisdu*, the rabbit. Clever, but no hero.

"Let me show you something," Yonaguska said.

He reached into his pack and pulled out this wampum belt. He handed it to me and let me hold it.

"See this, J.D.," he said. "The long white strip down the middle is the Tennessee River and the path of peace. The zig zags along the sides are the raids of Cherokee into Iroquois territory and Iroquois into Cherokee territory. Back and forth, we raided each other, until finally we made peace with this belt.

The white path, the path of peace, that is what we all

want. But in every village, we have the White Chief and the Red Chief. Because both are needed at different times. There is always a balance. This is *tohi.*"

"Tsali told me I'd walk an Unspeakable Road," I blurted out. "What does that mean?"

"He didn't tell me that," Yonaguska said. He frowned and took a puff from the pipe. "Maybe that's what we'll learn in the cave."

Sequoyah looked up from his carving. "The belt tells stories," he said. "What if we could find a way to tell stories like the whites, with markings? Look at this." He reached into his pack and pulled out a book and cracked it open. "See these markings?" he said. "These markings make words."

He handed the book around the circle and my uncles flipped through the pages curiously.

"Do you know what the words say?" Yonaguska asked.

"No," Sequoyah said. "I don't speak the whiteman's language."

"I do," I said. "Give it to me. It says Poor Richard's Almanack." I looked up. "I don't know what an Almanack is. But Richard is someone's name." I opened it to a page. "Better slip with foot than tongue," was what it said in English. As I translated it for them, I felt both ashamed and proud to know English.

"I think this could be powerful for us, if we could find a way to do this," Sequoyah said. "Look at this." He held up the thin plank of cedar he'd been carving. He'd cut strange symbols into the soft wood.

"See," he said. "This one, Ꮵ This is tsi. This one, W, this is la. Tsi-la. That's you, J.D.

I grinned.

We passed the plank around the circle.

"Can I do it?" I asked, when it came to me, and Sequoyah nodded.

I pulled out my dagger and tried to imitate one of the signs. It's hard to carve a circle into wood. My hand slipped, and the knife gouged into my palm. Fat drops of blood fell on the snow.

"You bled on my words," Sequoyah complained. He was just teasing me. He cleaned the board with a handful of snow, but there was still a smear.

Yonaguska found a strip of deerskin and wrapped my hand. "I don't know about this," he said. "I don't even want to speak the whiteman's language. I don't want to imitate his ways."

"How different is this from the notches we use on trees to mark directions? Or the stone carvings our ancestors made? We could keep our stories alive forever," Sequoyah said.

"I keep the stories," Yonaguska said. "When I tell a story, it's like a living tree. If you use these markings, the story is like the dead piece of wood. I think this writing is a kind of death or a kind of lie. Because nothing living stays the same."

"I'm with Yonaguska on this," Alickee said. "The white man's words dry up and blow away like leaves when the words no longer suit them."

"Talking leaves," Sequoyah said. "Why not?" Sequoyah's mind was always five steps ahead of everyone else.

"Dead leaves," Alickee retorted, and gave a disdainful "Humph."

We were passing the pipe around the circle again when we heard a clatter of hooves, the return of the hunters. Bigwitch emerged from the woods with a deer carcass slung across the shoulders of his horse, followed by Watts and Gola. Agili and Junaluska weren't with them. Bigwitch's cheeks were streaked with blood. His big grin faded when he saw the pipe in my hand. He'd never been allowed to smoke it.

"Look, father," he called out. "I killed the deer. I'm a man now, a hunter." He pulled the deer, it was a small doe, off the horse. He carried it in his arms like a child and laid it at his father's feet.

"Well done, son," Yonaguska said. "Did you thank her for her life?"

Bigwitch glanced back at Watts, who strode up behind him.

"I blooded him," Watts said. "I made him a man."

"I'm proud of you, son," Yonaguska said, ignoring Watts. "But kneel down and say the prayers. She has sacrificed herself for us."

Yonaguska hastily returned the wampum belt to its pouch and laid aside the pipe. But not before Watts saw them.

Bigwitch knelt down awkwardly, bent his head over the doe and muttered a prayer. Yonaguska knelt beside him, his arm on his shoulder. Bigwitch stroked the dead doe's head. He wasn't a bad boy or man. He was torn between trying to impress his father and trying to impress Watts.

Meanwhile, Agili and Junaluska rode up. They had headed in a different direction and come across a brood of grouse, which they dumped in a heap by the fire. We would eat well that night.

"Now, son, we must cut out the tongue and offer it to the fire." Yonaguska handed Bigwitch a knife, and he opened the deer's mouth and grabbed the tongue and sawed back and forth. Tongues are tough, hard to cut. When he got it loose, he threw it on the fire, and the smell of cooked meat rose up in the camp.

Yonaguska scooped up a handful of snow and used it to wipe the blood off Bigwitch's cheeks, just like Sequoyah had cleaned the wood. This annoyed Watts, who took it as a slight against his manhood ceremony.

Watts spotted the strip of deerskin on my hand, some blood soaking through it, and found his target. "Did you try to cut off another finger, *tsisdu*? Good thing you're learning the medicine ways, clumsy as you are. Because you'll never be a hunter. Real men hunt."

"What about you, Watts? Everyone knows you are fed by your wife and your mother-in-law," Alickee said. "And word has it, you've been known to dabble in stealing horses."

No one had ever said that aloud, and everyone froze. Those were fighting words.

"I'm sure that Watts brings home some meat," said Agili, trying to avert a fight.

But Alickee wasn't stopping. "Bigwitch killed the deer, Watts. What have you killed this whole trip?"

"Why do all of you defend this half-white runt?" Watts snapped. He rose and paced around the fire, puffing out his round shoulders and fat stomach. "You're going to teach *him* to be a medicine man? You let *him* smoke the pipe, you show *him* the wampum belt? His blood is cursed. It will taint this journey, you'll see!"

"I'm half-white, too," Agili said. "Are you telling me my blood is cursed?"

And like the coward he was, Watts backed down. "No, cousin, I am not speaking of you. Just this scrawny *tsisdu*, always in the way. And here is Bigwitch, he has become a man today, and no one cares."

Bigwitch looked away. He didn't want to be part of this. Even he knew it wasn't really about him.

Alickee stood up and went to Watts. He chanted something in the Natchez language and made an upward scooping motion his hands, like he was pushing something bad toward Watts. The blood drained from Watts' face, and he backed away. I wasn't the only one who thought Alickee might be a wizard. We all suspected he had a kind of magic you didn't want to fool around with.

"Next time, the knife," Alickee said in Cherokee.

Watts walked away into the woods and didn't return until the feast was done and we lay in our blankets. I heard him chomping on the bones of the grouse, the only thing we left him.

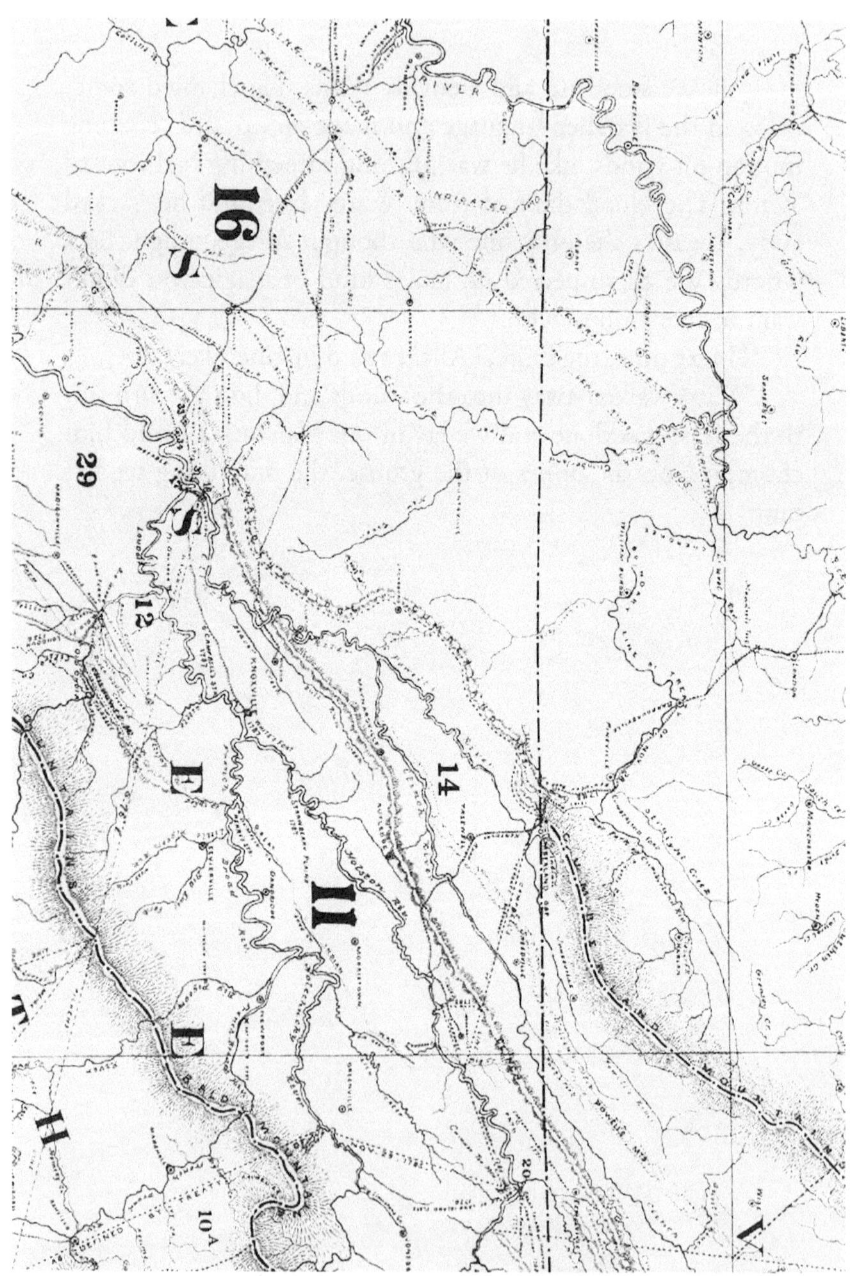

Former territorial limits of the Cherokee, 1884: Road to Kentucky.

Chapter 10

Step Down, Snow

Interview Ten: James Mooney and James Daugherty Wofford
March 17, 1891; Tahlequah, Cherokee Nation

[Mooney's Notes: Wofford has spread his copy of the Royce Map across his table. He traces their route to Kentucky across the colorful map with his finger.]

See, here is Kituwah, right here in the purple section near where it says Charleston. We travelled east along Rutherford's War Path, all the way to the French Broad River, where the map says Asheville. From there the Catawba Trail follows the French Broad north to the Catawba Gap. This is the main pass through the Smokies. On the other side of the mountains, we followed the French Broad to where it intersects here with the Nolichucky River and turned north on the Warrior's Path.

Just before the Catawba Gap, we came to the hot springs, and Yonaguska said they were holy and we should go to water there. He said that during the earthquake a lake of fire rose out of the springs, and it was an entrance to the Below World. I was afraid to go in, afraid of being swallowed up. But Yonaguska said there was medicine in the water and that it was better even than a sweat lodge.

The water smelled odd, like something rotten. We

stripped and climbed naked into the hot water, which felt so good after days of traveling in the cold. It reminded me of how Atagahi Lake felt in my vision. Yonaguska said the words for going to water, and we plunged together seven times.

I watched Sequoyah and wondered if he was hoping that the water would heal his injured leg. But he seemed absorbed in his own world, as always, thinking of things beyond my understanding.

Then he looked up and said, "I talked to a man who was with our people on the St. Francis River in Arkansas when the earthquake happened. It was much worse there. The river flooded its banks and destroyed their village, and many people drowned. Right before it started, animals came out of the woods. Panthers, foxes, and wolves came into villages. There was a roar like thunder and the ground caved in beneath them. The forests shook like rivercane in the wind, and afterwards trees lay splintered on the ground. I wonder what made the earth so angry."

"Tsali told me that it was because we have abandoned the old ways," Yonaguska said. "Many of our people who have gone to Arkansas were traditional Kituwah people. Maybe they should not have gone west. Maybe it's wrong for us to abandon our home. The earth is crying out and we're not listening."

We camped nearby, and I woke that night to the sound of thunder and peered out of the tent at thick snow falling. I'd never heard thunder during a snowstorm. It echoed through the mountains like the voice of a god. Lightning flashed across the white peaks.

"Thunder-snow," Yonaguska said, peering out with me. "The Thunder Boys are restless tonight. I don't know what this means. It's a strange omen for our journey."

All night, the thunder and lightning pierced my dreams. I dreamt of strange beings, men with the wings of birds and panthers with the talons of eagles. In the dream, I was walking through the snow with a band of people. We were pursued by enemies, and I was trying to get them to safety. But so many fell, bleeding in the snow, and I couldn't help them. I woke up weeping, and then I was ashamed, afraid that Yonaguska would hear my crying like a child.

But that dream. It was a shadow of the thing that later happened. I saw it then.

The next morning we came to the Painted Rocks at Catawba Gap, where the French Broad River flows in a narrow gorge through the mountains. There was a guard house there, left over from the wars with the Americans.

On a high cliff at the end of the pass were paintings from ancient times. Enormous reddish-orange designs, some figures of humans, deer, fish, and birds. Men with the wings of birds and panthers with the talons of eagles. The monsters from my dream. Monsters so ancient I had no name for them.

"This is what I mean," Sequoyah said. "These are talking pictures. They tell a story. If you used the same shape to say the same word every time, you could tell many stories."

"I think these two," Yonaguska said, pointing, "might be the Thunder Boys. And this one," he pointed to another form, "might be the great frog who swallows the sun and the moon. There is the moon," he said, "and here is the sun."

Alickee drew near the cliff and reached up to touch the sun circle. He traced his fingertips around the circle. "Our people were ruled by the children of the Sun, until the French came and enslaved us. But one day the Sun will avenge his people."

"I'm not waiting for a god," Watts scoffed. "It's the warriors who will bring us victory."

"There are no greater warriors than the Natchez," Alickee snapped "We were not defeated because we were not brave. We were outnumbered."

"I wonder what happened to the ancient ones who painted these?" Sequoyah asked. "Were they the same ancient ones who built the mounds? Will we, too, be forgotten one day? Will anyone remember our names?"

We stepped through the threshold at the end of the pass, out of the mountains and into the flat land. Into the landscape of dreams and legends.

We followed the French Broad a short way to where it intersects with the Nolichucky. A great chestnut tree stood at the crossroads, and a patch of bark had been peeled off and the exposed wood painted with red and black symbols I did not understand. It was the marker and the turning point.

We turned north on the Warrior's Path—*Athiamoiwee,* The Path of the Armed Ones.

This same war path became the road the settlers took into Tennessee and Kentucky. For them, the Warrior's Path was the Wilderness Road. But the more of them that came, the less it was wilderness.

Each time we saw a settler's wagon in the distance, we headed off the road and into the woods. It was slower that way, but safer. Because it was mid-winter, we saw only a few. When we came near homesteads, we skirted them. We camped out of sight from the road and took turns keeping watch in the night. Sometimes we'd hear the howls of wolves and screams of panthers, and Bigwitch and I would bury ourselves deeper in the bearskins and closer to Gola. We were on our way to becoming men, but we were still boys.

The first few nights I was sore from the long days of riding, but each day my body hardened and grew stronger. My horse Gata and I learned each other so well that it only took a slight pressure from my knee to tell him what I wanted. When you ride all day, you dream of riding all night. Your body is still moving, galloping, galloping, across the landscape.

Each day farther from home, it was like a long cord being stretched further and further. My uncles were a familiar comfort, but I still felt a little lost and lightheaded, disconnected from my source. I missed my mother, although I never would have admitted it.

The land was very flat after we crossed through Catawba Gap, flatter than I had ever seen before. The horizon was so much wider and the sky so much bigger, the clouds a dizzying dance above. At night the stars went on forever, with no mountains to block the view. The flat land made me feel exposed and vulnerable, like a turtle that has lost its shell.

And yet it was magnificent, seeing the wider world for the first time, all blanketed in snow. Even in the dead of winter, there were many strange sights. We saw great flocks of passenger pigeons, flocks so dense they blocked the sun, wheeling and twisting. Their wings thundered, their cry loud and harsh, as they swooped close to the earth. Their necks gleamed, bronze or golden or almost purple. It was easy to shoot them with a blow gun. I felt sad to strip their beautiful feathers, but grateful when we feasted at night on their roasted flesh.

Riding the Warrior's Path, I also imagined the heroic deeds I would perform, if we encountered the Shawnee or Spearfinger or the Stoneclad giants. I was eager to prove myself.

I kept an eye out for the *Tsunil' kalu'*, "The Slant-eyed

people," a race of giants twice as tall as ordinary men. They looked like the *Tsul'kalu'*, but they lived far to the west. The Thunder Boys also lived in the direction of the setting sun, which was the direction of death. The direction in which we were headed.

My uncles laughed when I told them my fears, but I think they secretly shared them. Only Alickee and Agili had ever been this far west.

The temperature began to drop, a hard freeze colder than I had ever known at home. The creeks and rivers were frozen in places. When we reached the Holston River, we weren't sure if the layer of ice was thick enough to hold us. We threw large rocks and branches out onto the ice and it did not break, and finally Junaluska volunteered to tip toe out and see if it would hold his weight, then his horse. Carefully, we crossed, relieved to reach the other side.

On the other side of the Holston, the Kentucky Road forked off to the west, and we took it, passing Buffalo Track Rock, still marked by the hooves of long-ago buffalo.

On the evening of our fifth day of travel, we reached the Cumberland Gap, which we called Cave Gap. Finally, mountains again, what we called the *Alligewi* and you call Allegheny. We were nervous about passing through the narrow notch between the mountains. Rock walls rose steeply on both sides, and the road was barely wide enough for two riders side by side.

"The buffalo made this road," Yonaguska said. "We used the buffalo's road, and now the settlers are using our road."

"The Shawnee used to ambush settlers coming though this gap," Alickee said.

"So did we," John Watts said, grinning. "Doublehead and the Bench used to scalp settlers and eat them. Once someone asked Doublehead what he thought of whites, and he said 'too salty!' What do you think of that, white boy?" John asked, turning to me. "Can I have a taste?" He flashed his ugly pointy teeth.

"It's bandits we have to worry about these days," Agili said. "Horse thieves. If our horses are stolen, we have no way to get them back. We're not even supposed to be here, and by law our word means nothing."

The Gap was the one place in our journey where it would be impossible to veer off the road if we spotted other travelers. The road had been widened by the famous settler Daniel Boone to allow settlers with wagons to pass more easily into the Kentucky wilderness, but the pass itself was still very narrow. It was the only way into Kentucky for settlers from the Carolinas and Virginia, so we were more likely to see them.

We spent that night in a cave on a ridge above the entrance to the gap. A spring flowed out of the cave and made a waterfall that had frozen solid. It was very beautiful, this curtain of icicles, and we slept in the cave next to the frozen spring. From the roof of the cave icicles also hung. It was the kind of cold that hurts your lungs to breathe, and we made a fire in the cave. The light from the fire danced on the icicles and melted them and made shadows in the shape of daggers on the walls of the cave. We huddled inside tents and furs.

I wondered what might live further back in that cave. Wolves, panthers, mountain lions? Or Spearfinger and her murderous hand? If we followed the cave back into the mountain, it might lead to the Underworld, to the Uktena or Tlanuhwa, a giant hawk with metallic feathers and eyes that flung lightning bolts. I slept close to Gola that night.

The next morning, we started through the pass, my uncles keeping their guns and bows at close reach. The road was rocky and steep in places, slippery with snow and ice, and the horses had to pick their way carefully. Rockslides, probably from the Madrid earthquake, had dumped heaps of boulders in places.

We stopped in our tracks when we saw a wagon coming from the other direction. Settlers should have been going the way we were going, into Kentucky, not out. But this wagon was bumping and lurching toward us across the rocky path, pulled by two skinny and sorry looking mules. My uncles readied their weapons, but as it got closer, we saw that the driver was a boy not much older than me.

He saw us and kept coming, then halted in front of us. He looked like he didn't much care if we killed him or not. He was too tired and hungry to care. His clothes were tattered and thin, no protection from the vicious cold. Yonaguska looked at me and nodded, and I rode up close to the wagon.

"Don't be afraid, we mean you no harm," I said, and the boy looked up in surprise as I spoke to him in his language. "Where is your father?"

"My father is dead," he said in a flat voice. "He took a fever and died, and now my mother is sick too. She's in the wagon. You better stay away from us, or you could get it too."

I turned around and yelled this news back to my uncles.

John Watts cursed.

But Yonaguska had the heart of a healer. He rode up and told me to tell the boy he would try to help his mother. I guess the boy figured that if we were going to kill them we would have done it already, because he made no protest, just shrugged.

We dismounted, Yonaguska grabbing his medicine

pouches, and we walked around to the back of the wagon.

"Stay back," Yonaguska told me, and I kept my distance while he climbed into the back of the wagon. We heard a weak cry, and Yonaguska shouted to me to tell her we were friends.

"Madam," I shouted, "my uncle will help you. My uncle is a medicine man."

I could hear her soft protest, and then I heard Yonaguska singing over her as he worked his cure. *Now, very quickly, Snow, you have just come to step down! Now, very quickly, Frost, you have just come to step down! Now, very quickly, Ice, you have just come to step down. Now, very quickly, you have just come to cool it!*

After a little while, he climbed out of the wagon. "She is sleeping now. The snakeroot will break her fever. Tell this to the boy."

I told him and handed him a bundle of food that Agili had handed to me.

"You are very strange savages," he said. And flicked the reins and drove his wagon on.

Chapter 11

The Horse Thieves

Interview Eleven: James Mooney and James Daugherty Wofford March 18, 1891; Tahlequah, Cherokee Nation

[Mooney's Note: Wofford again has the Royce Map spread out across the table and shows me the rest of the route.]

And then we headed west, into the Darkening Land. Deep into Kentucky, *Gan-da Giga-i*, the "bloody ground." Across the Barrens and into the Great Cave and the Below World.

We followed the Kentucky Road to Flat Lick, right here between Pineville and Barboursville. From there, we crossed the Laurel River here at Moddrel's Fort and traveled west on a hunting path to the Green River and Mammoth Cave, near Liberty here. It was not a happy journey.

I guess we were practicing going west, although we didn't know it then. On the Trail of Tears we came through Kentucky here, at Hopkinsville. Whitepath and Fly Smith both died there. We buried them there. I guess it was the bloody ground, to them and to so many others who died there. We camped at Princeton, right here, and then had to camp here, on the other side of the Ohio River from Golconda, waiting for the river to melt enough to cross into Illinois. It was the worst moment of the Trail.

On that first journey, Flat Lick was where our troubles began. Before Kentucky, I'd never seen a prairie. But here the waving grasses, still bluish-green in mid-winter, were so tall they could hide a man on horseback. And there was hardly a stick of timber big enough to make a fence rail, as far as the eye could see.

After we crossed at the ford of the Cumberland River, we came close to the town of Flat Lick and camped on the outskirts. It was a big town and we wanted to stay well clear of it.

Flat Lick was a salt lick, and buffalo used to gather there by the thousands to lick the brackish earth. But now they, like the Shawnee, were gone. Other game, deer and elk, still came from many miles for the salt, and hunters came for the game. The earth was so grubbed up that not much grew there. Only a few scraggly trees.

We camped near Stinking Creek, which was called that because hunters used to throw the remains of their kills into the creek. The water in that creek had the rotten egg smell of mineral springs.

That night Yonaguska started coughing a bit, and I saw Junalaska and Agili exchange worried looks.

"I think some whiskey might help with that cough, cousin," John Watts told Yonaguska. He didn't care about Yonaguska being sick. I think he just wanted to get Yonaguska drunk and watch him unravel.

I could see the struggle in Yonaguska's face. He always wanted whiskey, and he always knew he shouldn't have it. He was getting sick, so he had an excuse. Whiskey was the best thing for a cough, and it warmed you up like nothing else.

Yonaguska nodded.

And there was only one person who could get it, me. Agili and I were the only ones who spoke fluent English. Watts spoke some broken English, but if Watts or Agili showed up in the town, there'd be all kinds of questions.

I didn't want to bring my horse, because the bandits who rode the Warrior's Path might be right there in Flat Lick. So I walked the two miles to town.

It wasn't hard to find the tavern. I just followed the sound of loud laughter and fiddle music. Agili had given me a beaver pelt to trade for the whiskey. When I entered the tavern, heads turned. No one expected to see a boy with an Indian face in that place. I'd been around groups of white men all my life in Wofford Settlement. Hell, I'd lived with Ebenezer. But this was a much rougher cast of men. Loud, boisterous, dirty, and drunk. Even a couple of ladies of uncertain reputation, dressed in bright frocks.

I walked up to the bar and brought out the beaver pelt.

My voice was squeaky as I blurted out, "Trade this for a jug of whiskey, please."

"Well, I'll be damned," the barkeep said. "A little Indian boy that speaks English. He stands on his hind legs, too!"

The crowd laughed and hooted, and the barkeep took that as encouragement. "Do an Indian dance for us, little Cherokee. Do a War Dance. Where's your tomahawk, little brave?" And he danced around, whooping a silly imitation of a Cherokee war cry.

"I just want some whiskey please," I said. I thought about Alickee slitting this man's throat, or the Colonel beheading him with his long sword. I thought about how much better both my Cherokee and my white family were than these drunken fools. But I had to get the whiskey for Yonaguska.

"You going to drink it yourself?" the barkeep jeered. "I knew you started young, but I didn't think it was that young."

I wasn't sure what to say, because I didn't want them to

get too curious about our group.

"My father is a white man," I said. "We're traveling the Wilderness Road to claim a homestead."

"Why didn't he come in himself?" the barkeep asked.

"He has a fever," I said. And everyone in the tavern drew back.

"Get on out of here," the barkeep said, snatching up the beaver pelt and slamming a jug on the bar.

I took it and ran.

When I returned to the campsite, Yonaguska seemed fine. They'd made a fire and were roasting a couple of rabbits someone had caught. They hooted with glee when I showed them the jug.

"Well done, grandson!" Alickee shouted, and I felt proud.

That night, with my uncles drinking and laughing, I drank for the first time, not a lot, but enough to give me a taste for it. It was so much fun, drinking with men, singing songs, and telling stories. Even Alickee and Watts were for that moment friends. Yonaguska was quieter than usual and not drinking as hard as usual, and we were all relieved about that.

A seed was planted that night that seemed harmless enough and took a long time to grow. Whiskey is sneaky as a snake. It promises happiness and the price comes much later, when it's too late to stop and the damage is done.

Do I still drink? No, not for many years. But in my darkest hour, when other people needed me, I drank. Worse than my father, worse than my mother, worse than Yonaguska.

But that night, I felt so proud to be a man among men, or so I thought. Watts told gruesome stories about how Dou blehead and the Chickamaugans had terrorized settlers in Kentucky. Doublehead took scalps and roasted and ate the flesh of his victims. Watts' father, Chief Young Tassel Watts, tried to keep Doublehead from killing women and children in the famous raid on Cavett's Station. But Doublehead had smashed a boy's head with an axe.

When it came time to go to sleep, Yonaguska told me and Bigwitch to sleep with Alickee and Sequoyah, not with him. "In case I cough," he said, "I don't want to wake you."

Deep in the night, Alickee sat up suddenly. I opened my eyes and he put his finger on his lips and pointed outside. He motioned for me and Bigwitch and Sequoyah to stay put. He grabbed his knife and crept out of the tent. I lay on my belly and peered out through a tiny slit in the bottom. In the flicker of the firelight, I saw Agili, who'd taken the night watch, outside our tent, beckoning. Agili and Alickee crawled silently to Junalaska and Watts' tent. The four men crept toward the grove of scrawny trees where we had tethered our horses.

I couldn't see what was happening, but I heard the muffled cries and thumps of a struggle, and the whinnying of the horses. Then I heard Alickee and Watts yell. Bigwitch and Gola and I scrambled out of the tent and into the grove.

There were three whitemen on the ground, men from the tavern, scruffy and dirty. Their throats had been cut, and in the scant light of a crescent moon I saw pools of liquid forming beneath them. Their blood was the absence of light. That was the first time I saw men killed by violence.

And Alickee and Watts knelt beside them, taking their scalps.

Watts looked up at me and grinned. "You wanted to be a man, little *tsisdu*. Men kill."

Alickee beckoned me. "Let me show you how it's done."

He grasped a hank of the dead man's hair with one hand and cut a deep line across his forehead. He sawed around the hank of hair, placed a foot on the dead man's neck, and yanked, then held up the bloody bundle.

That was the moment I learned that people we love can also be monsters. I'd yet to find out that I could be a monster, too.

Bigwitch stayed and watched. Gola was lapping up the blood on the ground.

I walked away from my grandfather's lesson. I didn't even want to look at him. But Agili called me back to help them hide the bodies. We dragged the corpses closer to Stinking Creek, to a place where deer carcasses had been dumped. I had one leg of a man, Junaluska the other, and the dead flesh felt like a waterlogged tree. We hacked shallow graves in the ground and dragged the bodies in, then covered them with the bloated remnants of the dead deer. The stink of the offal and the sulphurous water was such that the smell of the dead men would not be noticed.

Yonaguska had not come out of his tent during any of this, and when I opened the flap to wake him, I saw that he was drenched in sweat and deep asleep. "Uncle," I said, but he did not wake. I ran to get Alickee, who cursed when he saw him and knelt to rouse him.

When Yonaguska rose to pack his things, I could see that he was shaky on his feet. Bigwitch and I helped him take down the tent and stow his blankets in his bag. We mounted quickly and rode by the weak light of the moon.

At dawn, a river appeared in front of us. It was the Laurel River, right here by Moddrel's Fort.

[Mooney's Note: Wofford points to the spot on the map.]

First we had to get across the river. There was no good way. There was no such thing as bridges back then. You crossed at fords. We had been lucky that the Holston River was frozen over, and the Cumberland River was small and shallow above the Cumberland Gap. This river was not wide but there were steep rock cliffs on both sides and many rapids. The water was freezing cold but not frozen. The last thing that Yonaguska needed was to get soaked with freezing water.

The horses picked their way carefully down large boulders to the ford. The rocks were icy, and the horses' hoofs slid several times. We crossed single file, with me and Yonaguska at the rear. The water was up to the horses' shoulders, and our legs were submerged in the icy water. Bigwitch had tied Gola to a rope and was pulling him along. The dog did not like the water.

The bed of the river was rocky and it was hard for the horses to keep their footing. We had almost made it across when Yonaguska's horse Tooantuh stepped in a hole and lost her balance. She pitched sideways and Yonaguska slid into the water.

If you have ever watched a person almost drown, and for me this was the second time, you know that time slows down and you feel like you are frozen and watching helplessly, unable to move, until finally your body reacts. Yonaguska was already sick and didn't have the strength to fight the water. I jumped into the water and so did Junaluska and Bigwitch, who were in front of us. The current was strong and it was hard to stand on the rocky bottom. Yonaguska was washed down a few yards but clung to a slippery boulder.

"Father," Bigwitch cried out, and tried to get to him, Gola scrambling after him. But the current was too strong.

Junaluska yelled to us, "You two get the horses! I'll get Yonaguska!" He plunged deeper into the river.

I grabbed Gata's reins and Bigwitch grabbed Tooantuh's and Ooneley's reins and the rope attached to Gola and led them to the bank. Alickee wrapped us in sleeping furs.

We watched from the bank as Junaluska reached Yonaguska and grabbed his arm and pulled him through the rushing water, against the current, back to the ford. The boulders were so high on either side of the river that the ford was the only place to get out. It looked like they might both be swept away, but Junaluska did not waver, and finally they made it to land. They both collapsed to the ground, and Sequoyah rushed to wrap them in blankets. Junaluska recovered quickly, but Yonaguska was shivering uncontrollably.

"We've got to make a fire and get him warm," Agili said. The main road continued north, but a smaller road, a hunting path, cut off to the west. There was a blazed tree with Shawnee symbols. Alickee studied it and said, "This is the way we must go. This will take us to the Great Cave."

We traveled a little ways west along the hunting path, until we were out of sight of the main road. I gathered fallen limbs and we made a blazing fire, not even worrying that the smoke would give us away. If Yonaguska didn't get warm, he would die. We stripped him, and Agili and I stripped, and put on dry clothes. But Yonaguska could not stop shivering. We realized we would have to set up tents and let him sleep.

The journey that had seemed so exciting had turned into a bad dream. That night, all of us but Yonaguska sat around the fire, but there wasn't much to say. I took some of Yonaguska's snakeroot from his pouch and made a tea for him to drink, and I sang the prayer against fever that he had taught me. There was nothing else to do.

That night, Alickee took me aside. "Grandson, I would regret spilling the blood of a deer more than I regret spilling those men's blood."

"It's not that you killed them," I said, trying to keep the disgust out of my voice. "Why did you have to take their scalps? When the whites say we are savages, I tell them we are not. But maybe we are."

"My father was a Frenchman's slave. He emptied their chamber pots, until the night he slit their throats. I've seen my people wiped from the face of the earth. My father saw his own mother raped in the temple. No god saved her. A little vengeance, grandson. I take what I can. And who is the real savage?"

"Do you see me that way? Is half of me your enemy?"

"Your father is my enemy. I hated him and hated my daughter for going with him. But you are one of us."

"What do you do with the scalps?" I asked bitterly.

"I hang them on my wall, like something I have woven. And I count them, over and over. Thirty-three."

"When will it end?"

"When the world ends."

Chapter 12

Mammoth Cave

Interview Twelve: James Mooney and James Daugherty Wofford
March 18, 1891; Tahlequah, Cherokee Nation

[Mooney's Notes: It's a cold day and even with a roaring fire in the hearth, Wofford's cabin is cold. He has an old wool blanket wrapped around his shoulders, a pattern of red, black, and yellow stripes. A little threadbare in places. He pulls it closer around him to keep out the wind that whistles through cracks in the cabin's chinking.]

Now I will tell you about the day I got my name.

As we rode further west, Yonaguska was getting weaker by the day, sweating even in the cold, barely able to eat or sit on his horse. But we were closer to the cave than to home. At least at the cave there would be shelter. We rode on, further and further west, toward the setting sun, toward darkness.

We followed the hunting trail west for three days. The country north of the Cumberland River is craggy and wild, with huge boulders, steep ravines, dense thickets. The hunting trail was faint and there were times that we thought we lost it, only to find it again.

On the third day, the landscape changed into what they call "the Barrens." It was a bleak plateau with only a few stunted trees and low grass. Alickee said this was because the Shawnee had used fires to hunt for so long that all of the trees were burned away. However it happened, it seemed like we had left the land of the living.

We could see that the earthquakes had also hit the Barrens. There were craters and cracks everywhere, worse than at home. It looked like the earth might swallow us whole.

When we passed a stomping ground where the grass had been recently trampled, Alickee got excited. "We're in buffalo country now!"

The road forked north and the blaze on the tree pointed to the Great Cave. The sun was setting but we decided to keep riding and get Yonaguska to the shelter of the cave that night. We gathered branches to make torches and a fire when we reached the cave.

We traveled in the dark for several hours. The road led down a steep ravine, and finally we saw the entrance to the cave, a rocky arch with a spring at the top. Water spilled down like a veil across the opening, and a kind of mist hung around it.

In front of the cave, there were three great bonfires burning. Suspended over the fires were giant steaming cauldrons. And stirring the cauldrons were black slaves. One whiteman barked orders and about ten slaves were carrying buckets out of the cave, stirring the boiling pots, and scraping a salt-looking substance out of pots and into barrels. A foul smell filled the air.

We didn't know what we were looking at or what to do. We had to get Yonaguska somewhere safe and warm. We didn't know if the overseer or the slaves would be hostile. We couldn't comprehend what they were doing or why they were doing it in the middle of the night. It seemed like some kind of insane wizardry, some terrible medicine.

If there was a moment that I became a man, this was it. I knew that I was the only one who could communicate with these people. I rode out into the open, toward the whiteman who was shouting at the slaves. As I approached him, my uncles rode forward so that they too could be seen.

One of the slaves was the first to see me and shouted something. All heads turned and work stopped as they gaped at us and we gaped at them. The red-faced whiteman reached for the pistol in his belt, and my uncles drew their muskets.

"Stop," I said. "Please. We mean no harm. We're on a hunt and my uncle is sick. We just want to shelter in the cave for the night."

"Indians been gone from here for decades. Who the hell are you?"

"Cherokee from Kituwah," I said. "Hunting buffalo."

"You're a little late to the party," he drawled. "Get on out of here or I'll fetch some more whitemen to get you out."

"Please, my uncle is very sick. Let us shelter for the night."

By the light of the flames, everyone could see that Yonaguska was slumped forward on his horse, clinging to its mane.

"Bloody savages! Go back where you came from! I don't want my slaves to catch a fever."

I turned to my uncles and shook my head.

Junalaska said, "Tell him we're not asking him, we're telling him. And that before anyone he sends for could arrive, they will all be dead."

As I translated his words, Agili rode between the fires, the slaves scampering out of the way, and my other uncles followed. We all rode into the cave, past the cursing overseer. Gola growled and bared his teeth at the angry man.

We passed through the veil of the falling water and the mist. The cave seemed to be drawing in its breath, as if the mighty lungs of the earth were inhaling.

The cave was so large that we could ride our horses inside, the ceiling far above our heads. In the dim light from oil lamps on the walls, we saw two massive wooden vats, a maze of wooden pipes, and a tall wooden tower. There must have been thirty slaves in there, shoveling dirt out of carts pulled by oxen and into the vats. Water spilled out of the wooden pipes into the dirt-filled vats.

When you enter the Below World, you know to expect trouble. And we had clearly found it. Bad spirits lived there. We thought we might find the Uktena, or the Stoneclads, but this was worse than any monster. Later, when I learned about the Christian idea of hell, I knew I'd already been there.

The slaves were thin and dressed in dirty rags. There were both men and women. They barely even looked at us and didn't stop working. Even the sight of Gola didn't scare them. I think they were too tired to be curious or frightened. They did not talk or sing, just worked without ceasing, hauling and pouring their buckets of dirt. I understand now what mining is, but at that time we had no way to understand what they were doing. It was the first time we had seen these kinds of machines, and the first time we had seen men labor to the point of exhaustion. It made no sense to us.

There was no white overseer inside the cave and no one seemed to be in charge. Yet they kept on. I slipped off my horse and walked over to one of the men shoveling dirt into the vat.

"What is this place? What are you doing?"

Without stopping or even turning his head, he answered me in few words. "Saltpeter mine. Gunpowder. For the war."

I translated to my uncles, and they nodded. "The Americans are fighting the British again," Agili said. "I never knew where gunpowder came from. They dig it out of the earth. It is a thing of the Below World."

"But why," I asked the man, "Why are you working in the middle of the night?"

"Half of us work the night, half of us work the day. We sleep and eat in here. Haven't left the cave since the earthquake."

"They're not allowed to leave," I told my uncles. "They live in here."

None of us could fathom it, but Alickee's body trembled with anger. He remembered his father's stories about life as a slave.

"Ask him where we can go to rest," Junaluska said.

"This cave go down to the innards of the earth," the man said. "River down there. Two dead Indians, dried up like smoked meat. Fawn Hoof, we call the lady, 'cause she got a necklace of hoofs. We don't go down that far. Not fooling with dead Indians. Maybe they your people?"

A shiver prickled down my spine, and I told my uncles about the woman with the fawn hoofs, just as Tsali had prophesied. "But she's dead," I said.

"The dead can speak," Alickee said.

"Just follow the passageway," the man told me. "Down and down and further down."

The passage narrowed on the other side of the chamber, and we had to dismount, but it was tall enough for the horses to go through. Junaluska and Agili supported, really almost carried, Yonaguska.

The passageway was heaped with piles of dirt, and a few slaves were hacking at the walls with picks, heaving dirt into carts pulled by oxen.

We came to a second large chamber, no lamps, completely dark. Sequoyah had prepared some makeshift torches, and when we lit them we saw people sleeping on the cave floor. Men, women, and children. You could smell that they used the privy in there. They couldn't leave. They had no blankets and slept on stone. It was warmer in the cave than it was outside, but it was still damp and cool.

I saw a boy about six years old curled up in a ball, trying to stay warm. I'd never seen a child that skinny. I reached into my saddle pack and pulled out the blanket I carried, an old striped blanket my mother had given me. I spread it over the sleeping child, tucked it around him.

"Tsuskwanunnawata," Sequoyah said. "Worn Out Blanket." And from that moment, that became my Cherokee name. I wanted the name of something brave and fierce. Instead, I got the name of a blanket. Worse than that. When we are grieving for someone who died, we dress ourselves in worn out blankets. Like in the Bible when they talk about sackcloth and ashes. And the name also means a striped blanket. I have always wondered if that was part of the reason Sequoyah gave me that name. Because I am a striped thing, neither one color nor the other.

That was the day I became a man and the day I became a mourner. And ever since then, slavery was something I hated. That's why I fought for the Union, not because I cared about the country that stole my country, but because I wanted slavery to end.

We passed through that sad chamber and into more darkness, descending deeper and deeper into the cave. Strange growths hung down from the ceiling and up from the floor, like icicles made of stone. It seemed like the land of the Stoneclads. Boulders loomed like statues of giants. The earthquake must have shaken loose the piles of rocks that blocked the path in places.

Hundreds of sleeping bats hung from the ceiling, and I was terrified they would wake up and swoop down. Rats as big as rabbits scurried past our feet.

We heard water, and came to another large chamber with a spring and a pool, where our horses stopped to drink. Then another chamber lined with white crystals, white as snow in the dim light, carved into the shapes of flowers and fruits. Rock-blooms. Another chamber with black rock speckled with white crystals, so that it looked the starry night sky.

Finally we came to a deep black river overarched with stone. And in a niche in the wall there was the woman sitting up, her arms crossed across her chest. We had arrived at the land of the dead.

Her skin was dried and shrunken but everything was intact—her hair, her teeth, her fingernails, her clothing. Her flesh was hard and dry, and you could see her ribs poking through her clothes. Two small cords around her wrists held her arms in place. Her hair was short and dark red. She was dressed in deerskin decorated with leaves and vines and wore moccasins of woven bark. Around her neck hung a cord strung with five or six red fawn's hoofs. And a second cord from which hung the claw of an eagle.

Next to her was a satchel made of woven bark. We opened it and found head-dresses made from the quills of large birds, hundreds of strings of beads, the jaw of a bear, and two rattlesnake-skins, one with fourteen rattles upon it. I rubbed at my missing finger when I saw those.

"This was a Beloved Woman," Sequoyah said, and each word echoed hollowly off of the walls, Beloved Beloved Beloved. A song answered from the spirit world, repeating it again and again, fainter and fainter.

In a smaller niche next to her was the dried-up body of a child, a young boy. He, too, was seated with his knees drawn up to his chest, and coarse dark hair sprouted above his eyeless skull.

Sequoyah held a torch up to the markings on the wall above Fawn Hoof Woman—circles and lines and figures of humans and animals. Zig zags that looked like lightning, a spiral like a coiled snake. A winged figure, some kind of bird.

"Maybe these could tell us something about the woman," he said. "Who her people were, why she is buried here. Maybe even a message for Yonaguska, what we are supposed to do."

I have carried the image of Fawn Hoof Woman around with me all of my life, because she seemed an omen of what was to become of all the Indians, not just a dead person but a dead culture. A curiosity. I heard that many years later they displayed her at the World's Fair and at the Smithsonian. So disrespectful, such a sacrilege. And when I talk to you, Mooney, I wonder: am I just another Fawn Hoof Woman, remnant of a dead culture? But our culture is not dead, some of us will not let it die. And I talk to you so our ways will not be forgotten.

We spread furs and blankets and made a small fire with the wood we'd brought. Junalaska and Agili lowered Yonaguska gently to the floor. He closed his eyes and sank into a deep sleep. Gola curled up next to him. There was nowhere to tie the horses, but where could they go? We were all exhausted and settled down for the night.

Chapter 13

The Buffalo Hunt

Interview Thirteen: James Mooney and James Daugherty Wofford
March 19, 1891; Tahlequah, Cherokee Nation

[Mooney's Notes: Wofford is stroking a buffalo hide blanket he has placed on the table. It looks like a child's blanket. He buries his fingers in the coarse brown hair. It seems to hold a memory that pains him deeply. He does not meet my eyes.]

I will tell you now how we killed the buffalo.

There was no way to know when morning came, but when we woke we stirred the fire and lit torches and ate. Yonaguska did not wake, just tossed and moaned and sweated. We debated what we should do. We had come this far, and we had to kill the buffalo. Tsali had been right about Fawn Hoof Woman. We couldn't ignore his other prophecy. But Yonaguska could not be moved. No one said it, but we were all afraid that he would die here. Bigwitch was despondent.

We decided that Sequoyah would stay in the cave with Yonaguska, while the rest of us went on the hunt. He wasn't much of a hunter because of his leg. I was torn. I didn't want to leave Yonaguska, but I wanted to be the one that killed the buffalo. And I thought maybe if we killed the buffalo, it would give us strong medicine to help Yonaguska recover. Bigwitch was also torn between staying with his father and going on the hunt. It was Alickee, actually, who told him he should come. The more hunters, the easier it would be to corner the buffalo.

In the flickering light of the torches, we prepared ourselves for the hunt by going to water in the underground river. It was strangely warm and came up to our waists. The river bottom was smooth rock. All water is sacred, but this river was surely holy, flowing through the Below World. It was impossible to know which way was east, so we just faced Fawn Hoof Woman and plunged seven times.

When I went under, I saw that there were fish in that river and they had no eyes. The fish were white as bone and they had eye sockets, but the sockets were empty. I guess since they lived their lives in darkness, there was nothing to see, no need for eyes. It made me think of the slaves in the chambers above who never left the cave. If they stayed there long enough, would they also lose their eyes?

Sequoyah stayed on the shore and said the prayers. He lit a bundle of tobacco and waved the smoke over Yonaguska and toward us. He offered the smoke in the seven directions, and prayed to the river, the Long Man, *Yunwi Gunahita*, and to the fire, the Ancient Red. He sang the hunting prayer:

Give us the wind!
Give us the breeze!
O great terrestrial hunter,
We come to the edge of your spittle
Where you repose.
O Ancient Red,
Let our trails be directed,
Let the leaves be covered with clotted blood.

As we prepared to leave, Sequoyah took from Yonaguska's medicine pouch the leaves that make the White Drink and brewed a tea over the fire. It would make Yonaguska throw up but he hoped it would purge the sickness from his body.

Junaluska, Alickee, Watts, Agili, Bigwitch, and I started back out of the cave with our horses, Gola trotting behind us. Bigwitch insisted he come.

When we rode through the chamber where I had given my blanket to the boy, sleeping slaves still lay curled on the stone floor, but the boy was gone. We rode out of the cave and into the daylight. It was as if the slaves had never stopped working since the night before, except that the overseer was nowhere to be seen. But I saw the little boy. His job was to scrape the white crystals out of the cauldrons and into buckets. He looked up in sad wonder as we rode past, and I met his eyes. To this day I wish I could have taken him with me, out of that place.

In the daylight we could see that the Green River was just beyond the cave entrance. I wondered if the underground river somehow connected with it. We decided to ride along the river, looking for stomping grounds in the river cane.

We rode through the clammy mist, the effects of the earthquake visible everywhere: sinkholes, rockslides, a section of riverbank that had caved in. It was odd to think that somewhere beneath our feet were the caves and the underground river and Yonaguska, living or dying.

Alickee told us that to kill a buffalo you have to shoot or spear it just behind the shoulder blade, to penetrate the lung. The most skilled buffalo hunters can do it on foot, he said.

"But grandson," he told me, "You stay on your horse. We can't risk you getting trampled."

After a couple of hours, we came to a salt lick scattered with bleached buffalo skulls and bones. A buffalo graveyard. A blustery wind stirred the sparse dry grass and it seemed like we had reached the end of the earth, the Darkening Land.

But a little further on, Alickee spotted some fresh buffalo dung. Our spirits soared as we realized we were close to our goal.

We smelled them before we saw them. The rank smell of wildness, a smell that was already gone from where I lived. None of us but Alickee had ever even seen a buffalo. They were a legend to us, just as surely as Spearfinger or Tsul'Kalu.

The biting wind was blowing against us, so we were able to spot them without them sensing our presence. It was astounding to see the legendary beasts in the flesh. There were only about ten of them, but their sheer size, their massive heads and horns, were almost too much to take in. We had ridden into the world of tales told over campfires.

The fear that pounded through my body was not only because of the buffalo. There was a pack of wolves stalking them. The wolves had backed the buffalo up against the half-frozen river and were circling and snarling, darting in and darting back as the buffalos stamped and blew at them, threatening to charge.

"Get your bows ready," Alickee whispered. I fumbled with the bow I had strapped to my saddle blanket. My hands were shaking but my spirit was sure that I would be the one to take the buffalo.

As we got closer, I saw more clearly the magnificence of the animals. Their heads and chests were massive, their legs tiny in comparison. Their great humps and shaggy manes rose in bunches above their shoulders. From tufted heads grew curved horns that could maul a wolf or a man to death. Long beards hung below their hairy muzzles, and mangy bunches of hair sprouted in patches along their sides.

Our horses grew alarmed, bucking and whinnying. But Alickee said, “Let’s go,” and we kicked them into a gallop, Alickee on Ayita leading the way.

The wolves saw us first and turned to bare their teeth at us. They were thin. It was mid-winter, and this was food they needed. I’d never been this close to a wolf and it sparked a different kind of fear than I’d ever known. For the first time, I felt like prey.

The hair on Gola’s back stood straight up. To him, this was a pack of enemy wolves.

We charged forward, and the wolves danced back, leaving a hole through which we rode, me whooping a war cry I’d never heard but found inside myself.

The panicked buffalos bellowed and snorted as we rode close, looking for the one with only one eye. But they all had two eyes, which confused us. Was this not the herd we were supposed to find?

We formed a perimeter around the buffalo, backing them up toward the riverbank.

I felt like my moment had come. I disobeyed Alickee and slid off Gata and drew my bow. If there was no one-eyed buffalo, we could at least take the biggest, and that is what I aimed for. But I found myself surrounded and half-blinded in a cloud of dust. And when the wolves saw me on the ground, the lead wolf saw me as easier prey than the buffalo.

I saw the wolf come toward me and could not move. I saw his face as he lunged, his snapping jaws, his long, sharp teeth, the luster of his grey fur and the coldness of his amber eyes.

Gola darted forward and got between the wolf and me.

The wolf charged and sunk its teeth into Gola's neck and slammed him down hard by the neck.

Bigwitch screamed and jumped off his horse and ran toward Gola.

An arrow pierced the wolf's neck. It was Alickee's, and he was next to me, pulling me out of the churning herd of buffalos.

"Get back on your horse," he shouted, pushing me toward Gata.

Bigwitch was kneeling by Gola, in danger of being stomped by the milling buffalo or attacked by the wolves, and Junaluska jumped down and grabbed him by the neck and tried to pull him away. But he was screaming and crying because Gola wasn't moving. His neck was broken.

The buffalo were stamping and pawing, snorting and bellowing. Then the bull lowered his head and charged John Watts, who had stayed outside the fray, not even trying to help Bigwitch.

Watts wheeled and fled, and all of the buffalo stampeded through the gap, the bull chasing that coward Watts. We all wheeled around and chased the bull, Alickee in the lead on Ayita. Buffalo are fast, much faster than you would think. The bull caught up with Watts and slashed his horn across the belly of Watts' horse. Blood spurted from its side and it fell, throwing Watts to the ground.

Watts should have been a dead man. But just as he fell, Alickee reached the bull. That fearless stallion Ayita rode alongside of it, shoulder to shoulder, and Alickee rose up in the saddle and plunged his lance behind the bull's shoulder blades, deep into his chest. Junaluska, Agili, and I were a few paces behind, and all three of us loosed arrows into the bull's flanks.

But it was Alickee's lance that killed it. He'd hit the lung and buffalo only have one lung. That's the secret to killing a buffalo. It was gasping for breath, wheezing and choking and whistling, a horrible sound. Life and death hung in the balance. And then the buffalo faltered, his front legs caved, and he fell to the ground with a grunt. He twitched and heaved, drew one last crackling breath, and was still.

John Watts rose from the ground, dirty and furious, and strode over the to the dead bull. He had an arrow in his hand and he drove it into the dead buffalo's eye. "Now it's a one-eyed buffalo," he said.

Alickee jumped off Ayita and grabbed Watts' shirt and put his face about one inch from Watts' face. "This buffalo was brave and strong and gave us his life. You aren't worthy to touch him. You stay away from him." And he shoved Watts hard in the chest, so hard that he stumbled backwards.

Then Alickee fell to his knees before the buffalo and chanted a prayer. *Yunsu, buffalo, my brother, my friend. Forgive me.* I saw that he wept. The blood of the buffalo was on him.

Watts' horse was still alive, its innards spilling out its gored side. Junaluska got a musket and shot him in the head. Watts had walked off in anger and shame. The shot drove away the rest of the wolves watching from a distance, and the rest of the buffalo had disappeared.

Bigwitch, who had stayed behind with Gola, rode up. I could tell by the look on his face that Gola was gone. I felt terrible for him, and I respected him more after that. He had risked his life to try to save his dog. If I hadn't disobeyed Alickee and gotten off my horse, Gola wouldn't have been killed. It was my fault.

Before we butchered the bull, we made a fire. Alickee

sprinkled sprigs of tobacco on the dead buffalo, then cut out its tongue and offered it as a sacrifice to the fire. Agili said a prayer asking for the buffalo's forgiveness:

Yunsu, buffalo, we thank you.
We ask your forgiveness.
O great terrestrial hunter.
O Ancient Red.
We ask your forgiveness.

I knelt beside the buffalo and ran my hands over its fur. It smelled terrible, but it smelled of power.

I was ashamed of my failure and my disobedience, and that I had to be rescued. But Alickee said, "I won't scold you, Tsuskwanunnawata. Sometimes being brave and being stupid are the same thing. You held the line and you got an arrow in the bull." That was the first time he had called me by that name. I wanted my name to be Buffalo Killer, not Worn Out Blanket. I wanted my manhood ceremony to be one of triumph, not failure.

But Alickee bent and dipped a finger in the blood from where the spear had penetrated its eye. He made a streak of blood down my nose. "To honor the buffalo's sense of smell." A streak of blood over each eye. "To honor the buffalo's vision." And a streak across my forehead. "To honor the spirit of the buffalo. And to say that Tsuskwanunnawata is a hunter and a man."

Then he smeared the blood on Bigwitch's face as well. "You have won honor, today, Bigwitch," he said. "You and your dog Gola will always be called brave because of this day. We will tell stories of the boy and the dog who fought the wolf." Bigwitch looked at the ground, tears streaming down his face.

Then we split the carcass lengthwise, gutted it, and severed the hide and gristle and bone from the meat. We carefully wrapped the liver and kidneys for Yonaguska. We cut sections of each leg, the ribs, the backbone, and the brisket. And we kept its great head and horns.

We had brought bags to carry what meat we could, but now we only had four horses, and one would have to carry two men. We could not take all the meat. It would not keep all the way back home anyway. We decided to cook what we could back at the cave and give the rest to the slaves. In fact, we decided we would give the slaves a feast. It wouldn't be hard to tie up that blasted overseer.

We also needed to bring as much of the hide as we could, to make the shields that Tsali had prophesied. And the horns, to make the headdress.

Agili told me to cut off and keep for myself a piece of the hide, so that when I had sons someday I could wrap them in it. It is very good luck to swaddle a boy baby in buffalo skin. So I did, and here it is.

[Mooney's note: Wofford again strokes the buffalo hide blanket as if it is a child.]

The year we walked the Trail to Oklahoma, my wife was pregnant with Mattie Ann. It was the coldest winter I have ever known. We were in Kentucky again, trapped on the Kentucky side of the Ohio River, unable to cross for two weeks because the river was jammed with blocks of ice. Many perished there from hunger and cold, and Mattie Ann was born right there. Even though she was a girl, we wrapped her in this buffalo blanket. It was the warmest thing we had. But there was nothing warm enough to save my wife. She died there. I carried Mattie Ann all the way to Oklahoma. Polly Tucker was nursing a baby and fed Mattie from her breast. But Mattie didn't live to the age of 20. She was always frail, a child of the Trail.

So I can't say it brought me luck.

Alickee said we could chip powder from the horns and give it to Yonaguska. It would make a powerful medicine. When he mentioned Yonaguska, we all grew silent. In the heat of the kill, even I had forgotten that he could be dead. Bigwitch had just lost his dog, and now his father might be dead, too.

Chapter 14

The Friendship Dance

Interview Fourteen: James Mooney and
James Daugherty Wofford
March 19, 1891; Tahlequah, Cherokee Nation

[Mooney's Notes: Wofford hands me a copy of The Cherokee Advocate, *pointing to a headline that reads "Wounded Knee Survivors Continue Ghost Dance." He shakes his head and stares at his hands, not even looking at me as he speaks.]*

The buffalo are gone from the West now, too. That's why the Lakota and the Kiowa and the Comanches are doing the Ghost Dance. Wovoka now is like Tsali was when I was a boy. He has visions and tells the people how to bring back the old ways. Now people are dancing everywhere, all day and all night, waiting for the Messiah. It hurts me to think of them dancing, because I don't believe the Messiah is coming, not now. I don't believe the buffalo will come back.

And now the soldiers have killed people for dancing, at Wounded Knee. It's not enough to take the land and kill the buffalo. Now they are trying to kill a dance.

[Mooney's note: I find myself telling Wofford about visiting the Ghost Dance grounds in January and February, and how the Kiowas and Comanches let me into their dance. I carry with me the photo I took of the Arapaho man kneeling while another man lays hands on him, and I show it to him. I tell him about record-

ing the Ghost Dance songs on discs for Berliner's gramophone, and he is very curious how a rubber disc can hold a song. I sing him one I learned from the Comanches: "The place whence you come, Now I am longing for. The place whence you come, Now I am ever mindful of."]

I have sung for you before, and now you have sung for me. Thank you for that. I think as long as a people have a dance in them, they are not dead. I pity the people who have no dance, or who laugh when others dance. Or think they can kill a dance. Because the dance, like this fire, it never goes out. It will outlast all of us.

I will tell you now about another dance.

After we killed the buffalo, we loaded up all of our horses with as much meat as they could carry and headed back. Since I was the lightest, John Watts had to ride behind me. His body was stiff with anger.

"We should make him walk," Alickee said. "Or better yet, leave him here." But we didn't.

When we neared the cave, we dismounted and crept silently through the woods. The overseer was sitting down, his back leaning against the side of the cave. In the blink of an eye, Agili had him tied up in with strips of leather, one strip over his mouth. His muffled cries went unheard.

The slaves looked on, terrified that something bad was about to happen. But Alickee said, "Tell them to go in the cave and gather their friends. Tell them it is time for a feast."

I told them that and told them to take the cauldrons of saltpeter off of the flames. It was time to cook buffalo.

While the others pulled the bags of meat off the horses and, together with the slaves, set to roasting it on the fires, Alickee and Bigwitch and I rode into the cave to check on

Yonaguska and bring the buffalo horns.

Again we rode deep into the darkness of the cave, as the wondering slaves headed to the mouth of the cave, some for the first time in over a year. We lit our torches and rode deeper and deeper in, to the banks of the underground river where Yonaguska lay.

When we reached the chamber, Yonaguska was still laying on the blankets, but his eyes were open, and it looked like his fever had broken. He was too weak to rise, but his eyes met mine. I was relieved beyond words that he was alive.

We dismounted and Bigwitch ran to embrace his father. Alickee pulled down the satchel with the buffalo head, set it on the ground before Yonaguska, and opened it.

Yonaguska reached out a hand and touched the horns and the thick fur of the head.

"You have done well," he told us in a shaky voice.

Alickee said, "We thought the powder of the horns might make a powerful medicine. And we brought you the liver and the kidneys. You will grow strong again!"

"Yes," he whispered. "Sequoyah can chip some powder into a broth for me. But my sickness is broken, and Fawn Hoof Woman spoke to me."

Alickee and I wanted to hear what she had said, but Sequoyah said Yonaguska was still too weak and needed to rest. We told him about the buffalo feast and the slaves, and he urged us to go while he stayed with Yonaguska.

I knelt and kissed the forehead of my uncle, then Alickee and Bigwitch and I rode back out to the feast.

The smell of seared buffalo was delicious. Some of it was grilled on spits over the fires, the fastest way to cook it. But Agili and Junalaska had also dug pits in which they placed rocks heated in the fire. They put meat wrapped in hide on the rocks and piled dirt on top. This meat had to cook overnight, but we could carry it home with us.

They smashed the bones with hammers the slaves brought them, to get at the tasty marrow. The slaves brought them cauldrons of water in which they threw the bones and scraps of meat to make a soup.

It was one of the best moments of my life, pulling the chunks of meat off the spits and sharing it with the gathered slaves. I made sure to give some to the boy with my blanket. I asked him his name, and he whispered "Corey." I have never forgotten him.

As night fell, we all sat around the fires. Agili and I were the only ones who could speak English with the slaves, but a bond beyond words had been forged.

Alickee began to sing, and Agili and Junalaska and John Watts joined in. It was a Friendship Song, really not possible to translate, but it goes something like *Hey yay yo, Ha way ya. Ha way hey ya ne ho ya ne. Ha way hey ya ne ho ya ne. Way ha!*

[Mooney's note: Wofford sings the song for me in his raspy voice.]

The Friendship Dance is a spiral. Alickee was the leader, and each of us rose and took the hand of one of the slaves and got them to join hands with each other. At first it was a long line, but Alickee formed us in a circle, then made a circle within the circle, and another one within that, spiraling always inward and chanting the song.

Do you know why dances always go in a circle? Because time is a circle, not a line. When whites go on a journey, they go in a line. They go as far as they can go. But the real journey is in the circle. Each time you go around, you go deeper in. And you understand how all things come around and go around.

That night outside Mammoth Cave, the people's eyes shone with wonder and joy in the firelight. I think that Heaven must be a Friendship Dance.

When we finished the dance, one of the oldest slaves, his name was Toby, began a song in what had to be an African language, because I could not understand it, but it didn't matter. Toby would call out some words, and the rest of the people would respond. I remember, it sounded like *Koko koyi, Koko koyi*, something like that. The words repeated, and soon many people took up the song. One man beat a rhythm using some sticks, and Alickee brought out his drum and caught the rhythm and drummed along with it. I took out my flute and learned their song. I know it still.

[Mooney's note: Here Wofford picked up his flute and played a song that was bright and rhythmic, short bursts of sound like a whistle. Then he resumed his tale.]

A few of the slaves stood up and started a dance. Like our Friendship Dance, they formed a circle, but rather than spiraling in, they just kept moving counterclockwise, shuffling and stomping their feet and clapping their hands, singing and shouting. Their bodies were bent slightly forward, like this

[Mooney's note: Wofford stands and bends forward].

And they would stamp and scuff their feet like this.

[Mooney's note: Wofford demonstrates the dance steps, sliding his feet back and forth on the wooden planks].

I will always remember those people and their dance. They were captives, held in a cave, digging out gunpowder for a war they had nothing to do with. They were held in darkness, cold and hungry and weary.

And yet, they danced.

The next morning, Yonaguska told us his vision.

"I died," he said, "and I went to the Above World. It was as if I was snatched up in the talons of an eagle and carried higher and higher, beyond the stars.

I landed in a meadow of the greenest grass, on the summit of what seemed to be a holy mountain. There were many colors, so bright it was hard to see. Fawn Hoof Woman was there, but she was alive. And the boy child was there, too, and alive. She held him on her lap. She was radiant with *I:gagadi, The Light that defeats the Darkness.*

Beside her was the Fire, the Ancient Red. With her was the bear whose jaw she has, the eagle whose claw she has, the two rattle snakes. Grazing in the meadow were many deer, does and bucks and fawns. All were at peace with one another. Nothing could be harmed or destroyed in all that holy mountain.

'What must you tell me?' I asked Fawn Hoof Woman.

'A great trial will come,' she said. 'A day of great suffering. Your people will walk into the Darkening Land. Many will die.'

'Can you not stop this?' I cried.

'I can stop nothing,' she said. 'I can only mourn. I have seen a bitter winter and a long road. A river filled with chunks of ice, the people camped on the riverbank, unable to cross. Women will die in childbirth, and elders will sicken and die. But the Cherokee people will not die. In years to come, they will be reborn.'

'What must I do?'

'You must keep the fire burning. You are the Firekeeper. You must pass it on to the next generation. You must never leave the mound.

And one more thing. You must never drink the rum again. It is unworthy of a holy man. And you must tell your people not to drink it. It will be their ruin. Return, and tell them what I have said.'

And so, I returned from the Above World. My heart of flesh is now a heart of fire. My ribs are the cave in which the fire burns and cannot die."

After that, Yonaguska was never the same. He seemed from that time on only part human, and part spirit. His body became more fragile, but his spirit was more powerful. And he never touched alcohol again, nor did he allow his people to.

He stayed at Kituwah. When the day of the Trail came, I could not entice him to leave, nor could he entice me to stay.

That is why there is an Eastern Band.

When Yonaguska described his vision of Fawn Hoof Woman, I thought about my mother and about mother-love. I thought about Selu, and how she let her sons kill her. And Selu was the source of the corn that feeds us all. I saw for a moment, although in my young man's arrogance I soon forgot, that holiness isn't about power. Maybe holiness is meek as an unloved mother.

And now they keep Fawn Hoof Woman in a museum and display her to the gawking eyes of tourists. Of, for shame, Mooney, for everlasting shame.

Part 4

Wofford's Settlement, Georgia,

Spring/Summer/Fall 1815

Chapter 15

Nacoochee Mound

Interview Fifteen: James Mooney and James Daugherty Wofford
March 20, 1891; Tahlequah, Cherokee Nation

[Mooney's Notes: Wofford is reading the Cherokee Advocate again. The headline this time: Jerome Commission Presses Allotments.]

It's happening again. They're taking our land. They want to divide the Nation into 160-acre allotments, just like they did in Georgia. The men with the surveying chains have arrived. Divide and conquer. Measure and conquer. It's just another way to claim the land for themselves.

Back in the East, they started surveying our land in 1831. But even before that, even before the gold was discovered, there were Intruders. The Woffords were Intruders, my father and uncles and grandfather were Intruders. Even worse were the Pony Club types, so called because they were horse thieves. They also stole slaves and livestock, anything they could get their hands on. They were lawless ruffians. And I became their enemy early on.

That spring of 1815, I rode back to the Settlement filled with pride. Yonaguska had given me Gata, the same horse I rode to Kentucky, and I was looking forward to showing him off. I was looking forward to telling my family stories about my Cherokee uncles and grandfather, who fought under Andrew Jackson in the Creek War and were the heroes of the Battle of Horseshoe Bend. Agili, Sequoyah, Alickee, even John Watts—they were all at Horseshoe Bend. It seemed for once like my Cherokee family and white family were on the same side.

But I was also troubled by Yonaguska's vision and how he and Alickee rejected everything about the whites. Yonaguska was training me to be a Cherokee medicine man, the keeper of our most sacred traditions. And here I was riding back to Wofford's Settlement where my grandfather would train me in his philosophy and Reverend Meeks would train me in his religion.

I was everybody's Indian but my own.

The encroachment of the whites on the Cherokee Nation was most visible in the expansion of the Unicoi turnpike. It was the same route I traveled every year between the Valley Towns and the Settlement. But that spring of 1815, it was being expanded. It went through what was still the Cherokee Nation, but after the War of 1812, our leaders agreed to let the settlers use the road. There was a company, a partnership of whites and Cherokee, who were widening it and building ferries and fords over the creeks and rivers. They were making it so wagons could pass through. The Cherokee leaders and partners had cut a deal that they would let the Turnpike come through Cherokee territory if they could be innkeepers and tollgate keepers and make money off if it. The Cherokee Nation was also supposed to be paid an annual rent, which we never got.

Looking back, it was the beginning of the end for us. It opened up north Georgia and Tennessee to more and more Intruders.

All the local men, the Woffords, McCrackens, Hollingsworths, Vaughans, and LeCroys, were working on the road that summer. There were three whitemen from Tugaloo who built the road, James Wyly, Devereaux Jarrett, and Ben Cleveland. They used their slaves and local white men to do the work.

In the mornings, my grandfather would hold his school under the chestnut tree. About noon, he would consult his pocket watch and tell us school was over. It was time to ride up to the turnpike. And he and I would ride to where the men were working on the road. Sometimes Tony would come too. Jimmy wasn't allowed to go, because Uncle Nathaniel said that since Benton and Charles were out working on the turnpike, he needed Jimmy on the farm to do the chores. This didn't sit well with Jimmy, and I felt pretty bad about it. But there was nothing I could do.

The Colonel was the County Surveyor, so he brought his measuring chains, to make sure that the road was the correct width. Measuring things was a passion for grandfather. He meant to bring order and progress to a land he thought was wasted on the Indians.

I would work with the rest of the men, and grandfather would stretch his chains across the road. And shout orders at everyone else. Even though I was only 13 that year, I could do a man's work, and I did.

I helped to build the road that my people walked to Fort Butler in 1838. That was the fort where the soldiers held us before we began the journey to Oklahoma. I helped to build the Trail I walked.

One afternoon when we got there, the men were burning stumps and piles of logs. In the winter they girdled the trees, cutting a strip of bark all the way around the bottom of the trees to kill them. By the summer, the trees had either fallen on their own or were easier to knock down. These weren't the trees of today, remember. This was a forest that had never seen an axe, and the trees were as wide across as a man is tall. When a tree like that fell, the earth shook.

That day the men were working near the mound in the Nacoochee Valley, by the headwaters of the Chattahoochee. There was a Cherokee town at Nacoochee, but after battles with the Creeks, many of the Cherokee had moved to Chota, on the other side of Yonah Mountain. Here, you can see it on the map. Here's Nacoochee, here's Mount Yonah.

The closer we got to Nacoochee, the stronger the smell of smoke. Ashes hung in the air. It was so humid that your hair would stick in sweaty clumps to your face and neck. The heat of the fires and the thick smoke made it that much worse. I could barely make out Yonah Mountain through the smoke.

We rode up on Wyly's slaves and the men from the Settlement pulling out stumps with teams of oxen. The men hammered iron hooks into the smoldering stumps and attached iron chains from the stump to the team of oxen.

One slave pulled at a leather strap hooked to the oxen's yoke, while another cracked a whip on the grunting beasts. Other slaves grubbed out the remains of stumps with pickaxes.

Jimmy's brother Charles and the two Hollingsworth brothers, my father's white wife's brothers, were using horses to drag logs to a tremendous bonfire. They hollered and slapped the struggling horses. Sparks cracked like gunshots in the heat.

The girdled trees that still stood were white ghosts. It was a landscape robbed of color. A valley of ashes. Oaks and elms and chestnuts lay like fallen giants. The sun blazed overhead and the very ground burned beneath our boots.

We walked over to where my half-brother Will and my cousin Benton were raking up ashes, which they saved for potash, heaping it in metal troughs it would burn you to touch. Will and Benton were covered with soot streaked with trickles of sweat. They grunted in greeting but continued to shovel. I picked up a shovel and helped, while grandfather made a speech, like he always did, something flowery and grand as his big loopy signature.

He pointed at the trees and said, "How the mighty have fallen! O brave new world, that has such people on it." Grandfather was always mixing together the Bible and Shakespeare and God knows what else. "Come here, J.D.," he told me. "Let's count the rings to see how old these trees are."

I knelt on top of the giant stump and started counting. "A thousand years," I said. I thought about what that tree had seen, the memories it held. Drought and flood, snow and heat, herds of buffalo, the ancient ones building mounds and writing on stone. How easy it was to kill so much.

"Heave ho, my lads," grandfather shouted above the fray. He pulled his surveyor's chains from the pack on his horse and commenced to measuring the road.

Benton asked me to fetch them some water from the creek. I took a bucket from their wagon and walked to where the road crossed Sautee Creek near where it flowed into the Chattahoochee. Next to that was the mound with the remains of the Nacoochee council house.

Five men were digging in the dirt at the foot of the mound. I recognized three of them. There was Lucas LeCroy, a Revolutionary War comrade of my grandfather's, and his son John LeCroy. And there was Joseph Wofford, the son of the Tory brother the Colonel had disowned. Joseph had married a Cherokee woman and lived among the Cherokee along the Etowah River, two days ride from the Settlement. The Colonel tolerated him visiting the Settlement because he wasn't even born when the war happened. He and Jimmy's brother Charles had struck up a friendship. But really Joseph was a bit of a scoundrel, like his father. I did not know the fourth man at the time, but later came to know him all too well. His name was Joel Leathers, and he was a thief. And the fifth man I came to know as Absalom Cleveland. He was a lunatic.

They were digging for treasure, and they seemed to have hit upon something. They were shouting with excitement and gathering around one spot.

I knew I should walk away, but I could not.

I splashed across the creek and shouted, "Stop it! Stop it!" They all turned to look at me with scowls of contempt.

"Look, little Indian," Leathers taunted. "We found one of your ancestors."

In the hole lay a skeleton curled in fetal position. It was surrounded by a square of stones. I looked down at its skull, its rib cage, the long bones of its arms and legs, its intact finger bones clutching what looked like conch shell beads. There were pieces of pottery, mostly broken, tucked around the body, and Leathers held in his hand what looked like the head of an axe.

"It's copper!" he crowed. "Keep digging, there's bound to be more!"

"Stop it!" I screamed. "This place is holy!"

"Afraid of ghosts, little brave?" one of the LeCroys mocked. "We're not."

He speared his shovel into the skeleton's neck, and with

a crack the skull rolled off to the side. That crazy Absalom Cleveland picked up the skull and began talking to it. He poked his fingers into the eye sockets and wiggled them. He pranced around with the skull, bobbing and dancing.

I climbed into the grave. "Get away from here," I was screaming.

Grandfather, Will, and Benton must have heard me scream, because as Leathers and the LeCroys were pulling me out, me kicking and punching, Will pulled us apart.

"For God's sake," grandfather boomed. "What are you playing at, J.D.?"

Filthy, snot-nosed and crying, I tried to tell them.

"Nonsense," grandfather said. "No such thing as spirits." He bent to look at the skeleton. "But oh, what a fine specimen." He knelt by the grave.

"Fascinating! Fascinating!" he said. "See how perfectly preserved the bones are. I believe these ancient Indians were shorter than what we see now. I wonder if this was a man or a woman?"

He rummaged around a bit in the crumbled stones and pulled out another object. It was a small skull made of hard black stone, with one eye made of a milky blue stone I later came to know was opal.

Grandfather held it in his palm like it was not cursed, like he could palm death and go unharmed. "Those were pearls that were his eyes," he murmured. "Rich and strange, rich and strange."

I sank to the ground and wept as they all poked at the ancient skeleton. Will came and sat next to me. "I'm sorry, little brother," he said, patting my back. "Don't weep now. There's a good lad."

The treasure hunters were not finished. After grandfather

was satisfied with examining the skeleton, the diggers went at it again, and I heard a cry of glee. Leathers was holding up a string of bright beads.

"It's pure gold!" he shouted. "I knew it! I knew we would find some gold! Not even tarnished!"

Everyone stared, dumbfounded. This was a treasure beyond belief. I had heard my mother say that Cherokee had found gold near the Valley River, but I'd never seen any. Stories were passed down of the Spaniard DeSoto and his men passing through the Nation, looking for gold, but never finding any.

Here it was. And like the road we were building, it was only the beginning. Fifteen years later, the source of this gold was discovered, not far from the mound, and it brought hordes of miners into what was left of the Nation. Gold sealed our fate.

"You will be cursed," I told them. But no one was listening. "It will be the death of you," I swore. But no one cared.

I could hear the hum of the ancestors, like a nest of angry wasps. I could hear their voices in the way the water slapped against the rocks of the Chattahoochee, and the buzz of the crickets in the tall grass. I looked to the mountains, Alec to the north and Yonah to the south. Surely, I thought, the Nûñnĕ'hĭ held council. Surely the Spirit People, the Rock People, the Tree People, would rise up and say, Enough!

But these men, they prospered. And the curse just fell back on me, like my prayer was a slow bird that a lazy hunter shot right out of the sky.

Chapter 16

A Horse Named Warrior

Interview Sixteen: James Mooney and James Daugherty Wofford
March 20, 1891; Tahlequah, Cherokee Nation

[Mooney's Notes: Wofford is studying a letter written in Cherokee.]

This letter is from Redbird Smith. He's writing to all the Keetowah Society members. Now you know I can't tell you much about the Keetoowah Society, Mooney. This is not for you to know. I can't even tell you what Keetowah means. But I can tell you this: we walk the path set out by God, the *tohi. The earth is the LORD'S, and the fulness thereof; the world, and they that dwell therein.* No one owns the earth but God.

Can you believe that I'm 90 years old and they're still trying to take our land? It wasn't enough that they took our land in the East. Now they want this land too. Dividing it up into little squares, just like they did back East. They tell us if we take an allotment, we will be landowners, we'll be rich. No thank you. No Keetowah Cherokee will accept allotments.

See this, here.

[Mooney's Note: Wofford points to a spot on the Royce's map he still has spread across the table.]

This is the Tugaloo-to-Coosa Road. This was a very old

road from Tugaloo, which was a Cherokee mothertown like Kituwah, to the ancient Mounds at Etowah. The road follows the Etowah River to where it becomes the Coosa River near the Alabama border. When Tugaloo was destroyed by my grandfather and General Williamson during the Revolutionary War, many of the refugees took this road and settled near the Etowah Mounds. See here, it goes right though Pine Log village and down to the Etowah. I didn't know that area at all as a boy, but later I came to know it well.

One day my grandfather sent me and Tony right here, where the Tugaloo-to-Coosa Road crosses the Unicoi. The Hollingsworths were working at the intersection. Jacob and Thomas Hollingsworth despised me. My grandfather knew this, and I was angry that he sent us to them. But I was glad to have Tony along.

When I got to where they were working, the Tugaloo men were all there—Mr. Wyly, and Ben Cleveland, and Devereaux Jarrett. The Hollingsworth brothers and Wyly had served under Ben Cleveland's command in the Creek War, and they all liked to tell war stories and brag and impress Cleveland. That crazy Absalom Cleveland was his uncle, and I'd heard that his father "Devil John" was also crazy, but Ben was a straight and narrow man, a soldier.

Wyly, on the other hand, was a stout man with mutton chop whiskers and a loud voice, partial to checkered waistcoats and a big gold watch hanging from a chain. He was at that time the sheriff of Franklin County. Devereaux Jarrett was a rake with a big black moustache. The Tugaloo men did not know me, but the Hollingsworths sure did.

When I slid off my horse, Thomas called out, "Well, if it ain't the little halfbreed and his pet Negro!" He was showing off in front of his former captain and the other wealthy men.

I kept my mouth shut. I was a man among my mother's people, but here I was a boy, and a half-Indian boy at that. And Tony had to be careful to not get whipped by those fools.

Wyly's slaves were digging out boulders with pickaxes. "Go get you an axe, half-breed, and dig with the other coloreds," Thomas said.

I did as I was told, Tony and me both picking up tools.

None of the whitemen were really working. Jacob and Thomas were making a pretense of supervising the slaves, yelling at them to dig harder, dig deeper, while Wyly, Jarrett, and Cleveland puffed on cigars. The Hollingsworths were bragging about their feats during the Creek War. A village they had sacked and burned, all the women screaming and crying.

"Those Creek women," Jacob sneered, "They sure put up a fight."

Tony and I were digging around a huge boulder. It weighed a ton and Tony and I were digging with all our might to dislodge it. I picked up a shovel to try to get up under it, but the boulder was so heavy that the wooden shaft snapped.

"You useless bloody savage," Thomas yelled, and hauled off and struck me across the face. Thomas was a big man but I punched him in the gut, not enough to fell him, but enough to hurt.

"Why you goddamned heathen," he roared, and struck me another blow that knocked me down. The other men were laughing and whooping as he kicked me in the ribs.

He didn't see the man ride up behind him until the man lashed a whip across his back.

He cried out and turned to see a blonde-haired, blue-eyed gentleman on a beautiful black stallion. The man was dressed in a good black suit and a fine white linen shirt, a black cravat around its pointed corners.

"You leave the boy alone," the blonde man roared.

Two other men rode up right behind him, one white and one Cherokee, and behind them three slaves were leading a small herd of horses.

"Martin," Wyly called out in a fake hearty voice. "Please, it's all a misunderstanding. We've been waiting for you. Enough, Thomas, let it go." Thomas and Jacob stood and glared as the new arrivals dismounted and shook hands with Wyly, Jarrett, and Cleveland.

"And who might you be, young man?" Martin asked. He brushed me off and slapped me on the back.

That was how I met one of my truest friends.

"James Daugherty Wofford," I said. "Grandson of William Wofford, son of Benjamin Wofford, son of Nancy Natchez, grandson of Alickee and nephew of Yonaguska, Sequoyah, John Watts, and Agili."

I addressed the latter part to the Cherokee man. But to my astonishment, Martin answered me in Cherokee. "I know your grandfather and your uncles. I am honored to meet you. Oh yes," he said, noting my confusion. "My mother is Susannah Emory, and her mother is Eughiotee. I am Cherokee."

He turned to Wyly, Jarrett, and Cleveland. "This boy is the nephew of great warriors, men who fought the Creeks at Horseshoe Bend. You should treat him with respect."

It was worth getting beat to see the expressions on the Hollingsworths' faces.

It turned out that the other Cherokee man was Black Watt Adair, and the white man was John Bell. They were all wealthy Tugaloo men, partners in building the road. Martin and Adair were a very different kind of Cherokee from my own family in the mountains. Mountain Cherokee were mostly fullblood, spoke only Cherokee, and kept the traditional ways. Adair and Martin were from the South Carolina side of the Tugaloo and were mixed bloods who were educated at white schools and owned large plantations. And slaves. They were Lower Towns Cherokee, the new elite, embracing the white ways. The whiteman Bell was married to Black Watt's sister Charlotte Adair.

There was little difference between Martin and Adair and Wyly, Jarrett and Cleveland. They all planned to open inns and toll booths along the new turnpike and make a profit. For a short while, this worked. But before long, we were all pushed west, first to the northwestern corner of Georgia, where Martin and Adair were part of the building of New Echota. Then a thousand miles west to Oklahoma.

In 1815, Martin was everything I wanted to be. A Cherokee who made a success of himself in the white world. Martin planned to open an inn on the turnpike at Nacoochee, and he also planned to breed and sell horses. That day, he and his slaves were bringing the first of his herd to the new site. They were Spanish mustangs, magnificent animals, all pintos—brown and black with white patches.

"Let me show you something, J.D.," Martin said. "Freddy," he called out to one of his slaves, "bring up Warrior."

Freddy brought forward a horse that was completely white except for a patch of brown across his ears and forehead. We call this a Medicine Hat horse, rare and lucky in war.

"I bought Warrior from a Florida trader," he said. "He'll be the stud for my herd." He stroked Warrior's strong neck. The horses had all been marked with a purple double lightning bolt on their flanks, Martin's sign. "J.D., why don't you ride Warrior, and help us settle the horses at the new homesite."

To ride a horse like that! I was a Cherokee again, a man again. My uncles had taught me well, and I mounted Warrior with confidence and effortlessly turned the herd.

I glanced at Tony, who'd been trying to stay out of the way since the fight with the Hollingsworths. "Can I bring my friend Tony, too?" I asked.

Martin raised his eyebrows at the word "friend."

"Best you leave him here to help with the digging," he said.

And God forgive me, I left him there.

"Tony," I heard Thomas Hollingsworth call out as I headed down the road, "You get back to digging out these rocks with Mr. Wyly's boys." I looked back and saw Tony pick up the axe that I'd been using and start hacking at the dirt around the boulder we'd been trying to move. He didn't even look at me.

I felt a hook of shame lodge in my heart, a hook as heavy and sharp as the ones we hammered into the stumps to pull them out. Tony and I were blood brothers, Thunder Boys. But the first time someone offered me a shinier fruit, I took it. I betrayed our friendship.

Chapter 17

Shoe Boots

Interview Seventeen: James Mooney and James Daugherty Wofford
March 21, 1891; Tahlequah, Cherokee Nation

[Mooney's Notes: Wofford holds another letter written in Cherokee.]

Redbird Smith has invited me to the Keetowah Stomp Grounds for a meeting about allotments. The Keetowah do what is right, no matter the cost. We opposed slavery. That's why we founded the Society in the first place. And now we oppose allotments. We will never sell out.

Back in the East, before the Society was founded, people who had the Keetowah spirit opposed slavery. Alickee and Yonaguska both taught me that, but many of my friends and uncles did own slaves. It was a division from the beginning. And many people opposed Cherokee marrying Africans, but it did happen, like this story about Shoe Boots I'm about to tell you. And like Tony's grandparents, although I don't know if Red Fern and Izzy were married.

Now we call the blacks who walked the Trail Freedmen. And some of us fought in the Civil War to make them free. Some of the Freedmen themselves fought. But I'm getting ahead of my story.

One morning at the Settlement, while we were having school under the chestnut tree, a Cherokee man I'd never seen before rode up with two white men. I recognized the whitemen—it was the Indian Agent Return Meigs, and Joseph Wofford.

Back then, the U.S. government appointed "agents" to deal with the Indians. It was Meigs' job to keep the peace between the Cherokee and the Intruders. Meigs was in his 50s at this time, with a slender, athletic build, a high forehead, and an air of great intelligence. He came from Connecticut and spoke with that Yankee accent. Like the Colonel, he'd fought in the Revolution and believed in Jefferson's plan to "civilize" the Indians. He was supposed to encourage the Cherokee men to take up farming, and the Cherokee women to take up spinning and weaving. He was also supposed to keep Intruders off of Cherokee land, although that proved impossible. The Colonel knew Meigs well and considered him a friend. He'd helped negotiate the treaty to buy Wofford's Settlement.

The Cherokee man was very tall and very dark. He was wearing a red British military coat with great epaulettes, a cocked hat with a long feather, and heavy European-style military boots that reached above his knees. A long sword hung from a strap across his chest. His appearance was imposing, and he knew it.

"Well, if it ain't old Shoe Boots," the Colonel cried. And that is how I met one of the heroes of Horseshoe Bend, a legendary figure among the Cherokee.

The Colonel welcomed Shoe Boots and Meigs and that ruffian Joseph, and led them to the front porch, where Aunt Peggy brought them some cool drinks. The Colonel dismissed the other young people, but he let me stay because I could help translate what Shoe Boots was saying. He told me to tell Shoe Boots who my uncles and grandfather were, and

Shoe Boots grew very excited when he learned I was related to Agili and Alickee. Fine warriors, he crowed in Cherokee. He grasped my arm in friendship.

Both Meigs and Joseph spoke some Cherokee, but I was the one most fluent in both languages, so I translated Shoe Boots' story for my grandfather. It turned out that Shoe Boots was the father of the Cherokee woman named Dorcas who John LeCroy had married and brought to the Settlement a couple of years back. They had a baby named Thomas. I'd heard that Dorcas didn't speak any English, so I'd gone over there and spoken to her in Cherokee a few times. But I didn't know that she was the legendary Shoe Boots' daughter. I also didn't realize that Joseph Wofford's wife Anna was related to Shoe Boots in some way, I think maybe his niece.

Like I said, Joseph was a bit of a scoundrel, and so was John LeCroy. The two were thick as thieves, I think because they *were* thieves. They traveled in the same disreputable crowd. Shoe Boots explained that Joseph and LeCroy had convinced him to sign a paper, which of course he could not read. He thought the paper just meant he was agreeing to allow Dorcas to marry LeCroy. But after he signed it with an X and the marriage took place, he was told that the paper stated that he was giving all of his slaves to LeCroy. What made it worse was that Shoe Boots was married to one of his slaves, a woman named Doll, and some of the slaves he had signed over were his *children*. LeCroy and Joseph took possession of the slaves, but Shoe Boots went to Meigs to complain. Meigs was furious and had the agreement torn up and Shoe Boots' slaves returned.

But recently LeCroy had gone back and taken two of them, a man named Frank and a little girl named Lizzie who was Shoe Boots' own daughter. Shoe Boots was here with

Meigs to get his daughter and Frank back, and he wanted the Colonel's help. He said he knew that the Colonel was the Chief of this place, which was true. Joseph was pretending it was all a big misunderstanding, but I'm certain Shoe Boots knew that he was being two-faced.

When I translated all of this for the Colonel, he glared at Joseph. He was embarrassed that a Wofford would be part of a trick like this. "It would be an honor to assist you," the Colonel had me tell Shoe Boots. "And I apologize on behalf of my family."

The Colonel had Peggy bring some whiskey, and all the men raised their cups and drank. The Colonel got out his pipe, Shoe Boots got out his, and they all had a nice drink and smoke. After a few whiskeys, they commenced to telling stories, careful to choose only those that would not offend the other.

The Colonel bragged about my uncle Nathaniel and my cousin Benton and half-brother Will fighting in the recent Creek War. They found common ground in talking about how much they hated the Creeks. Nathaniel and Benton and Will had been part of the Georgia militia and fought under General Floyd at Autossee and Calabee. The Colonel had helped build and supply Fort Daniel, about thirty miles south of the Settlement, to make sure the Creeks didn't cross the Chattahoochee.

I translated this to Shoe Boots, and then translated his tales of the Battle of Horseshoe Bend, although it was hard to keep up with the flood of his words. The Cherokee, he explained, wanted revenge on the Creeks for all of the Cherokee towns they had burned in the past. Hundreds of Cherokee warriors signed up to fight with Andrew Jackson. My uncles and grandfather Alickee were among the best, he said, with a grin and a pat on my knee.

Shoe Boots said his own war power came from a scale of the Uktena, and I had to explain to my grandfather how rare and powerful that was. Shoe Boots drew from beneath his shirt a medicine pouch and pointed to it, indicating that the scale was in there, but of course he would not take it out and show it to whites. He said that he also had a giant tortoise shell given to him by the Shawano, and that he used this medicine against the Creeks. He put the Uktena scale into the waters of the Tallapoosa and bathed himself before the battle, and he broke off a piece of the turtle shell and burned it, then drew a black line around his men with the coal. Together with Junaluska and some other warriors, he had crossed the river at night to steal the Red Stick canoes and led the Cherokee back across the river to break through the Creek defenses. The river turned red with the blood of the defeated Red Sticks. Because of his magic, he said, he was not wounded and none of his men were killed.

In fact, he said, he was invincible. He was so strong that he could throw a corn mortar over a house, and with his magic power he could clear a river at one jump. This was a few whiskeys in, and he stood and did his famous rooster crow, flapping his arms with a great cock-a-doodle-do. This was why he was also known as The Cock.

My grandfather was highly entertained but blanched a bit when Shoe Boots got to the part about the victory dance, with eighteen enemy scalps stretched on hoops and fastened to poles. But he shouldn't have been disturbed. Benton had shown me a bridle rein he'd made of human skin flayed from the body of a dead Creek warrior. Benton also told me that Andrew Jackson's men had counted the number of dead Creek warriors at Horseshoe Bend by snipping off the tips of their noses. What would a pile of bloody nose tips look like?

I thought then about the eagle that my grandfather had desecrated. Why does every war end in desecration? But it hasn't stopped any of us.

The next day I went with my grandfather and the other men to retrieve Shoe Boots' daughter Lizzie, and the other slave named Frank. My grandfather had sent for Sheriff Wyly to accompany us.

The LeCroys lived a few miles from us, on Hunter's Creek. There was old Lucas LeCroy, who fought in the Revolution with my grandfather, and his sons John and Luke Junior. Grandfather had some debt of allegiance to Lucas from the war. That's why he tolerated the LeCroys.

When we rode up to their homestead, John LeCroy came out on the porch with a musket. With him was Joel Leathers, the man from the Nacoochee Mound. Leathers always wore buckskin leggings and a buckskin shirt, even though he didn't have a drop of Cherokee blood. He wanted to look wild and dangerous, but really he was just mean.

"Put down your weapons," Wyly called out. "There'll be no shooting here today."

"It's a free country," Leathers snarled.

Shoe Boots shouted threats in Cherokee, and the door opened and Dorcas came out, holding baby Thomas, and behind her came Lizzie. The two were sisters, and one the slave of the other. But Dorcas was a shy, gentle girl who had no desire to own her sister. That was all LeCroy. She took Lizzie's hand.

Shoe Boots, not caring about the muskets, rushed up on the porch. "Kahuga," he shouted. That was Lizzie's Cherokee name. But as he embraced the thirteen-year-old girl, he pulled back and placed his hand on her belly, where a bump was visible beneath the fabric of her dress.

It wasn't hard to figure out who the father was. Shoe Boots hauled off and punched LeCroy. Grandfather and Wyly and Meigs ran to break it up and wrestle the guns away from LeCroy and Leathers.

"You don't own Lizzie and Frank," Return Meigs shouted. "Turn them loose, or Sheriff Wyly here will lock you up."

"That's a fine thing," Leathers sneered. "White folks locked up, and Indians and slaves go free!"

"That baby's mine," LeCroy shouted. "I own it."

Joseph Wofford was there and pretending to be on Shoe Boots' side, but the two-faced bastard had been in on the trick to get Shoe Boots' slaves transferred to LeCroy in the first place.

I stayed out of it while they all argued. I got curious when I heard the faint sound of horses whinnying, like they were scared. The LeCroys each owned a horse, but not a herd. I snuck off behind the cabin and followed a short track through the woods that led to a corral. And sure enough, over a dozen horses were milling and stomping in the field.

They were Martin's mustangs. There was no mistaking the bright purple double lightning bolt on their rumps. That dye was impossible to wash off.

And there was Warrior, his white coat glistening in the sun. I hopped the fence and went to him, and he nudged my shoulder with his nose in recognition.

Then he neighed in alarm, and I turned around to see Leathers approaching.

"You," he spat. "Get away from my horses."

"These ain't your horses," I told him. "These are John Martin's horses. I know his mark. I've ridden this horse."

"This here's a white man's country," he said. "Cherokee

got no rights here. No judge will take the word of a damned Indian."

I was resting my arm on Warrior's neck, and his proud beauty gave me strength.

"Mr. Wyly," I yelled. "Mr. Meigs! Grandfather!"

By the time Leathers had climbed the fence, the other men ran up.

"These are Martin's horses," I cried. "Look at the marks!"

Wyly had seen the horse the day I rode Warrior. "Joel Leathers," he said. "You're under arrest."

Leathers looked at me with pure hate. "You'll pay for this, Wofford. You best not forget, because I won't. Not ever."

Wyly rode away with Leathers in custody, and Shoe Boots rode away with Lizzie and Frank on two extra horses he had brought, while LeCroy looked on in rage.

Chapter 18

Tugaloo Crossroads

Interview Eighteen: James Mooney and
James Daugherty Wofford
March 21, 1891; Tahlequah, Cherokee Nation

[Mooney's Notes: Wofford has a book on the table, Lyrical Ballads by Wordsworth and Coleridge. He shows me the name written in big swooping letters on the first page: William Wofford. His grandfather. He opens it and reads a poem to me.]

A slumber did my spirit seal;
I had no human fears:
She seemed a thing that could not feel
The touch of earthly years.
No motion has she now, no force;
She neither hears nor sees;
Rolled round in earth's diurnal course,
With rocks, and stones, and trees.

This poem always makes me think of Alfie. She died way back in '46. Eight years after the last time I saw her. Alfie was the most alive person I ever knew. She made me feel alive. Me and Jimmy. We were all great friends, back then.

There was a big Fourth of July celebration that summer of 1815 at Tugaloo Crossroads, and we all got to go—me,

Jimmy, Tony, Alfie, and the rest of our crew. Only Meley Jane didn't get to go. She was staying with her mother. I'd only been to Tugaloo a couple of times, and it seemed like a great city at the time. It was a day's ride from the Settlement, on the border with South Carolina.

Grandfather always loved the Fourth of July, because he got to relive his glory days from the Revolution. But that year there were special festivities because of the recent defeat of the British in the War of 1812. Also, Tugaloo was the starting place for the new turnpike, and a new inn had just opened. They were going all out with a fair, a parade, and even fireworks.

For us young people, this was about the most exciting thing that had ever happened to us. Alfie had never even been to Tugaloo. She'd never been anywhere but the Settlement. We all piled into the backs of wagons. Alfie's father went, and my father and uncle and grandfather, and Benton and Will and Charles. And Tony was allowed to go.

We followed the road toward the Tugaloo, which was called Wofford's Trail, and could have reached the Crossroads in one day, but the Colonel wanted to stop at Robert Brown's house at the foot of Currahee Mountain. He knew Brown from the war. Brown's wife Jane was Cherokee, related somehow to the Cherokee Walkers, Wards, and Leatherwoods who lived in the Currahee hills before the Woffords came. Currahee Dick, Richard Henson, lived there too. His wife Peggy was Jane Brown's sister.

When the surveyors cut that line between the Cherokee Nation and the state of Georgia, it wasn't like all the Cherokee stayed on one side of the line and all the whites on the other. It was too late for that. The families were so intertwined and tangled. You couldn't draw a line through the middle of a family and say you on one side, you on the other. You couldn't draw a line inside your own self. When the Removal came, everyone had to choose, and for some it was an impossible choice.

That night Bryant Ward was there, the one who was married at one point to the Cherokee Beloved Woman Nancy Ward, and his white son John Ward, who was also married to a Cherokee woman, Catie McDaniel. And Catie's mother Sookie, we called her Granny Hopper, was there.

My father's woman Laughing Gal was also there. She was a woman you didn't soon forget. She was tall and big-hipped, wore men's trousers and a man's hat, and smoked a pipe. She talked really loud, and she could drink any man but my father under the table. She helped my father run the still, and later she opened a tavern on the Etowah. The white women in the Settlement were all afraid of her. If my father's white wife, Will's mother Mary, saw her coming, she ran the other way. Even Alfie was a little scared of her.

The Cherokee women who were there that night sat on the porch, speaking in Cherokee, telling stories of the old days. It might be true that most of the Cherokee men were gone from that place, but the Cherokee women were not. I liked listening to them, hearing them speak my mother's tongue.

And the men drank the whiskey my father had brought. That's part of the reason we stopped there. My father's whiskey was famous in those parts, and he supplied the Browns and all the other families near Currahee and Tugaloo.

Me and Jimmy and Alfie and Tony ran around with the Brown children, chasing the fireflies that rose up out of the grass in the warm dusk, cupping them in our hands and peering through our fingers at their glowing tails. We caught June bugs, those bright green beetles, and tied a string around their leg and held on to them as they flew around in circles. And we chased each other, playing tag in the tall grass. At the Brown's, no one cared that Tony was a slave. He wasn't treated any different.

I sat on the porch steps and listened when I heard Bryant Ward start telling stories about Nancy Ward, *Nanye-hi*, and the Battle of Taliwa. In the famous battle against the Creeks, Nanye-hi accompanied her first husband Kingfisher. She hid behind a log and chewed on his bullets to make the edges more jagged. There were about five hundred Cherokees and twice that number of Creeks. The Cherokee were at first outmatched and fell back. But when Kingfisher was mortally wounded, Nanye-hi sprang up, snatched Kingfisher's rifle, and killed the man who killed her husband. Then she joined the fight and rallied the Cherokee to victory. She was only seventeen when this happened. After this battle, the Creeks ceded all the land north of the Chattahoochee and the Etowah to the Cherokee.

Ward was an old man by this time, but he relished the tale of his famous wife. I'd heard that Nanye-hi and her daughter Betsy sometimes visited the Wards, but I never met them. I wish I had. I liked the feeling that I lived where she had once lived, and maybe she had walked the same trails in her white shawl of swan feathers, dreaming the thoughts that only a Beloved Woman could have.

The next day, we traveled Wofford's Trail to where it intersected with the new turnpike, and followed the Unicoi to Tugaloo Crossroads, where Toccoa Creek enters the Tugaloo. Tugaloo was a Cherokee mothertown, like Kituwah, and the ancient mound was still there along the riverbank. The Cherokee town was burned by Williamson's men in 1776, my grandfather among them. In 1815 settlers were pouring in by road and river to seek their fortunes to the west.

Tugaloo was the biggest town I had ever seen. The main street was lined with shops and businesses with painted wooden signs proclaiming their wares. Mr. Jarrett's general store, a blacksmith shop, an apothecary, a cabinet maker, a gunsmith, a cobbler, a wheelwright, a tanyard. Wagons, buggies, and stagecoaches were jostling for space and kicking up dust.

It was loud and overwhelming, if you were used to the countryside. The clang from the blacksmith's shop, the tap-tap of the cobbler's hammer, the scritch-scratch of saws on wood. The smell of tannin and new leather and sawdust and ale and many horses.

We pulled up behind Traveler's Rest, the new inn, which sat just above the river. It was run by Joseph Martin, who was a cousin of my Cherokee friend John Martin, but white. They were both nephews of the famous Revolutionary War hero Joseph Martin, who had married Nancy Ward's daughter Betsy. There were Martins and Wards all up and down the Tugaloo, some white, some Cherokee.

When we hopped out of the wagon behind the inn, I saw the stepping-stone was a boulder covered with ancient markings, a lot like the Painted Rock I'd seen on the journey to Kentucky. There were circles and squiggles and what looked like animals. I guess Joseph Martin thought it was quaint. But it seemed rude to step on something that had once been sacred. Like wiping your boots on the slabs of stone Moses brought down from the mountain, with the Ten Commandments.

The inn sat on a hill above the Tugaloo River, which was a much bigger river than our Middle Broad. The Tugaloo was wide and deep and crowded with boats. It separated Georgia from South Carolina, and settlers from the coast came in on flatboats. On the riverbank below the inn, fair stalls had been set up. There were makeshift corrals with cattle, horses, and sheep. Tables piled high with produce and goods. And beyond the stalls was the mound, with a small building on top.

The new inn was two stories, with a tavern at one end, and about a dozen bedrooms for guests. Grandfather had rented one room for the girls, one room for the boys, and one room for him and my father and Uncle Nathaniel. Alfie's father was going to camp out in the woods.

We carried in our bedrolls and satchels. It was dinnertime, and the boys were allowed to go down and eat in the tavern, except Tony, because he was a slave. In Tugaloo, the easy friendship between me and Jimmy and Tony suddenly shifted. It was awkward leaving him there in the room, while Jimmy and I went down to join the men. The Colonel had food sent up to the girls, because a tavern wasn't a proper place for a girl, and Tony got some of that. But it wasn't the same.

Still, Jimmy and I felt proud to sit with the men and drink ale and listen to their talk. The men in the tavern were drinking heavily, boasting and arguing and hurling insults, some joking, some not. I was worried about my father because he was already a bit spliffy from the night before. Laughing Gal was right there beside him, in her men's clothes and stove pipe hat, and no one dared to say a word about it.

Ben Cleveland was there, telling stories about the Creek War and the Battle of Autossee. Cleveland was usually very stern, but he was in his cups that night and on a tear.

"Chief Mad Dog and his band of savages were upon us," he roared. "But we drove them back across the Tallapoosa.

We burned that town to the ground!"

Black Watt Adair was also there and not to be outdone. "That's nothing!" he shouted. "I was at Horseshoe Bend. We put an end to the Red Sticks, me and Junaluska and the Ridge and the Agili." I was beaming with pride as Black Watt named my uncle. "We snuck across the river in the dead of night and stole the canoes. The river ran red with the blood of the Creeks we killed."

"That's nothing to be proud of," Charles said bitterly. Every head at the long table turned to look at him. "Why should Cherokee kill Creeks for the whites? Just getting more Indians out of the way."

"And who the devil are you?" Black Watt said. "Who have you ever fought?"

In fact, Charles was old enough to enlist in the Creek War, as Benton and Will had, but he didn't do it. He saw it as a whiteman's war. It's too bad, because Charles would have been a great warrior. He was a head taller than any of the other Woffords, and his spirit was fierce. Charles wanted to be a Cherokee, but he didn't know how. No one had taught him. Uncle Nathaniel had forbidden Aunt Lydia even to teach their children Cherokee words. Charles was angry most of the time, most of it directed toward his brother Benton. They were like Cain and Abel, those two.

"This is my son Charles," Nathaniel told Black Watt apologetically. "Forgive his rudeness. He fancies himself a Cherokee because his mother is half Cherokee, but he knows nothing about it."

"A man with a Cherokee mother is a Cherokee," Black Watt said. "But someone ought to tell him how Cherokee men behave. With honor, with courage. The Creeks have long been the enemy of the Cherokee."

“My mother is not a Cherokee,” Benton said. “Our mother is white. We are all white.”

“You’re a liar and a traitor,” Charles snarled back at him. “You know our mother’s mother. Her name is Susannah and she’s a full-blooded Cherokee. Just because you look white, you deny the blood that runs through your veins.”

“And just because your skin is dark, you fancy yourself an Indian,” Benton snapped. “You’re a Wofford, though you don’t deserve the name.”

Uncle Nathaniel was sitting between the two of them like a fence. My father got up and lurched over to Charles and put his arm around him. He clumsily patted Charles on the back. “It’s alright my boy. We’re all part of this family.”

But Charles reached across and shoved Benton so that he fell backwards to the floor. Charles was the Wofford you didn’t want to fight. He was a natural athlete, always the fastest runner in a footrace, the one who could lift the heaviest weights, throw a ball the farthest. And deliver a punch that would knock you out.

Uncle Nathaniel and Black Watt grabbed Charles by the shoulders and hauled him, thrashing, out of the tavern.

Benton got up and resumed his seat, trying to pretend that nothing had happened. But his red white face spoke his anger.

“Do you remember, Benton,” Cleveland said, trying to smooth it over, “the Battle of Camp Defiance? The savages were hiding in the swamp like cowards. When they sprang at us from the undergrowth, you fought like the devil.”

“The Creeks got what they deserved,” Black Watt was quick to agree. Everyone was on the same side again, and Jimmy and I leaned forward and ate it all up, all their tales of valor. I ignored my father, who was getting sloshed at the other end of the table. I wished he was more like Cleveland or Adair.

A short time later, a boy poked his head in the door and shouted, "Charlie Wofford is challenging any man to a cudgel fight. Place your bets!"

And the tavern emptied out as men rushed into the street, a few to fight, most to watch and bet, Jimmy and I among them.

Oh yes, cudgel fighting was a sport back then, and Charles was the best. The goal of a cudgel fight was to break your opponent's head open with a stout stick. When blood was drawn, the crowd would shout "a head!" The blood had to run at least one inch to count. Cudgeling was a bit like sword fighting, and Charles had benefitted from the Colonel's lessons.

There were a lot of strangers in Tugaloo that day, so they didn't know that it was foolish to go up against Charles. You can be sure that Benton didn't volunteer. He stayed inside the tavern. A burly farmer from across the river stepped up, and bets were placed. The large crowd formed a ring around the two fighters. Joseph Martin, the tavern keeper, was referee. Charles scowled at his opponent, his rage itching for a target. I think he was seeing Benton as he gave that poor fellow the drubbing of his life.

The farmer was stouter than Charles, but Charles was faster, more agile, and fueled by fury. He rained blows upon the man's face and skull. A crack across the forehead, a smack to the jaw, a whack on the top of the skull. The man was blinded by the blood, and the crowd roared, "a head, a head!" Joseph Martin and a couple of other men had to pull Charles off the bleeding man. The locals won their bets and collected their money from the strangers. No one else volunteered to fight, and Charles stalked off alone into the night.

The next morning, I wanted to go see the Tugaloo mound, and Jimmy and Alfie agreed to come with me. Tony had to stay behind to help the Colonel and my father and Uncle Nathaniel do some trading at the fair.

It wasn't far from the inn. Even in the early morning, it was hot and buggy along the river. Like always, I carried my blow gun slung on a strap across my shoulder, and my satchel with my flute and my knife.

We scrambled up the side of the mound and saw that there was a kind of gazebo at the top, which looked like it had been built recently, maybe for the fair.

Yonaguska had taught me that Tugaloo was the most important mothertown after Kituwah, and that it also had a fire burning inside the mound. It made me sick to think I was standing on the place where the council house once stood.

Alfie bent down and picked pink fireweed and made a bouquet fit for fairies. Fireweed only grows in burned places. Beauty from ashes. She pinched the small stems between her finger and thumb. There was no shade on the mound, the only trees a few saplings. Alfie had forgotten to wear her bonnet, and sweat was glistening on her nose and the sun was bringing out her freckles.

Jimmy was kicking at rocks and picking them up and throwing them off the sides of the mound.

"Stop it, Jim," I said. "Don't you know that people died here?"

"People die everywhere," Jimmy said.

"Our own grandfather," I said. "He came here, he told me, with Colonel Williamson. He killed the people that lived here. They burned the village to the ground."

"I don't like it," Jimmy said. "But there's nothing I can

do about it."

We looked out over the river, the canebrakes filled with birds. I caught a glimpse of green. It was a Carolina parakeet, just like the ones the Colonel had.

I took out my flute and played a sad song I made up in my head, a song about a mother bird who lost her chicks. It was almost like my song called the parakeet, because it flew up and perched in one of the small saplings on the mound.

"You know what they used to call this valley?" I asked them. "Valley of the Green Birds. Estatoe. So many birds there were. The people travelled in their long canoes up this river and came to Tugaloo to trade food and skins and baskets and tools. But no one ever sold a living bird."

I blew a wrong note on my flute on purpose, a note as harsh as the green bird's cry, and the bird took to the sky and flew low over the river. In the distance, dark bodies worked in new fields along the riverbanks, planting cotton where the canebrakes used to be. Where many things grew, now only one thing would grow.

I heard the crunch of boots on dirt and turned to see a portly man lumbering up the side of the mound. His hair was loose and messy and he carried a long hunting musket. It was Absalom Cleveland. He was followed by a skinny, mottled cur.

He grunted as he reached the top, and when he looked up and saw us he stood stock still, staring. He was staring at Alfie. I didn't know much about lust at that point in my life, but I saw the way he was looking at her, Jimmy did too, and we both moved closer and put a protective arm around her.

Absalom walked closer, leering. He raised his gun and pointed it at us. "You'll be going now," he said. "You'll be leaving the lass with me."

Jimmy pulled Alfie close, shielding her with his body. I rose and held my hands out, palms down, and walked slowly toward him. The dog bared its teeth and Absalom squinted into the gun sight.

As I got closer I saw his unkempt beard, his tangled hair, the food stains on his loose shirt. He swayed slightly like he was standing on the deck of a ship.

I knew what I had to do.

I began to speak in Cherokee, total nonsense, but he didn't know that. I chanted, moving closer and closer to him.

"Are ye one of them?" he asked. "Ye've come back, have ye?"

"I am the guardian spirit of the mound." I chanted in English, and I started to dance. I danced in a circle around him, spinning and stomping and singing in Cherokee.

The dog's ears were laid back in fear, and the big man fell to his knees and moaned. A string of drool hung from his mouth. He wailed like a small child.

"This mound belongs to the spirits," I chanted in English. "You can never come here again. Now go!"

Absalom pushed to his feet and ran clumsily down the side of the mound, the dog right behind him.

Jimmy released Alfie and we all just looked at each other for a minute. Then Jimmy chanted "I am the spirit of the mound" in a mock eerie voice. We laughed and couldn't stop laughing. Jimmy started to dance around in a circle and Alfie and I joined in, and we danced circles around each other and laughed and laughed until we collapsed on the ground.

"What were you really saying in Cherokee?" Jimmy asked.

"Your mother is a whore and your father is a whoremaster," I said, and we all collapsed in laughter again.

“I hope we didn’t anger the real spirits,” Alfie said, and I felt a pang of guilt at that.

She was still holding her small bouquet. She separated it into two bouquets and handed one to Jimmy and one to me. “For my gallant knights,” she said. And both of us blushed and shoved the fireweed deep in our pockets.

[Mooney’s Note: Wofford opens Lyrical Ballads to a different page and shows me the dried flowers, just brown stems and leaves now, but once, I know, the vibrant pink of fireweed.]

I can’t touch them now, they’d fall apart. But I keep them still, so I always know where they are.

Chapter 19

We've Been Set Free

Interview Nineteen: James Mooney and James Daugherty Wofford
March 22, 1891; Tahlequah, Cherokee Nation

[Mooney's Notes: Wofford has an old broadside spread across the table. When I look closer, I am surprised to see that it is an early copy of the Declaration of Independence.]

Look what I got right here. This is a collector's item, one of the first batch ever printed. It was one of my grandfather's great treasures. It's funny that I was the one to inherit it. This was my inheritance from him, that and everything else in his cabinet of curiosities that no one else wanted. They wanted the land. I wanted the rocks and plants and books and papers. I wanted these words. I still read them every Fourth of July, just like he did. And I wonder if they'll ever come true.

I saw my first slave auction that Fourth of July in Tugaloo. After our scare with Absalom Cleveland on the mound, we went down to the fairground. It was crowded with visitors in town for the celebration. On the banks of the river, settlers clambered off of flatboats and heaved trunks filled with goods into wagons. The Unicoi was already attracting a stream of Intruders.

Along the row of livestock sellers, I saw John Martin with his now-recovered herd of Spanish mustangs in a makeshift corral. His slaves Rup and Fred were watering and grooming the horses, while Martin negotiated with potential buyers.

"Osiyo, J.D.," he called out as I approached. "Or should I call you Tsuskwanunnawata?"

I grinned and grabbed his arm in greeting. His gold ringlets hung past his shoulders, as pretty as a girl's. He was the whitest Cherokee I ever knew.

"I was in the Valley Towns trading," he said. "I heard stories of the boy who rescued the drowning child from the river, and the great buffalo hunt. You are famous, my boy!" He slapped me on the back. "I'm going to need some help with the horses at Nacoochee. Do you think your grandfather could spare you to work for me sometimes?"

I swelled with pride. "When can I start?"

"You could exercise them for me right now, if you want." He opened the gate of the corral and beckoned me in. "Pick one and ride."

I chose the nearest mustang, mounted bareback, and headed through the gate. I had to take the fairgrounds at a slow trot, and I'm not going to lie, I wanted to be seen. Jimmy and Alfie, who had walked on while I talked to Martin, turned in wonder as I trotted past. I waved at them and also at the Colonel and my father and Uncle Nathaniel, who were making their rounds at the fair, Tony trailing behind them. When he saw me ride past, he gave me a huge grin. But I felt a pang of guilt, riding Martin's horse past Tony, just like I rode away and left him that day on the Unicoi.

I trotted up to the main street and threaded my way through the crowd of wagons and carriages. At the edge of town I broke into a canter and then a gallop down the new turnpike. I loved to go fast and feel my leg muscles tight against the horse's sides. It's like flying, tearing through the air, released from the earth and the creep of human feet.

When I returned to the fairgrounds, I saw a crowd gathered around a platform. It wasn't time for speeches yet, but as I got closer I saw that it was a slave auction. I saw my father and Nathaniel in the crowd. And Tony with them. I saw Alfie's father, who had told us that he was going to buy a slave to help Alfie's mother with the housework. I saw Benton and Will. And I saw John Martin.

Next to the platform huddled a group of about twenty slaves. On top of the platform, a whiteman in checked trousers and a clashing striped waistcoat was shouting. Next to him stood a young black man wearing nothing but linen trousers. The slave trader had greased him up to show off his strong muscles.

"Who will give me $700 for this fine specimen of a Negro?" the slave trader barked. "The bidding starts at $700."

"$725," Martin called out.

"This Negro is a skilled cotton hand. Yessirree, none better! He can plant it, he can harvest it, he can work a cotton gin."

"$750," yelled Benton.

The Black man had no expression on his face. His gaze was fixed far above the crowd, into the nothingness.

"Turn around, Henry," the slave trader said, and the man turned his back to the crowd. "Not a mark on him. Never been whipped. This here's an obedient Negro."

Benton and Martin continued to bid against each other, and Martin won the bid at $850. The Black man climbed down from the platform, and Martin led him by the arm to the corral. I followed on the horse and slipped down.

"My father needs me," I told him. "I have to go." Oh, how I wanted to ride those horses all day long. But it didn't feel right anymore.

I walked back over to the auction and found Tony, standing next to Jimmy. Alfie was standing next to her sister Mary Polly. I wanted to say something to Tony, but I could think of nothing to say. At the Settlement, we all pretended slavery wasn't that bad. More like just having servants who were part of the family. That's the lie we lived with.

We all watched as a young woman not much older than Alfie climbed up the platform. She was a pretty, round-figured girl, her hair in neat plaits, a trembling smile on her face. She kept looking back at another slave in the group to be sold. The older woman was silently crying. She must have been the girl's mother.

"This here's Easter," the slave trader said. "She's fourteen years old and she's a good girl. A good hand around the house, and good breeding stock. Who will give me $350 for Easter?"

"$375," Alfie's father called out. "But let me get a good look at her."

James McCracken climbed up on the platform. "Open your mouth," he said, and the trembling girl opened her mouth while he inspected her teeth. He squeezed Easter's buttocks through her dress and looked down the back of her dress to make sure there were no scars.

Alfie's face was red with shame.

"$400," a man in the front row shouted.

"$425," said James McCracken, and the deal was sealed. He led Easter down and presented her to Alfie and Mary Polly. "This here's my daughters," he told Easter. "You do as they say [']til we get home to their mother." He walked off and left Easter with the girls.

Easter curtsied but kept looking over her shoulder. "They

sellin' my Ma now," she said. "Might I watch who buys her?"

"That would be just fine," Alfie said, very formal and very awkward. She'd never owned a slave before and was trying to figure out how you were supposed to act.

Easter's mother climbed up on the platform. She was powerfully built and very strong in the way she carried herself, but the tears still streamed down her face.

"You stop that crying right now," the slave trader hissed into her ear, like no one would hear it, but everyone did. "You wipe those tears or I'm-a wipe '[']em for you."

He turned to the crowd with a big fake smile. "My apologies, ladies and gentlemen. Renata here's just a bit out of sorts cause we done sold off her daughter. But this here's a first-class slave. Strong as an ox and still in her breeding years. She can cook and clean and she can work in the field as good as any man."

Renata stood there while men called out numbers, and they settled on $750. It was Mr. Jarrett who led her away.

"She won't be so far," Alfie told Easter. "The Jarrett place is only two days' ride from our place. Why, you can come and see her any old time you want."

Easter looked at Alfie. "You got a lot to learn, Miss," she said. "It don't work like that."

Jimmy and Tony and I followed my father to where my grandfather was watching a demonstration of a cotton gin. My grandfather knew that buying a cotton gin was the key to his grand plan to make his fortune growing cotton. We stood and watched as a man showed the onlookers how it worked. It was a wooden machine with two rollers in the middle turned by a crank. The man stuck a wad of cotton in one end and cranked. The first roller had hooks that pulled out the cotton seeds, and the second roller had brushes that smoothed the cotton out. When it came out the other end, the cotton was white and fluffy as a cloud.

The man held it up to show the crowd. "This here is white gold," he said. "Used to be, the uplands cotton that grows around here took too long to clean. Wasn't worth the effort. All that's changed now. This gin makes short work of that uplands cotton. You get some slaves to plant and harvest, and you got yourself a plantation. You got yourself a big white house with some columns, just like they got in Charleston and Savannah."

"I'll take it," my grandfather said, and that was that.

Benton and Will fetched the wagon to carry it. Benton had just bought two slaves, Allen and Ben. They would be the start of his own cotton plantation. It was never as big as those ones in Charleston and Savannah, but he got pretty rich using slaves to work his cotton.

The Colonel was gleeful. "We're on our way now, my boys," he boomed. "King cotton will make us kings."

He forgot that the whole point of his revolution was not to have any more kings.

Jimmy and Tony and I watched as they loaded it up.

"Crane," Jimmy said. "I'm real sorry about all this. This ain't us."

"I know,' Tony said. "It don't matter none."

But it did.

That night the Fourth of July festivities began with a parade. All of the surviving soldiers from the Revolutionary War marched in their old uniforms—blue coats with red trim and gold buttons, white vests and white breeches, black leather caps with a tassel on top and a silver crescent with the motto "Liberty or Death."

My grandfather marched at the head, and my father behind him played the drum just as he had in the war. Others played fifes and drums and sang along to "Yankee Doodle Dandy." All of the Colonel's old war comrades, Jacob Hollingsworth and George Vaughan and Captain Little and Captain Grant, were there.

Behind the soldiers of the Revolution, the soldiers of the recent Creek War marched—Captain Cleveland, Captain Wyly, the Hollingsworth brothers, John Vaughan, William Grant, Nathaniel and Benton and Will and Mr. Jarrett. Black Watt Adair did not march. There was no Cherokee contingent.

Bringing up the rear was Absalom Cleveland, the madman from the mound, dressed in his late father's Revolutionary War uniform and leading a white albino bear on a chain. The Bear had been burned. One side of his face and upper body was a web of scars where no fur grew, and he was missing his eye on that side. The socket was sealed shut with a ropy scar.

There was a metal ring around his neck where the chain attached. It looked too tight. The Bear lumbered along on all fours, sometimes stopping and rising on two legs to look at the people who were looking at him.

Absalom was marching in an exaggerated manner, lifting his knees too high as if mocking the march, and pulling at the Bear each time he stopped. The Bear's one good eye, a pink albino eye, scanned the crowd. It seemed both indifferent and menacing.

In one hand Absalom carried a whip, and when the Bear stopped, he cracked the whip on it. The Bear let out a moaning bark.

Ladies shuddered and little boys threw rocks at him, which he swatted away like flies.

No one else recognized the Bear, but I did. The madman had captured the Chief of the Bears, the Great White Bear of Kuwahi, who healed the wounded in his magic lake. The Bear that Tsali was looking for, the Bear that could bring back the old ways. The Bear I'd seen in my vision. The Chief of Bears, led on a chain, mocked by an ignorant crowd.

This madman had burned him out. No, we had burned him out. I thought of the smoldering stumps along the new turnpike, the fires we lit to clear the way for wagons.

I still had my blowgun with me from that morning's walk. I stood behind a post on the porch of Jarrett's store. Thwip-thwip. I hit Absalom in the neck. He howled and grabbed his neck, and the people thought it was part of his shenanigans. Thwip-thwip. I hit him in the hand that held the chain. I saw the blood bloom on his hand as he dropped the chain, but no one else noticed.

They were too busy watching the Bear, which, free from the chain, stood on two legs and bellowed, then turned and loped down the road into the woods, dragging the chain behind him.

Seeing that he was gone, the crowd turned and followed the parade, while Absalom ran after him, howling and bleeding.

Yonaguska told me a story once about a hunter who got lost, and a bear took him in and fed him and made him part of the family. The man stayed with the bear so long, he began to grow hair all over his body. He was becoming a bear. His people found him one day and killed his bear father for meat and took the hunter home. But he couldn't live among his people anymore. He died.

Sometimes I have been that bear-man. Sometimes I have wanted to die.

The parade made its way down to the fairgrounds, and I followed. They marched all the way to the mound. That's what the gazebo was for. It was festooned now in ribbons and banners and flags, all red, white, and blue.

My grandfather and the other important men of the town, Wyly and Jarrett and Ben Cleveland, climbed the mound and stood on the gazebo. It was a tradition to recite the Declaration of Independence on the Fourth of July, and since the Colonel knew it by heart, he was chosen for the honor.

"We hold these truths to be self evident," he recited. "That all men are created equal, and endowed by their Creator with certain inalienable rights, among these life, liberty, and the pursuit of happiness." And on he went. He truly believed these things, and if he saw any contradictions in his own life, he never admitted it. He just looked the other way.

I wondered then if he thought about the Cherokee village that was here, the village he himself had burned during the Revolution. He was standing on the mound, king of the hill. Finders keepers, losers weepers, that's what people say. Already at that time, no one remembered what the mound was for, or the people that lived there.

He recited the entire Declaration of Independence, even the long boring parts. And he ended with a rousing speech of his own, about how he traveled to the White House to meet Thomas Jefferson, how the British had just been defeated again in the War of 1812, and how we were all on the brink of the greatest prosperity the world had ever known. How Wofford's Settlement was just the beginning of Georgia's expansion and triumphs.

"We've been set free," he shouted, and everyone cheered.

There were more speeches and prayers, and then a 13-

gun salute. Finally, as night fell, the fireworks. None of us had ever seen fireworks before, and we watched in wonder as shells burst above us into great flowers of light. It seemed a holy thing, as if man had briefly done what only God can do—throwing stars around like playthings. Mastering the thunder and lightning.

Jimmy and Alfie and Tony and I huddled together like worshippers, heads thrown back to watch new stars light up the night. Then fade to black.

Chapter 20

Toccoa Falls

Interview Twenty: James Mooney and James Daugherty Wofford
March 22, 1891; Tahlequah, Cherokee Nation
[Mooney's Notes: On the table sits an oval-shaped, flat stone with a hole in the center.]

I'll bet you don't know what this is. Or maybe you do, since you're Irish. It's a hag stone. And I'll tell you how I got it, and why I keep it.

On our way home the next day, the Colonel wanted to visit the great waterfall on Toccoa Creek. He'd taken it into his head that he wanted to live there. A man named Gotcher had built a house next to the falls, and he wanted to buy it.

We were all excited. I'd been to the falls a few times before. The shoals on Nancytown Creek were nothing compared to the Toccoa Falls, which poured over a high cliff into a pool deep enough to swim in.

Toccoa was a famous place among the Cherokee, a sacred place. Rarely do you see water fall from such a height. There were many legends of the Spirit People who inhabited it. There'd been a Cherokee village of Taucoe, but it was wiped out when Tugaloo was wiped out.

We all piled into the wagon, the Colonel at the reins and the young people in the back. Tony got to come, and the Colonel let me and Jimmy take turns up front.

When we got there, the Colonel went to find Mr. Gotcher, and we all pulled off our shirts and boots and ran into the water, laughing and splashing. It had been so hot for days, and the cool water felt like heaven. We splashed our way to the curtain of water and stood beneath it. The water pounded the top of my head and got inside my nose and mouth.

Jimmy and Tony and I were wrestling and pushing each other's heads under the water, like boys do. I looked up and saw Alfie standing beneath the falls. She stood there in her wet chemise and pantaloons. I'd gone swimming with her a thousand times, but now I saw her new curves, the hint of breasts and hips. Her red hair stuck to her neck and shoulders. Our eyes met and something passed between us, like a veil had fallen and we saw each other for the first time.

I turned and saw that Jimmy had stopped roughhousing and was watching me watch Alfie. I saw the anger in his eyes.

"J.D., I dare you to jump off that cliff into the water," Jimmy said. "I bet you won't. I bet you're too scared."

"Jimmy, it's too high," I said. "Don't ask me to do that."

"So that's how it is," he said. "You tell all these stories about how brave you are, how you hunted buffalo and killed a man in Kentucky. I say jump, or you're a damned coward."

Everyone was listening now.

"Jimmy," I said. "Why are you doing this?"

"Because I'm tired of your bragging, that's why," he said. "I'm tired of your damned Indian lies."

No boy can take being called a coward. But I also felt that I owed Jimmy something, like our brotherhood required the sacrifice. Like I should let him win. I splashed to the shore, pulled my boots on, and started up the steep hill to the side of the falls.

Alfie followed me. Jimmy called after her, but she didn't turn around.

"Leave me alone, Alf," I said. "I have to do this. Go back."

"I won't go back," she said. "If you're going to do this, I'm doing it too."

"Don't be daft, Alfie. It's a death jump."

"Then we'll jump together," she said. Alfie was like that, so stubborn.

We clambered over boulders in our wet clothes. The sun was glaring, the insects biting. Both of us were sweaty and out of breath when we made it to the top. We stepped out onto a flat rock beside the stream, holding back from the edge. I looked at her and knew for the first time what it was to love.

"Elfie," I said foolishly, in my theatrical young man's rush. "Since I'm about to die, I need to tell you this. Even if I could live a hundred years, you're the only girl for me."

I called her Elfie because she was small and her ears were just a wee bit pointed at the top. But it was more than that. She was a spirit of the woods. She belonged in the forest and in the creeks. She was a wild creature crammed into a proper dress and a proper life.

I bent and kissed her, in the awkward and unforgettable way of a first kiss. It was a seal that never broke, though I walked a thousand miles away from her. She was mine and I was hers.

Alfie always wore around her neck a cord from which hung a stone with a hole at the center. This stone. That day, she untied the cord and placed the stone in my hand and curled my fingers around it.

"It's yours now," she said. "A hag stone keeps you safe. Even if you jump off this cliff, the hag stone will protect you. Will you wear it for me?"

I tied it solemnly around my neck, like a promise.

But before I got the chance to jump dramatically to my death, I heard chatter and laughter coming through the trees. Jimmy and Tony and Mary Polly and Charlotte pushed through the bushes.

"I couldn't let you do it," Jimmy said. "I'd have no one left to fight with."

"I didn't think you would," I said. "I knew it was all in jest." But that was a lie.

I saw Jimmy spot the stone around my neck, and I saw him look away.

We all took turns peering over the cliff. My heart was still beating too fast from my kiss with Alfie, and I couldn't meet her eyes.

"The Nûñnĕ'hĭ live here," I told my friends. "They're watching us right now. My uncle told me that a Nûñnĕ'hĭ woman lives beneath the water, and she beckons to men and they jump to their death. Listen," I said. "You can hear the Nûñnĕ'hĭ drumming right now." We all grew silent, and I swear I heard a faint drumbeat.

"I hear it," Alfie's sister Mary Polly squealed.

"You and your Nûñnĕ'hĭ," Jimmy scoffed. "You're just trying to scare the girls."

"Sing us a song, then, Alfie," Charlotte said. "For courage."

"It will be a sad song," she said. "A song about a man who's been captured by the Fairy Queen." And she began,

"But how shall I thee know, Tam Lin,
Or how my true love know,
Among so many uncouth knights
The like I never saw."

Alfie had a mountain voice, the lilt of Scotland still in it. Reedy like a flute, high and clear and true. I hear it to this day.

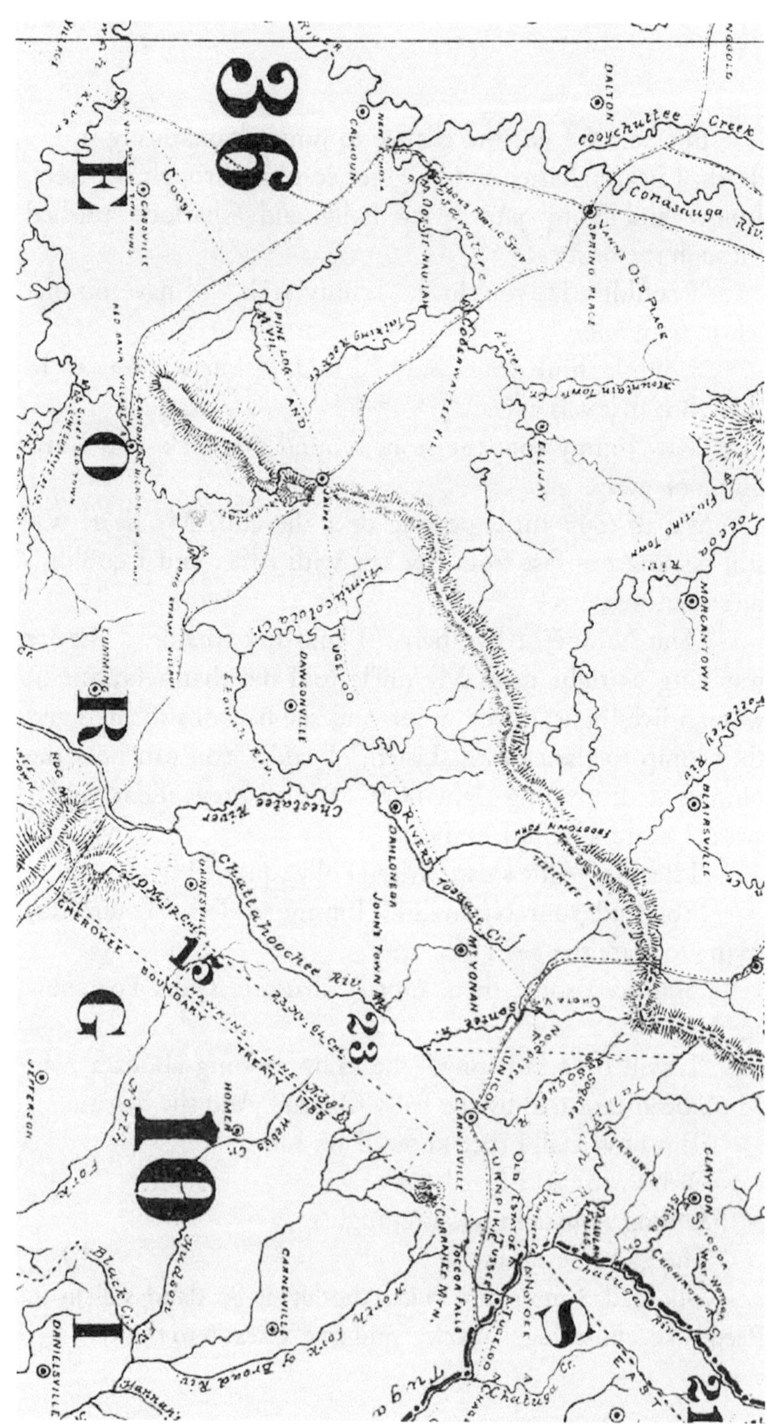

Former territorial limits of Cherokee, 1884: Hickory Log.

Chapter 21

The Ball Game

Interview Twenty-one: James Mooney and James Daugherty Wofford
March 23, 1891; Tahlequah, Cherokee Nation

[Mooney's Notes: Wofford reaches up and pulls a stickball stick off the back wall of the cabin. He hefts it in his hand for a moment before shuffling back and setting it on the table. The stick is wooden, about two and half feet long, with a little basket at the end adorned with bits of hide and colorful feathers.]

It's been many years since I have played. I was a good stickball player in my time, but not as good as my cousin Charles. In fact, Charles made this stick for me. You have to use hickory wood, because it's the strongest and toughest. These sticks take a beating, and give a beating too! You make the basket out of deer sinew, and you decorate it with bat skin and hummingbird feathers, because those are the fastest and lightest creatures. I'll tell you now about how Charles came to be one of the greatest stickball players, that summer of 1815.

Some mixed blood Cherokee from Hickory Log village wrote Reverend Meeks a letter asking for a Baptist mission and school. Meeks had just the missionary in mind—a young man named Duncan O'Bryant who'd been riding out with him on his visits to Cherokee villages. O'Bryant was an Irishman, just like you, Mooney. But a Protestant, not a Catholic. None of us had ever heard an Irish brogue before, and it was fun to hear him talk. Although sometimes you couldn't understand what he was saying.

Since neither Meeks nor O'Bryant spoke Cherokee, and since I was Meeks' pet Indian, he thought it would help to have me along.

Hickory Log was about 60 miles to the west, along the Etowah River. I'd never been there, none of us had, and when Jimmy heard I was going, he wanted to go too. Then Charles heard, and he wanted to go. Not because he was interested in spreading the Gospel, but because he had decided, after Black Watt's scolding, that he needed to learn how to be a Cherokee. I think Charles envied me, that I already knew how to be Cherokee, but he wasn't about to take lessons from a boy ten years younger than him.

The five of us set out in high spirits. I hadn't been on an adventure since Kentucky, and Jimmy and Charles had never travelled farther than Tugaloo. I was riding Gata again, using only my bearskin saddle. When we crossed the line out of the United States and into the Cherokee Nation, I felt a rush of freedom.

Reverend Meeks rode slow and calm, almost like he was riding on a donkey. With his long neck and small bright eyes, he always reminded me of a turtle. He was lanky, but his shoulders were rounded like a turtle shell, with that spindly neck and small head poking out from beneath his wide-brimmed hat. People underestimate the turtle, because he is slow. But don't forget the story of the turtle and the deer. The mind is more powerful than the legs. Some Cherokee resented Meeks and the other missionaries coming in and telling them to change who they were. But I always felt, with Meeks and later with Evan Jones, that we changed them as much as they changed us. They told us their stories, and we told them our stories, and it wasn't a bad thing to wonder together, where holiness lies.

Reverend Meeks was slow but solid. Duncan O'Bryant seemed a bit too delicate for the adventure at hand. He was small and slight and sat a horse like a girl who doesn't know how to ride. I kept being afraid he would fall off. Jimmy and I would look at each other and smirk when he lurched too far to one side or the other. But later I got to know him very well and he was a good man. He loved the people he served. He just didn't have the dash-fire of a Meeks or an Evan Jones.

I could tell that Charles would have liked to gallop all the way to Hickory Log, but that wasn't going to happen. Meeks plodded along, singing hymns, urging us to all join in. "O For a Thousand Tongues"—all eighteen verses! Charles and Jimmy didn't sing, but Meeks and O'Bryant and I harmonized. What better church than a road beneath the high arch of chestnut trees in bloom? A hot lush tunnel, flashing shafts of sun, patches of shadow, the road strewn with white petals. Chestnut flowers stink, rank and musky as spilled seed. I found myself thinking about Alfie, even as I was singing about "the glories of my God and King!"

The Alabama Road at this time was a rough dirt track through mostly forest. It had been Creek territory, and the Creeks were all gone. It wound through the headwaters of the Chattahoochee River, which had long been a borderland between Cherokee and Creeks, and now was a borderland between Cherokee and whites. We didn't see a single Cherokee village or farmstead that first day. We stopped for the night near Mule Camp Springs, where the Alabama Road comes together with the Federal Road, and the Chestatee River with the Chattahoochee. We saw a few Intruders there in a rough camp at the crossroads, but they saw me and Charles and kept their distance, because they weren't supposed to be there. We didn't know it then, but soon the Chestatee would be gold country, with prospectors pouring in from all over the world.

We crossed the Chattahoochee at Goddard's Ford and made camp on the western bank. Reverend Meeks said that Vann's Tavern was not far, just a few miles away on the Federal Road, but he didn't want to spend the money for a room or pay the toll to take the ferry across the river. He also didn't want to encounter the ruffians likely to be at the tavern. James Vann was dead by then, but his son Rich Joe Vann had taken his place. Even Jimmy and Charles had heard the stories about James Vann, who was rich as a king, cruel as a hangman, and drunk as a sailor. He had killed his own brother-in-law in a duel, and he was there when Doublehead was assassinated, although he was too drunk to help. He once tried to kill his own mother in a drunken rage, but he shot his horse instead. He was murdered while drinking at Blackburn's Tavern, and people still argue about who killed him.

There was a fish weir upstream of the ford where we crossed and camped, the first sign of Cherokee presence I'd seen, and I sharpened a stick and waded into the river and speared us a couple of fish for dinner. We cooked them over a fire, then sat back and looked up at the stars. Charles was starting to loosen up a bit, as if the farther we got from the Settlement, the easier he breathed.

"Do you know the story of the Seven Boys?" I asked. Nobody did, so I told them. "You see those seven bright stars all in a cluster? Once," I said, "there were eight young boys who liked to play the *gatayu'sti* game, where you roll a stone wheel around, pushing it with a curved stick. Their mothers got so tired of the boys playing this game that they served the boys *gatayu'sti* stones for dinner.

The boys were so angry at their mothers that they went to the Council House and performed the Feather Dance, praying to the spirits to lift them up into the sky. They danced around and around the Council House until they started to rise up off the ground. When the mothers came to find them, they watched the boys rise higher and higher in the air. One mother pulled her son back to earth using one of the *gatayu'sti* sticks, but he fell too hard and the earth closed over him. So only seven of the boys stayed in the sky. Those seven stars you always see, those are the campfires of the seven boys."

"You don't really believe that story, do you?" Jimmy asked.

"Let me ask you this," I said. "Have you ever been so angry that you wanted to run away? Have you ever wanted to float up into the sky?"

"I have," Charles said. I looked at him, stabbing at the dirt with the sharp end of the stick I'd caught the fish with. He met my gaze, and that was the first time we really saw each other, not as cousins, but as men.

To my surprise, O'Bryant reached over and patted Charles on the knee. "We'll all have wings one day," he told him in that lilting Irish tenor of his. "We'll all fly up into the sky, on wings like eagles."

You might think Reverend Meeks wouldn't like these kinds of stories, but he did, as long as they didn't have anything he thought was of the devil, like the Uktena or Tsul'Kalu.

"We call them the Pleiades," Meeks said about the stars. "The Seven Sisters. In the Greek tales, they're the daughters of Atlas, chased by the hunter Orion. Zeus turned them into stars to save them."

“I know you don’t believe that,” Jimmy said. “It doesn’t make any more sense than the Seven Boys. And what does that have to do with Jesus?”

“Jesus loved a good story,” Meeks said. “He told them all the time.”

I’d never thought of that.

The next morning, we set out at dawn and hit the Federal Road just a few miles up. If we had turned south it would have taken us to Vann’s tavern, but we turned northeast toward the Etowah. The Federal Road was a much bigger road than the Alabama Road at that time. Like the Unicoi, it was big enough for stagecoaches and wagons. And like the Unicoi, it opened the floodgates to white intruders.

At the Etowah we saw the first signs of a thriving community. But it looked more like Tugaloo Crossroads than the Cherokee Valley Towns. In fact, it was called Hightower Crossroads. There was a ferry across the river and buildings on both sides—a stables, a tanyard, a blacksmith. Blackburn’s Tavern was on the other side. Jimmy and I wanted to go across and see where Vann was killed, but Meeks said no, we needed to get to Hickory Log.

Hickory Log smelled like honeysuckle in high summer. Heavy vines draped the rough posts of the open stockade, muscadine grapes ripe for the picking. Hickory Log, *Waneiasvtlvyi,* spread on both sides of the river. There were about a dozen cabins and a seven-sided Council House. Barns, smokehouses, a blacksmith forge, pigs and chickens wandering about. In every direction stretched fields with tall stalks of young corn, all tangled with big yellow squash blossoms and curly bean tendrils. There was a field of sunflowers in bloom. Orchards with hundreds of peach and apple trees, hung with the first hard green fruit. Further out, pastures with cows and sheep. No fences around the fields, because we hold the land in common. The livestock wandered free, and that made them easy prey when the Pony Clubs got going.

This memory is both sweet and bitter. Hickory Log and all the towns along the Etowah became my world for many years. Along the riverbank and all of its creeks, Cherokee homes clustered, with people I came to know and love. There was nothing spectacular about the slow, gentle river, but it fed so many. The soil along its banks was flat and rich, and much corn grew. The fish were fat and plentiful, small game still thriving in the near mountains. The droughts and earthquakes of 1811 and 1812 had given way to some plentiful years.

For a time, the Etowah Valley was a refuge for us, there and New Echota just to the northwest. Many of the people there had fled the Lower Towns like Tugaloo and Estatoe and Keowee when they were destroyed by the Americans. The *gadugi*, the community spirit, was strong in that place. It seemed for a while like a place where we could stay.

It was a hot day, the end of July or beginning of August, and many of the Hickory Log people were working and playing near the river. Women sat on boulders, washing clothes, preparing food, weaving baskets out of river reeds. Some of the women wore long European style dresses, but others wore much shorter hemp skirts and deerskin tunics. Children played in the river, swimming and jumping in and out of canoes, wearing only breechclouts. Charles and Jimmy gaped in wonder. They'd never seen that much bare skin in their whole lives.

A few men sat in chairs in front of the Council House, and we dismounted there. We were looking for George and Moses Parris, and there they were. George Parris was an older whiteman, his son mixed blood. With them was another mixed blood Cherokee who introduced himself as Thomas Pettit, and two fullblood Cherokee, Atsekilla and Dighiegheski. The Parrises and Pettit were dressed like whitemen. Atsekilla and Dighiegheski wore European style trousers and loose shirts, but the rims of Atsekilla's ears were split off and wrapped with wire so that they formed great rings. Dighiegheski wore heron feather earrings. Both men wore their hair in topknots, and bluish tattoos were visible on their arms and necks. Jimmy and Charles had never seen traditional Cherokee, and it was a little bit funny to watch them trying not to stare.

Pettit, like us, had a white father and a Cherokee mother. In fact, his father knew our grandfather during the war. He shook our hands and called out to a young woman, his daughter Agnes, to bring us refreshments. She brought us some cool hickory milk and a plate of deer meat and hominy. Agnes was always a good-looking woman, her curves filling out a cotton blouse and a woven skirt that came just to her knees, revealing shapely brown legs and bare feet. She smiled at Charles as she handed him his cup and his bowl, and that was it. Charles was home.

The next morning was Sunday. Meeks had asked the Parrises, Pettit, Atsekilla and Dighiegheski to spread the word to their neighbors that they would be preaching in front of the Council House. A few dozen people came, spreading mats and blankets to sit on. It was a mixture of mixed bloods and fullbloods. Meeks asked me to stand up front with him and translate and sing. He wanted Jimmy and Charles to sing, too, but they fled to the edge of the crowd and wouldn't come any closer.

Meeks started the service but turned it over to O'Bryant,

since he was the one who might settle here as a missionary. That little man, he could preach the birds out of the trees! The Hickory Log people were entranced by his Irish accent and kept trying to say words the way he said them. He took as his text "Even the sparrow." God's son, he told them, walked on the earth ("arth," the people echoed) a long time ago. And he told us not to worry ("woo-ry," they said) about anything. God knows what we need. God knows when the sparrow falls and the lilies bloom. He's counted every hair on our heads. God holds the whole world ("hool warld" they repeated) in his hands.

O'Bryant pointed and waved with his hands, stomped his foot, and when he really wanted to make a point he did this little kicking thing, like kicking a ball. Even if you didn't understand a word he said, he was fun to watch. The couple of older whitemen knew to say "Amen" and the rest of the congregation picked it up and shouted enthusiastic "Amens" every once in a while.

I was translating everything, the linkester once again. The exhorter too. That's what we called missionaries back then. I wanted to be just like O'Bryant. I even tried the kicking thing. I admit, I liked that part. It was like acting out stories with Yonaguska. Later, after I went to the mission school in the Valley Towns with Evan Jones, I did become a preacher. I was good at exhorting, good at talking. Not as good at staying holy.

I translated what O'Bryant was saying so that it would make sense to Cherokee. But when I got to the part about God holding the world in his hands, that started some arguments. For traditional Cherokee, the world is an island suspended above the sea by four cords. How big did God have to be to hold the world in his hands? Were we saying that God was a giant?

O'Bryant and Meeks couldn't understand the argument. I was explaining in Cherokee that God lives in the Above World and that it's not his actual hands holding the earth. J.D. Wofford, thirteen-year-old theologian! Finally, Meeks stepped back in to end the service with a rousing rendition of "Rock of Ages."

After the service, women brought out food for a feast. It was just like dinner on the grounds at a Baptist Church, except that instead of fried chicken it was squirrel stew, wild grapes, grilled trout, *konuche*. Jimmy and I snickered when Agnes Pettit brought a plate to Charles, her long glossy hair loose down her shoulders and back. Charles' cinnamon face turned a rosy red when she pulled up a wooden stool next to him, her bare knee touching his.

Atsekilla and Dighiegheski and some of the other men were speaking in Cherokee about a stickball game planned for the following day. You could hear the Lower Town accent in the way the older men spoke, rolling their r's in the way of people from Tugaloo and Keowee. Almost no one talks that way anymore. They were talking about Hickory Log playing stickball against Pine Log village, but one of their best players had fallen off a horse and hurt his leg, and they were short one player. I saw Thomas Pettit point to Charles, and the other men nodded. Charles' muscular build was evident, and Pettit had noticed his daughter's interest.

Meeks and O'Bryant had told us we'd be riding north that afternoon, taking the Federal Road to the Moravian mission near the Vann plantation. Meeks had written to John and Anna Gambold, the Moravians who ran the mission at Springplace. They already had a few dozen converts, and he and O'Bryant wanted to get their advice about starting a mission at Hickory Log.

But when Pettit asked Charles if he wanted to play stickball, Charles was very excited, and so were Jimmy and I. Visit missionaries or play ball, what do you think young men would choose? It didn't hurt that it gave Charles the chance to show off for Agnes. Charles had no idea what he was getting into when he agreed. He probably pictured it as a team version of cudgeling. He was always up for whacking people over the head. He didn't realize that stickball is as much a ceremony as a game. Stickball is dead serious. Sometimes people are killed. There's a reason we call it *Anetsa*, "little brother of war."

Meeks did realize all that, and he was not pleased. He knew there would be prayers and dancing and all kinds of pagan revelry. He tried to talk Charles out of it, and then he tried to talk me and Jimmy out of staying too. But Charles was as happy as I'd ever seen him, and there was no way Jimmy and I were going to miss seeing him play.

"Don't eat from the table of demons," Meeks warned, shaking a long, skinny finger at me. I promised him I would not. Then Meeks and O'Bryant headed out, but we stayed in Hickory Log.

There was some debate about whether Jimmy and I would be allowed to watch the ballgame preparations. I explained that I was Red Paint Clan and *tsila* to Yonaguska. Dighiegheski was the medicine man in Hickory Log and had met Yonaguska. Both he and Atsekilla also knew my uncles and grandfather from the Battle of Horseshoe Bend.

Dighiegheski tested me. "What is the prayer for going to water? What plant breaks a fever?" Of course I knew these things, and I even told him the prayer for hunting buffalo. I told him about how we killed the buffalo and about the Great

Cave. So he agreed that I could assist him in the Ballplay ceremony.

It was harder to establish Jimmy and Charles' lineage. Aunt Lydia had told me that both her mother Susannah and her grandmother Ahnewake were Cherokee women of the Wolf Clan, and that was all I knew. Jimmy and Charles didn't even know that much. I'm sure Pettit was happy to hear this, because Agnes' mother Catherine was Bird Clan, so a marriage with Charles would be permissible. The Hickory Log folks were willing to accept Charles because they wanted him for the game and because he was a desirable match for Agnes. But Jimmy was too young and had no connection to his Cherokee roots, so Dighiegheski ruled he could watch the game but not the preparations, which were not open to non-Cherokee.

Jimmy was not unhappy about that. When it became clear that there was going to be some elaborate Cherokee ceremony that would last all night, he was not interested. It was decided that he would spend the night with the Parrises, who were not involved in the game.

That night, Dighiegheski dressed in the white deerskin of an *adawehi*, and he gave me a beaded tunic to wear. I helped him build a fire in a field on the other side of the river, using wood from a lightning-struck cedar tree. At one end of the field lay a great oblong boulder covered with markings—circles, rings, and waves. Dighiegheski placed his pots and herbs on this rock, and we mixed red, white, and black paints and prayed over them.

Near the fire we set up two forked poles with a long pole between them and hung the ball sticks for the dance. When darkness fell, the twelve players for Hickory Log, Charles included, were brought to the field. Atsekilla was one, and Buzzard Flapper, Teheniska, Snip. I don't remember all of their names. They would be allowed no food until after the game the next day, and they would stay up all night dancing. I watched as they stripped and left their clothes at the edge of the field.

Someone handed Charles a breechclout. He hid behind a tree and donned it for the first time in his life. He really couldn't understand anything that was going on, because it was all in Cherokee and completely foreign to him. It must have been like a strange dream. But he never hesitated.

All of the men had tattoos but Charles. We prayed over the players as we painted their faces and bodies. Charles stood there, the skin of his torso and legs several shades lighter than his face and arms. More exposed than he'd ever been in his life. Staring straight ahead, standing straight and strong. Dighiegheski took special care with him. He took ash from a charred cedar branch and rubbed it across Charles' forehead. He cupped Charles' chin in one hand and dipped his thumb in the red paint, bloodroot, and drew tongues of flame on Charles' cheeks. Someone touching your face is an intimate gesture. It's hard not to blink, but Charles did not. Dighiegheski painted wings, his hands rough and tender, on Charles' chest and back. He said to me, "Translate for him this story." So I did.

"Once," Dighiegheski said, "The animals challenged the birds to a great ball-play, and the birds accepted. The birds had the Eagle for their Captain, and the great Hawk Tlanuwa on their team, but they were still a little afraid of the animals. Then two little creatures hardly bigger than field mice arrived and asked to join the game. The Captain asked why they did not go to the animals, where they belonged. The small creatures said they had, but the animals had made fun of them and driven them off because they were so small.

The birds pitied the small creatures and wanted to take them in. So they decided to make them some wings. They remembered the drum they used in the dance. Its head was made from groundhog skin. So they cut off two pieces of hide from the drumhead and stretched them over two cane splints and fastened them to the little mice. One of them they called *Tlameha*, the Bat, and the other they called *Tewa*, the Flying Squirrel. The Bat was so fast, dodging and darting around the animals and keeping the ball in the air, that the Bear and the Terrapin never even got to touch the ball. The Bat sent the ball through the endposts and won the game for the birds. And that is why we tie pieces of bat skin to the ballsticks."

Then Dighiegheski pulled the middle of Charles' hair into a topknot and chopped off all the hair around the sides. He took a piece of batskin and some feathers and tied them to the topknot. "I name you Tlameha," he said. "Tell him," Dighiegheski said to me. But Charles already understood. His eyes were shiny with unshed tears.

Dighiegheski sat down at the drum and began to play and chant the ball-play song. The players chose ballsticks from the rack and circled the fire, swinging the sticks as they would in the game. Players use two ballsticks in Cherokee stickball, so they carried one in each hand. Charles followed the others, learning the steps as he went. Then from the trees emerged seven women in deerskin dresses decorated with colorful beads and feathers. Seven women for seven clans. Some wore bells on their ankles, others tortoise shells with pebbles in them, and they made their own music as they danced. Agnes was among them.

The men circled the fire and the women circled the men, coming close to them then wheeling and dancing away from them. Dighiegheski sang the ball-play songs and sometimes the women picked up the refrain and sometimes the men. The men clapped their sticks together and made motions of picking up and throwing an imaginary ball. Dighiegheski called out *Hi!* and the players responded *Hi-hï.* ' He called *Ehu'!* and the players called out *Hähï'!--Ehu'! Hähï'! Ehu'! Hähï'!* He called *Ahiye'!* and the dancers called out that same word, *Ahiye'.*

I had brought my flute and played along, and made up harmonies I didn't know I knew, a song that darted and swooped like a bat, or like a ball that is tossed back and forth between ball players. Like this.

[Mooney's note: Wofford picked up his cane flute from the table and played a lively, if somewhat discordant, song.]

The moon was full, the night was warm and humid, and the blazing fire made it even hotter. The green pine branches we threw on the fire made a pungent, piny smoke that swirled around the dancers. Every hour or so Dighiegheski led the players down to the river to practice going to water. Going to water at night is different because you can't see much, just the fireflies sparking in the rivercane, the great full moon rising in the east, the moonlight glinting on the river. Seven times under, seven times up. Pretending to die is good practice. You let the river take the fear and become one with the water. The immersion is fuller at night, because you are walking into something you cannot see, swallowed by the cool dark of the river. There is a trust required to enter what you cannot see.

Dighiegheski prayed a special going-to-water prayer for the ballplayers:

Yûnwï Gûnahi'ta, Long Man,
I come to the edge of your body.
You are mighty and most powerful.
You bear up great logs and toss them about where the foam is white.
Nothing can resist you.
Grant these men your strength that their enemy may be of no weight in their hands.
That they can toss the enemy into the air and dash him to the earth.
Now these men have ascended to the first heaven.
Now they have reached the second heaven.

As Dighiegheski said this he raised his hands slightly, and higher and higher as he named the third, fourth, fifth, sixth and seventh heaven. When he got to the seventh heaven, he stretched his arms up to the sky and said this prayer:

Now their feet are resting upon the Red Seats.
Red Bat, make them expert in dodging.
Red Deer, make them fleet of foot.
Red Hawk, make them keen of sight.
Red Rattlesnake, make them terrible to their enemies.

I know what you are thinking, Mooney. How could I preach about Jesus that morning and pray to a river and a bat that same night? You may not understand, but to me this was not a contradiction. Some of the most traditional Cherokee are Christians. We walk the white path and seek the face of God. No Cherokee, unless they are a witch, would eat from the table of demons. We eat from God's table. You are Catholic, Mooney. You understand ceremony. The water, the fire, the ash, the blood. These are all pictures of the Unseen. We are knocking on the same door.

The song and the dance, whether it's the Ball-play dance or any other one, it's a way to leave your thoughts behind and enter the spirit world. When you fast, when you stay up all night, when you become part of the rhythm of the dance, a veil between the worlds is torn. You lose yourself and find yourself. In the Bible, King David danced and sang before the Lord. Sometimes a dance can tell a story that words can't tell. It can tell pain, and it can tell joy. Sometimes a dance can heal.

For Charles, who had never danced in his life, his body had a use now, his face had a use. The dance gave his warlike spirit something to do. He was cured of the Great Black Loneliness that had followed him all of his life. He had brothers now who could love him without wanting him to be something different.

The last part of the Ball-play ceremony was the scratching. At dawn, Dighiegheski used the *kanuga*, a comb with seven sharp teeth made of turkey bone, to scratch sets of seven bloody lines on each player's arms, legs, back and chest. I could hear the teeth tear through the flesh with a rasping sound at every scratch, but not a single player flinched. Pain, too, can be a doorway. Blood trickled down their bodies and made them slippery, and they also chewed the leaves of the slippery elm and smeared the slimy spit all over themselves, to make it harder for the other team to get a hold on them.

Then the players, carrying their ball sticks in their hands, started for the ball ground. It was eight or nine miles north, near where Long Swamp Creek comes into the Etowah. The day was hot and the players had already stayed up all night and had nothing to eat, but we were all in that state where your body forgets its limitations. Eight or nine miles was nothing. I was very excited to see Long Swamp village, because this is where the Battle of Taliwa took place, where Nancy Ward helped defeat the Creeks. There was a mound there and it was a renowned ballground, where many famous matches were played.

Dighiegheski exhorted the players the entire way, promising them their enemies would be clunky as bears, slow and clumsy as the terrapin. Their adversaries would be driven under the earth, into the shadows of the Darkening Land, where they would perish forever from remembrance.

The players brandished their ballsticks and yelled and sang songs like this one:

What a fine horse I shall win!
I shall win a pacer!
I'm going to win a pretty one!
A stallion for me to ride!
What a pretty one I shall win!
How proud I'll feel when riding him!
I'm going, to win a stallion!--Hu-û!"

When we reached the ballground at Long Swamp, what a sight! There were hundreds of Cherokee assembled for the game, from all of the Etowah villages. It was the last game of the year. That night would be the Green Corn Ceremony, and no more ballgames until next year. I had never seen this many Cherokee in one place. People were milling about, placing bets with guns, blankets, horses, holding up their weapons, clothing, and jewelry to stake on the game.

The field was about three or four acres, with goal posts at either end. The ball had to go through the posts to make a run. It could be carried with the sticks, thrown, or kicked. The only thing you couldn't do was pick it up with your hands after the ball toss. You had to catch it with your stick first. But once you had it, you could put it in your hand. The first side to score twelve goals was the winner.

Each team brought its own drivers, what you would call referees. They were in charge of the ball toss and intervened if there was a fight or a dead ball. They carried long sticks in case they had to separate players or keep them from killing one another. The Hickory Log driver was George Still, an older man who lived at Red Bank and was held in high regard.

I spotted Jimmy in the crowd, chalk-faced and awkward, his arms hanging at his sides like he didn't know what to do with them. He stood next to the Parrises, Thomas Pettit, and George and Moses Sanders, another mixed blood family. To my surprise, I also saw Sequoyah. I remembered then that he lived at Pine Log. But I couldn't talk to him until after the game.

Dighiegheski let me walk beside him as we led our players single file onto the ball field. The crowd yelled and cheered. Our players lined up in the middle of the field, and as Dighiegheski and I walked to the sideline, I caught sight of Jimmy looking at Charles. Charles was not the same man he had been the day before. His face was painted black and red, his hair was gathered in a topknot tied with bat skin and feathers, and blood trickled from scratches all over his body. To Jimmy, he must have looked like an unholy mess. Jimmy's narrow face looked like spoiled porridge, like he wanted to run away but couldn't. To him, it was all a bad dream.

The Pine Log team filed out onto the field, carrying their ball sticks, led by two medicine men. One was very stooped and ancient and dressed in a coat of feathers like Alickee's. He was accompanied by a great gray wolf that was almost bigger than he was. The Pine Log players were also scratched and bloody. Each of them stood across from one of our men, to make sure the numbers were equal. Our driver, George Still, and their driver, Drowning Bear, stood in the middle. Silence fell as George picked up the ball. As soon as he tossed it in the air, there was a great clatter of wood against wood as the players scrambled to catch the ball with their sticks.

A Pine Log player caught the ball and headed toward the Hickory Log goal, only to be tackled by a half dozen Hickory Log men. Charles had never played before, but the game was pretty simple, and he caught on fast. He was in the heap, wrestling to get possession of the ball. When one of the Pine Log players picked up the ball with his hand, the Hickory Log players called out "*Uwâ'yï Gûtï! Uwâ'yï Gûtï!*" "With the hand! With the hand!' The drivers had to break apart the pile-up and toss the ball again.

Pine Log's best player was Cross-Eyed Watt, a behemoth of a man, the offspring of giants, I think. His head was as big as a pumpkin, and his eyes looked in two different directions. No one could stand in his way, not even Charles. He was not very agile but he could knock people out of the way for his teammates.

At first, Pine Log was winning this way. Cross-Eyed Watt would clear a path and Black Fox and Sawnee would score. But Atsekilla worked out a throwing strategy. When Hickory Log got the ball, Atsekilla would throw it to Buzzard Flapper, Buzzard Flapper would throw it to Teheniska, Teheniska would throw it to Snip, and Snip would throw it to Charles, and Charles would run it through the goal. Charles' talent was dodging and weaving. Like his namesake the Bat, he could dart quickly in one direction or another, evading the opponents in his path. Each time he scored, the Hickory Log crowd shouted *Tlameha, Tlameha*! The Bat! The Bat!

At one point, a player sent the ball over the heads of the spectators. All of the players charged into the crowd. They knocked over a woman with a baby, and her relatives started fighting with the players. The drivers had to intervene with their sticks and separate everybody.

When both teams were tied at eleven goals each, the game turned brutal. Pine Log players tackled Hickory Log players who didn't even have the ball and held them down to keep them out of play. Hickory Log players hit Pine Log players with their ball sticks. Charles' cudgeling experience came in handy as he bashed Pine Log players over the head. They tripped each other up, grabbed hair, tussled, and punched. Players who started the game trickling blood ended the game gushing blood.

Cross-Eyed Watt was in a rage. The Pine Log players had never seen Charles before, and it was like the Hickory Log team had brought out a weapon they weren't supposed to have, this sneaky *Tlameha*! I think he decided he was going to kill Charles. It wouldn't have been the first time a player was killed in a ball game. After that last ball toss, he ran straight to Charles and flattened him and pounded at his head. The crowd screamed, some in protest, some in encouragement.

Suddenly Jimmy pushed his way through the crowd and ran out onto the field. Before anyone could stop him, he flung himself on Watt's back like a squirrel taking on a bear. He bit Watt's ear and tore at his hair and jabbed his fingers in his eyes. The drivers rushed over and pulled Jimmy off. They had to drag him off the field kicking and fighting, tears streaming down his face. I heard shouts of *Tewa, Tewa*. If

Charles was the Bat, Jimmy was the Flying Squirrel.

Meanwhile, the other Hickory Log players piled on and pulled Watt off of Charles. For a horrible moment, Charles just lay there, and I thought he was dead. We all did. But then he sat up, his face streaming with blood, both eyes swelled almost shut, and his right arm hanging at an odd angle. He picked up one of his ball sticks with his left hand and limped to the center of the field for the next ball toss. The crowd roared in approval, even the Pine Log people.

Drowning Bear tossed the ball and Atsekilla caught it in his stick. He threw it down to the field to Snip. Snip ran toward the goalpost but stopped short and waited. Charles half-stumbled down the field and his teammates blocked for him until he neared the goal. Watt was dazed and slow and couldn't break the line, and neither could his teammates. Snip tossed the ball to Charles, and Charles, half-blind and barely standing up, caught it with the stick in his left hand and staggered through the posts. Hickory Log had won!

Those who had placed bets paid off, exchanging blankets, guns, and horses. Except for Cross-Eyed Watt, who sulked off the field, his ear dripping blood from where Jimmy had bitten it, there were no hard feelings. It was a game that everyone would remember. The story of that game was retold many times, both in Hickory Log and Pine Log.

The rest of the players headed down to the river for a final going-to-water, but Charles was helped to the sidelines by Atsekilla and Drowning Bear and tended to by Atawah, the elderly Pine Log medicine man, who was a renowned healer. Atawah's wolf Hah'kwal was always by his side, watching everything, guarding the old man. Some said Hah'kwal was part of his medicine, a Spirit Wolf.

Tsi-nv-wo-i, Atawah said, as soon as he looked at

Charles. *Shoulder.* Cross-Eyed Watt had pulled it out of joint. He spoke the word with a strange accent, which I soon learned was because he was Natchez.

Atawah was tiny and frail, one of the oldest people I had ever seen. But he was stronger than he looked. He told Charles to lay down on the blanket that Atsekilla had spread, planted his foot on Charles' shoulder, took hold of his hand, and gave it a hard yank. Charles screamed but there was a loud clicking sound as his shoulder slid back in place.

Atawah asked the younger Pine Log medicine man, Natsuwi, to fetch his bag. Then he looked over at me. "What shall we use, young man, to dress these wounds?"

"*Da'yewû* and *Saloli Gatoga*," I replied. Tassel flower and yarrow.

Natsuwi pulled out satchels with the correct herbs and handed them to me to make the poultices for Charles' eyes and shoulder. I tried to hide my left hand and arm as I prepared the medicine, mixing the dried leaves with a pine salve, the sharp smell tickling my nostrils. I didn't want them to see that I was missing my pinky finger or see the white trail of scars up my arm from the snakebite. But Atawah noticed.

"You've been scratched by a brier," he said, running his finger inside the long white groove on my arm. That part of my arm is numb. Sometimes I run my own finger along it, just to test it. An old habit. It's like seeing inside myself, what's beneath the skin. And wondering why it feels nothing, and why it's so ugly.

Of course, Atawah knew what the scar was from, but we do not name it. "You've been marked for something. It could be very good or very bad," he said.

I didn't tell him I had seen the Uktena. Then he would know it was an evil mark. "I will pray it is for good," I told him. But inside myself I knew better.

I helped Charles to sit up and we placed the poultices on his eyes and shoulder. Atawah used a length of cloth to tie his arm in a sling. He lit a small bundle of *tsola*, Indian tobacco, and waved the smoke over Charles, chanting in a strange tongue that must have been the Natchez language.

Agnes had already gone to brew Charles some white willow tea. She sat next to him on the blanket and held the cup to his trembling lips. He could not see her because the poultices covered his eyes, but he already knew her hands. She carefully dabbed at his scratches and wounds and rubbed in the healing salve. The wolf Hah'kwal had settled next to Charles, like it was his job to guard the wounded man.

I was also sitting on the blanket, and suddenly Jimmy stood over us. "I thought you were dead!" he cried, his voice cracking. "Why are you doing this? What are you trying to prove?"

Hah'kwal bared his teeth and growled. "Peace, Hah'kwal," Atawah told him, and the wolf settled but kept a wary eye on Jimmy.

"Little brother," Charles said hoarsely. "I am Cherokee. So are you. Come, sit with us." He patted the blanket next to him.

"Never!" Jimmy cried. And he ran off into the woods. I rose to follow, but a familiar voice behind me said, "Let him go. No man can choose another's path."

"Sequoyah!" I stood and embraced my uncle. Sequoyah approached Hah'kwal and gently stroked his head. I got the feeling that few people were permitted to touch the wolf.

"Atawah," Sequoyah said. "Did you know this is the grandson of Alickee?"

A warm smile spread across the creased face of the old

man. "I knew your grandfather's father, Yanaca Tahanka, Buffalo Killer. A great hunter and warrior among the Natchez."

"This boy went on the buffalo hunt with me two years ago," Sequoyah said. "He helped Alickee kill the bull."

Atawah peered into my face. "What is your name, my boy?"

"Tsuskwanunnawata," I said. I still felt a little ashamed of my name.

"That is a good name," he said. "A blanket is a needful thing. I see Alickee and Yanaca Tahanka in you. But your face is at war with itself. I don't know which side will win."

I saw that his wrinkled arms were tattooed with serpents and suns. "You must come to Pine Log," he said. "Hah'kwal and I can show you the place on the mountain where the spirits live. And the wolves."

I did go to that place later, with Natsuwi. But Atawah was gone by then. The wolves were still there.

The ballgame was followed by the Green Corn Ceremony, the Cherokee New Year. Many Hickory Log and Pine Log people spent it with the Long Swamp people that year, since they were already there. I found Jimmy and told him we would have to stay for the ceremony and could leave the next day. He spent the rest of the time sitting by himself, refusing to take part.

The women had set out a great feast in the courtyard of the Long Swamp Council House, which was built on top of the mound. They decorated the ceremony grounds in front of the Council House with arbors, trellises covered with saplings and vines.

We all climbed up the mound and entered the Council House, where the Long Swamp medicine man, Waitee, said a prayer over seven ears of new corn. It was a ceremony of giving thanks to Selu for the corn and for starting over. Waitee extinguished the old fire in the Council House and re-lit it to signify that all things were new. He placed seven grains of corn and a deer tongue in the fire. The people of Long Swamp took turns lighting torches from the new fire and carrying it to their own hearths. In all the villages, people would burn old clothing and pots and furniture. It was a time to restore the *tohi*, a time to start over.

A new fire was lit in the center of the courtyard. Judge James Daniel, wearing the wings of a raven in his hair but dressed in whiteman's trousers and a suit coat, recited the laws of the Nation and declared: "All crimes are forgiven. Let no man hold a grudge or seek vengeance. We share now the fruits of Selu."

I noticed that Daniel had several slaves who were helping with the feast. The Parrises and Sanders and Pettits also owned slaves. Most of the mixed-bloods did, and it got worse over time, as they grew more and more cotton. Daniel owned a whole plantation there at Longswamp, much nicer than my grandfather's house. His house was built on slabs of marble that his slaves mined near there. It would have made more sense for Daniel to thank the god of cotton than Selu, if there was such a god. The Almighty Dollar, that's the god of cotton.

Daniel and me, Charles and Jimmy, we were all living in the borderland. Some people chose a side and stuck with it. Others, like Daniel, like me, tried to have it both ways. Two-faced. You could even say Double-headed.

The feast that night was bountiful. There is no better taste than the sweet new corn, especially after a night and day of fasting. There was every kind of food you can imagine—

platters heaped with corn, squash, beans, blueberries, blackberries, huckleberries, muscadines, poke greens, *kanuchi*, venison, fish. *Con-nau-su-kah*, a drink made with grapes. We stuffed ourselves.

When the dances began, Charles and I just watched. Waitee drummed and Secowee, another Long Swamp man, led the dance. They danced the *ye-lu-le*, which means "to the center." It tells the story of how the Creator and the Thunder Boys gave the first fire to Kituwah, and from there the sacred fire was given to all the towns. That night there was a men's dance, a women's dance, a beaver dance, a ground hog dance, even a buffalo dance.

I don't know how any of the ballplayers stayed awake. I tried, but I drifted off, curled up on a blanket. Nearby, Charles rested, with Agnes at his side. I don't know where Jimmy slept that night.

The next morning Agnes brought Charles and me some corn, and we sat on the blankets and ate. The festival would last for four days, but our plan was to return to the Settlement that day. Our fathers thought we were with Meeks and O'Bryant, and they would not be happy if the missionaries returned without us.

Jimmy appeared with all three of our horses. He had brought them from Hickory Log to Long Swamp the day before, so we could ride home from there.

"Let's go," Jimmy said sharply, not looking at anyone.

I stood up, but Charles did not. "I'm staying here," he said. His good arm was wrapped around Agnes' shoulders.

"You can't do that," Jimmy said, looking at Charles now, scowling. "Look at you, all filthy and broken and dressed like a savage."

"Jimmy," Charles said, as gently as I'd ever heard Charles

speak. “This is in my blood. This is who I am.”

“What will you tell father and grandfather? You’re a Wofford. Your blood is Wofford’s blood.” Jimmy ran the fingers of both hands through his hair, like he wanted to tear it out.

“I am Wolf Clan,” Charles said. “My name is Tlameha.”

Jimmy turned and glared at me. “This is your fault,” he yelled. “You did this.” Flecks of spit flew out of his mouth. He swung up on his horse, his whole body trembling, and rode off.

“I’ll tell them,” I promised Charles. “I’ll make them understand.” Then I mounted Gata and followed after Jimmy.

Chapter 22

Barlow High Top

Interview Twenty-two: James Mooney and James Daugherty Wofford
March 23, 1891; Tahlequah, Cherokee Nation

[Mooney's Notes: Wofford is looking at a small framed portrait when I walk in, but he sets it face down on the table. Its gilded edges surprise me, at odds with so much else in the cabin.]

It was early that fall of 1815 when Meley Jane was taken. She often rode back and forth between her mother Betsy's house near Soquee, on the Unicoi, and Nathaniel's house at the Settlement. Aunt Lydia always welcomed her. Sometimes Nathaniel would ride back with her and stay with Betsy for a few days.

This time she rode back by herself. A couple of days later, Betsy came to collect her. That's when it was discovered that she was missing. All of the men in the Settlement went out looking for her, but they could find no trace.

That night, the Colonel remembered that the same afternoon Meley Jane had left, Carolina had also ridden out to deliver whiskey to the Browns. That was in the opposite direction from Soquee, but folks were upset and looking for someone to blame. The Colonel told Nathaniel, who latched onto the idea that it was Carolina who had taken her.

Nathaniel marched over to the little shack Carolina shared with Rachel and Tony and baby Hannah, pounded on the door, and yanked Carolina by the elbow into the middle of the yard, while the other men gathered around. It was an ugly piece of work, Carolina trembling before men who the day before had seemed like family.

Back in those days, if there was a crime, it couldn't have been a whiteman who did it. If there was a slave or an Indian around, that's who did it, regardless of the truth. I'm not sure how much that's changed, even after all this time.

When my father saw what was going on, he said, "Hold on just a minute, Nathan. Carolina rode east toward the Browns that day, and he delivered the whiskey. And we *know* him, we've known him all his life. He would *never* hurt Meley Jane or anybody else."

But Nathaniel said, "It ain't your girl that's missing, Ben. There was only one man that left the Settlement that day, and it was this negro." He spit on the ground.

I couldn't understand how Carolina, who I'd known my entire life and who my grandfather and uncle had known much longer, could suddenly become "this negro," as if nobody had ever seen him before.

Benton had to butt his head in, of course against the slave. "Meley Jane's my sister too," he said, even though he had never shown a lick of care for her before. "I say the negro did it. I say he hangs."

Aunt Lydia had come out to see what the ruckus was. Now remember, Carolina was her cousin. Slave or no slave, they were blood. When she saw what Nathaniel was doing, she called him out in front of everyone.

"Nathaniel Wofford," she said. "If you lay one hand on Carolina, I swear to you by the living God I will be your wife in name only for the rest of my life. The hand that hurts Carolina will never touch me no more."

This was one of the only times I ever saw Nathaniel lose his temper. "Wife," he said, "You're just jealous because Meley Jane isn't yours. If she were one of yours, you'd feel the same way."

That was a low blow and it wasn't even true. Lydia had always treated Meley Jane like one of her own, and she was just as worried about her as Nathaniel. She just knew, and she was right, that Carolina didn't do it.

"Uncle," I said. "There's all sorts of types that ride the Unicoi these days. You remember Joel Leathers and his men up there at Nacoochee. I know it's one of them that took her. Let me ride up there tomorrow and look for her some more."

"You leave at dawn, and you got three days," my grandfather said. "If she ain't found by then, this negro pays the price."

A voice rang out, and it was Jimmy's. "This ain't right," he said, "you all blaming Carolina. I'm riding with J.D." That was the thing about Jimmy. He loved justice. He would not countenance a lie. It cost him something to disagree with his father, but in his bones he knew Nathaniel was wrong.

"I'm going too," Tony cried out. He stood there with his hands fisted and tears streaming down his face.

"The hell you are," the Colonel barked. "You'll stay here with your Ma. For all I know, you was in on this with your Pa."

Tony trembled with rage and stared at the ground, but my father looked straight at his own father and said, "I'll lend him my horse. The boy has a right to clear his father's name. A *natural* right," he said, using one of the Colonel's favorite terms.

"If you go, boy, you'll get the whipping of your life," the Colonel roared.

The Colonel had never whipped a slave before. After that there was just silence, and Tony kicking at the dirt.

And so it was that day, between sons and fathers, brothers and brothers, husbands and wives. Some bonds were broken, others strengthened. It was never the same.

We left at dawn the next morning. I was happy that Jimmy was going, because things had been strained between us since Hickory Log. Strained between me and Uncle Nathaniel and my grandfather, too. I think they all blamed me for Charles' desertion. Maybe some of that strain got taken out on Carolina.

Tony went in spite of the Colonel's threat. The Thunder Boys to the rescue. But there was nothing grand about this adventure. We were filled with dread at what we might find, and what might happen. The monster this time was real, and it was human.

We crossed the border into Cherokee territory and rode north as hard as we could, turning west at the Chopped Oak on the Unicoi toward Soquee, where Black Watt Adair was building his new tavern.

Black Watt was outside building a porch when we rode up. I asked him if he'd seen Meley Jane.

"I know that sweet lass and her mother," he said. "But no, I haven't seen her at all." He stopped and thought a moment. "Oh no," he said. "I hope to God this isn't it. But that fool Absalom Cleveland rode through here yesterday, drunk as a skunk. Driving a four-wheel post-chaise, had to be his nephew Ben's good carriage and good horses. I thought what a waste, Cleveland's good carriage was bound to be ruined. I couldn't see anyone inside, just the fool and that mean dog of his. He stopped and asked me for some whiskey, and I sold him some, God help me, just to be rid of him. He stopped right over there," Adair said, pointing to the other side of the road.

I walked over and looked around, and my heart about stopped, because there on the ground was a green feather from Meley Jane's necklace.

"Jimmy, Tony, come here. He's got her. That lunatic has our Meley Jane!" The thought of that disgusting wretch touching her was unbearable.

I wondered why she didn't cry out, and the images that came to me were not good. Her mouth tied shut, a rope around her body. But somehow she'd managed to drop the feather. I was sure she'd done it on purpose. Meley Jane was smart. She was leaving a trail.

We rode on to Nacoochee and stopped to ask John Martin if he'd seen Absalom's chaise.

"Mid-day yesterday," he said. "Whipping the horses, driving far too fast on this bumpy road."

When we told him about Meley Jane, his face turned grim. "I'll wager he's taking her to the lair his outlaw friends keep up on Barlow High Top, near Quanassee," he said. "They've got a lookout up there so they can see travelers coming along the Unicoi and ride down on them. It's the same gang that stole my horses. Leathers was whipped and branded and then they let him go. That gang's been riding up and down the Unicoi, brawling and thieving. And this ain't the first girl who's gone missing, either."

Martin was a member of the Lighthorse Guard, the Cherokee police. If the outlaws were up near Quanassee, that was inside the Cherokee Nation, and he had jurisdiction. "That girl's Cherokee. Her mother is Betsy Terrell. I'm duty bound to make this right. Looks like we got ourselves a posse," he said. "I'll go with you and we'll get her back. You two are my deputies," he said, looking at me and Jimmy.

"Three," I said, and pointed to Tony. Now there was some history between Martin and Tony, from that time on the Unicoi when Martin rescued me from the Hollingsworth brothers but left Tony there to dig up rocks with the other slaves. I don't know if Martin remembered, but I know Tony did. And I still felt bad about it, that I had let that happen.

"Very well, three," he said, even though we all knew a slave could never be a deputy. Martin had such a blind spot, he couldn't see that Tony was no different from me and Jimmy. Martin had grown up and gone to school with rich white people. He was one of them, more than he cared to admit.

Barlow High Top was almost to the Valley Towns, not far from where Alickee lived. "I know someone else who can help us," I said. "My grandfather Alickee can hunt an outlaw as good as he can hunt a deer. They'll never hear him coming."

"Or a buffalo," Martin said. "I've heard about Alickee. We could use his help."

Martin saddled up Warrior, slung a thong of ox-hide holding his musket over his shoulder, and filled a bag with some rope to tie up the outlaws. We set out, following the Unicoi through the Gap and along the Hiwassee. It was the same road I travelled every fall and every spring, back and forth between the Settlement and the Valley Towns. I knew every twist and turn of it, the steep and winding passage up the ridge between Blue Mountain and Rocky Mountain. They call it the Unicoi Gap, but it's not much of a gap. It's hard going. I can't think of it without remembering leading hundreds of men, women and children through that gap to Fort Butler on the eve of the Trail. I'd dare anybody alive today to make that climb.

Jimmy and Tony weren't used to riding this far and this fast, and I could tell it was wearing on them, but they never flagged. Every hour it took us was another hour that Meley Jane was being hurt. We weren't too young to understand what rape was.

Twice more along the road, we found green feathers. So bright you couldn't miss them. She was showing us the way.

It was already dark when we saw Ben Cleveland's post chaise on the side of the road, tilting in a ditch, one of the back wheels broken. I climbed inside the coach, and sure enough, another green feather.

It was just a few miles east of Barlow High Top, and we figured Absalom had taken the horses and Meley Jane and headed up the mountain to find his friends. They'd see us if we got any closer, so Martin and Jimmy and Tony bedded down there for the night. But I rode on another ten miles by moonlight, all the way to Gulanyi, to fetch Alickee.

I stopped short of Alickee's cabin, not wanting to wake him, but of course he heard me and came out. You couldn't sneak up on Alickee. When I told him what had happened, his tattooed face twisted in rage. I remembered how he had told me that his grandmother had been raped by the French.

"We'll make them pay for this," he said. "We'll teach them what happens to a rapist."

We bedded down in his cabin to snatch a few hours sleep.

When I awoke at dawn, I could hear Alickee outside, getting ready. I lay still for a moment and studied the small cabin. I hadn't been inside it very many times. My mother was scared of her own father. Thirty-three scalps, he'd told me on the trip to Kentucky. And there they were, hanging from the walls. Hanks of hair, blonde, red, brown, black, long and short, coarse and fine. Sometimes a piece of parchment skin showed through on the edges, sewn with rough thread to wooden circles that looked like embroidery frames. It was a gallery of human pelts. I felt sick, but I bit it back. There was work to be done.

I joined him outside. He'd hung a pack on his horse Ayita, heavy with weapons. We mounted and rode toward Quanassee. But stopped when we got close enough that their lookout might see us. We took to the woods.

We came back out on the Unicoi a little bit past where Martin, Jimmy and Tony had camped, and circled back around to find them. Alickee and Martin knew of each other but had never met. It was an awkward meeting. They surveyed each other—the blonde and blue-eyed Martin in his fine suit, and Alickee with his bird skull earrings and strange tattoos. Martin was part of the new generation of Cherokee elite whose fathers were rich white men from South Carolina. Lower Towns Cherokee. And Alickee was a Chickamaugan—a compatriot of Dragging Canoe and the older John Watts, Young Tassel Watts, who fought the whites tooth and nail. They were the farthest extremes of what it meant to be a Cherokee. Alickee also knew that Martin owned slaves, and that made him distrustful.

But they did appreciate each other's horses. Alickee had never seen a Medicine Hat horse and was impressed by Warrior, and Martin admired Ayita and asked if Alickee would let him breed him.

Jimmy and Tony simply gaped at Alickee. I'd told them the stories, but nothing prepared them for his wild appearance. And he spoke no English, so as Alickee, Martin, and I made our plans, I had to translate for Jimmy and Tony.

We agreed we'd have to wait for nightfall to attack. This was frustrating, because the clock was ticking to get back to the Settlement before the three days were up. But Alickee and Martin both thought there might be as many as a dozen outlaws up there. Leathers rode with two other thieves named Billy Barlow and John Burke, and the LeCroys sometimes rode with them as well. And of course, Absalom, who wasn't much use as a thief or fighter, but he had his family's money.

Alickee said Billy Barlow had shown up in Quanassee a few years earlier with a Cherokee woman. As soon as he moved in, horses and livestock started disappearing. He lived on the top of a bald mountain which came to be known as Barlow High Top. There was a sinkhole at the top of that mountain, and Cherokee people knew it was a door to the Below World. Only a whiteman would be dumb enough to build a house up there.

The only road up to their lair was along Fires Creek, but they'd spot us if we went that way. Alickee and Martin agreed we'd have to climb the mountain from the backside, then wait for nightfall to make our move.

Alickee wanted to kill all of them, but Martin argued that killing whitemen would bring down the wrath of the whites not only on us, but on other Cherokee. We needed to rescue Meley Jane and bring Absalom back to face justice. Alickee just shook his head. I could tell he thought this was a foolish plan.

It was a long trek up the backside of the mountain. We followed a branch for a ways, but when it petered out we had to make our own path up the steep ridges. Our horses went part of the way, but we had to tether them when the going got too rough. Gata, Ayita, and Warrior could have kept going, but Jimmy and Tony were riding larger and clumsier settler's horses.

It was late September and still hot. The season of goldenrod and corn flowers. It got more and more humid as the day went on, like it was building up to a storm. The forest was dense with brush and underwood. We pushed through low branches, fought our way through thickets of rhododendron and laurel and patches of thorns and briars. Climbed over and around great humped boulders. The mountain hummed with cicadas and crickets and shrieked with the mockery of crows.

Jimmy and Tony and I had climbed mountains like this in the Leatherwood. We were all strong boys from the farmwork we did, and both of them were taller than me. We fell into our familiar rhythm, but this time there was none of our usual joking and playing. Tony strode on his long crane legs, Jimmy lumbered along like a bear, and I was the nimble rabbit.

It was Alickee in front, Martin right behind him, and me and Jimmy and Tony all together in the back.

Jimmy could be silent for hours, but Tony was a talker. "What do you think is happening to my Pa right now? Do you think the Colonel will be true to his word and wait?"

"I think so, yes," I told him. The Colonel prided himself on being true to his word. The problem was that he'd also be true to his word about hanging Carolina when the three days were up. But I didn't say that.

I'd explained to Alickee about the Colonel and Carolina, and Alickee was incensed on Tony's behalf. It confirmed everything he already thought about the Woffords, even though I told him my father didn't agree with the Colonel.

Alickee couldn't understand anything Tony said, but I translated. And Alickee said, "Tell him if the Colonel kills his father, I'll come down there myself and help him get his revenge."

I didn't really want to translate this for Tony. After all, the Colonel was my grandfather, even if he was dead wrong. But I did. And Tony beamed with pride, that someone like Alickee would place such value on his father's life. For no one else ever had before.

And I wondered again and again, where did my allegiance lie? To which of my grandfathers? To my family or to my friend?

I found myself explaining the Thunder Boys to Alickee and Martin. I was worried they'd think it was silly, but they didn't. I told them our names, Rabbit and Bear and Crane. And how our friend Alfie was Redbird. And Meley Jane, I told them, she was Little Dove. At that we all fell silent.

Martin's fine suit came off, piece by piece, as we climbed. By the time we got to the top, he was down to trousers and a light linen undershirt soaked with sweat. We were all scratched up and sweating, thirsty and hungry.

And Jimmy and Tony and I were thinking all the way up about those outlaws, and whether we were about to get ourselves killed.

"How many do you think there are?" Jimmy asked. "What kind of guns they likely to have?"

"These men are cowards," Martin reassured him. "Hiding up on a mountain, riding down on innocent folks. They ain't no match for us."

We stopped just below the treeline. The trees were shorter at the top of the mountain, deformed by the wind. Stubby pines and stunted yellow birches. Above us was barren rock and the strange sinkhole. We could see the outlaws' watchtower, built in the limbs of the lone tree that grew out of the rock. We caught a whiff of a foul odor, the stench of dead animals, and wondered what on earth they were doing up there.

There was a spring and a small creek that came out of the side of the mountain just below the treeline, and a crude whiskey still next to it. A bucket of corn mash that smelled rotten. But not as bad as the smell coming from the summit.

"We will go to water," Alickee said, "and prepare ourselves for the battle." The creek wasn't deep enough to immerse ourselves, but we stepped in up to our knees and splashed our faces and clothes. The water felt wonderful after the hot climb. Alickee asked me to say the words for going to water, and I did. Jimmy and Tony didn't understand the words, but I think they caught the solemnity of the moment. And I think they both saw me in a different light from that moment. They saw that I really was learning to be a medicine man. It wasn't one of my idle boasts.

Alickee had brought some face paint, and after we bathed, he painted our faces. I wondered how Jimmy would take this, since he'd been so upset to see Charles' transformation at Hickory Log. But he didn't protest. With the forefinger of his right hand, Alickee made seven stripes, alternating red and black, across our faces, and a long red stripe from our forehead down our noses, all the way down to our chests.

"Will you tell him," Tony said, "that my grandfather was a Cherokee named Red Fern? Will you tell him I belong to the Wolf Clan?"

I told Alickee. He turned to Tony and said "*Aniwaya*," and Tony repeated "*Aniwaya*." *Wolf Clan*.

Alickee said, "*Ditlihi*," and Tony repeated, "*Ditlihi*." He asked what that meant, and I told him *warrior*. Tony was about to burst with pride.

When it came to be Martin's turn to be painted, Alickee

looked at him questioningly, and Martin nodded yes. It was a sight, the red and black paint against Martin's blonde hair. I'm pretty sure Martin had never used paint before that. White skin, brown skin, black skin, all painted. All Cherokee.

Alickee took a feather from his pack, and I saw that it was an eagle feather, tipped with red. He tied it in his hair.

Alickee said a prayer for war over us:

How instantly we have lifted up the red war club.
Quickly our enemy's soul shall be without motion.
There under the earth shall his soul be, never to reappear.
He shall never go and lift up the black war club.
There under the earth the black war club and the black
    fog
Shall never be lifted from him.

When he said that prayer, I thought about Absalom, wanting his soul to go under the earth and never reappear. I wanted to kill him. We all did, except Martin.

We all had guns except Tony. If Tony shot a whiteman, he would be killed on the spot, even quicker than a Cherokee. He had no protection. That was the world we lived in. But I gave him my blowgun to use. After all the times me and him and Jimmy had practiced with it out in the Leatherwood, he was a crack shot with a blowgun.

Alickee's plan was that he would sneak up first and take out the man in the watchtower. He didn't say "kill" because Martin didn't want him to kill anyone. But I knew he would kill him. Then Tony and Jimmy would climb up on the roof of the cabin and set it on fire, while Martin and I barred the door. We'd let it get real smoky in there, then we'd open the door so they'd be blinded and choking as they came out.

We'd tie up the outlaws and ride off with Absalom and Meley Jane. Martin and I found a heavy log to drag up there and block the door.

I was worried about what Alickee would actually do once we got up there. I didn't think that Martin, Jimmy, and Tony were ready for Alickee's way of doing things. But I did know that if I was going to raid a nest of outlaws, Alickee was the person I most wanted to be there.

We didn't make a fire, couldn't give ourselves away. But we had some jerky and hardtack to eat. We had a couple of hours to kill before nightfall.

"Let me tell you a story," Tony said. Of course, I had to translate for Alickee as Tony spoke. But Tony did voices, a lot like Yonaguska, and I never had that talent.

"Talking about fire," Tony said. "Have you ever heard the story of why Fire and Rain are enemies? My grandfather learned this story in Africa, and he told it to me.

Once there was a Chief with a beautiful daughter, and all the men in the village wanted to marry her. Rain and Fire, they saw her too, and found her beautiful. Rain came a'courtin', and she fell in love with his cool water.

But Fire went to her father, the Chief. He roared at the Chief, 'I will have your daughter.' And the Chief was so scared, he said 'Yes, you can have her.'

The Chief sent for his daughter. 'I have something to tell you,' he said. 'You're going to marry Fire.'

'Oh no,' the daughter said, 'I've promised to marry Rain.'

'What are we going to do?' the Chief cried. 'Fire will burn us to bits.'

'I got an idea,' the Daughter said. 'Just you wait and see.'

The next day, the Daughter announced there'd be a race

between Fire and Rain. She would marry the winner. People came from miles around to watch the race. And when the Daughter said 'Go,' Fire took off, blazing and burning right up to the sky. But the Rain, he just sat there and yawned.

'Run,' shouted the Chief, 'or my Daughter will be burned to bits.'

But Rain just sat there and watched Fire show off. Finally, Rain kissed the Daughter on the cheek and disappeared. It looked like he had run away. Til the Rain began to fall. He formed big black clouds up in the sky, and he thundered and he lightninged, and he poured his water down. Rain put out Fire, and he won the race. He came back and took the Daughter's hand. They got married and they're together to this day."

I translated all of this to Alickee, who was delighted. "I would like to see this Africa," he said. "Just like with us, it's always a race between the fire and the water."

At nightfall, we edged closer. As we crept to the top, we could see that the watchtower had a platform like the crow's nest of a ship, and a rickety ladder up the side. There was some kind of enclosure underneath it. The moon was full but there were clouds coming in and it was getting harder to see.

We figured out that part of the smell was because they had a tanyard up there. We could see some skins hanging and great buckets where they were soaking pelts. We could smell the dung and urine they used to treat the skin and the offal from the carcasses.

We also saw small, crudely made wooden cages. They were keeping some kind of animals there as well, something that scratched and hissed and screeched in the dark. And another animal whose shrill cry sounded like a woman or a baby.

"Minks," Alickee whispered. "They stink worse than a skunk. And the shrill one is a fox."

The sloppy cabin was poised on the edge of the summit, its doorway facing the lip of the sinkhole, a dark pit in the moonlight. Who would build a cabin between the edge of a cliff and the edge of a pit? No Cherokee, that's for sure.

The outlaws' horses were tethered near the cabin, and I knew Absalom's dog had to be somewhere nearby, but between the smell and the noise, there was little danger our arrival would be detected.

While Alickee snuck over to the watchtower, I got close to the side of the cabin and peered through a chink.

I didn't see Meley Jane. But in the flickering lamplight I saw Absalom and his mangy cur, stretched out on a filthy straw mattress. Leathers, with two men I later came to know as Barlow and Burke, were seated around a crude table, drinking and playing cards, laughing and arguing. A slovenly Cherokee woman was with them, must have been Barlow's wife.

But the biggest shock was who else was with them. It was John Watts! There'd been rumors he was a horse thief, but no one knew he rode with the white Pony Club. When Alickee found out Watts was there, there was no telling what he would do.

I looked over at the watchtower and saw him creeping up the ladder. I saw that the lookout was a boy not much older than me. I watched Alickee draw his blade across the boy's neck, as I knew he would. Then he gave the signal.

First Martin and I dragged up the big log and blocked the door. Then Tony and Jimmy climbed silently up the side of the cabin and onto the roof, each with a handful of kindling and a flint. They looked for gaps in the roof-boards, lit their kindling, and stuffed the burning bundles in as far as they could go. It took a minute, but I heard the crackle as the flames caught, and the shouts of the men inside as they realized the cabin was on fire.

They tried the door and it wouldn't budge. Martin and I had the log up against it pretty tight. They were shouting and cursing, the dog howling. There was only one way out. Jimmy and Tony came around and helped us and we held the log there for a good few minutes, until all we could hear was coughing, and then we rolled it away and let them pile out.

Leathers, Burke, Barlow, and Watts all had guns, but so did Martin, Jimmy, and I. Tony ran off to the side with his blowgun. They pointed their guns at us as they coughed and got their breath, and we held our guns on them. We must have been a strange sight to them, all painted up like traditional Cherokee, two boys and a man with blonde curls.

The Cherokee woman took off into the woods, and we let her go.

And Absalom, blinded by the smoke, ran straight into the sinkhole, his dog with him. The sides were steep and slick and dog and man were flailing around down there, unable to get out. Absalom was screaming for help, the dog yelping, but we just left them down there for a while.

Leathers' forehead bore an ugly scar where he'd been branded for stealing Martin's horses. The letters HT for Horse Thief were burned into his face. I'm sure when he first saw us he thought we were a war party from one of the local Cherokee settlements. But then he recognized Martin and me under all our paint, and he spat out some words I won't repeat here, with a sneer of contemptuous bitterness. I'd never heard language that foul before.

"I see your face has been decorated, too, Leathers," Martin said. He was enjoying seeing Leathers' comeuppance. "Now where's the girl?"

"We ain't got no girl," Billy Barlow sputtered, and spat on the ground. "Just my ugly Cherokee wife, and she done run off just now. Y'all scared her with your Injun paint." I got my first good look at Barlow and saw that his face wasn't put together right. The top half was flatter than the bottom half, and one eye was higher than the other. His face looked like a loaf of bread that had gotten tilted and rose all lopsided. He squinted out of piggy eyes.

Burke was the looker of the bunch. He had thick, curly brown hair and a face as pretty as a girl's. You could tell that he'd been raised in wealth and then squandered it somehow, run away or been sent away for being a rogue. Even now, he swaggered like he had some kind of status. And when he talked, he talked like a gentleman, all courteous and honey-toned, like he was used to sweet-talking people into letting him get away with his crimes or their property.

"Now fellas," he drawled, "I'm sure we can work something out here. If it's the lunatic and the girl you want, you can have them. None of us touched the girl. We can't help the actions of a crazy man." And he smiled like we were all going to be friends.

"You're a liar and a scoundrel," I said. "Don't nobody believe a thing you say."

Watts didn't see Alickee yet, but he recognized me. "Why you little halfbreed bastard," he growled. "I'm finally gonna get my chance to see you dead." But then he looked over at the watchtower and saw the fallen form of the boy. He dropped his gun and sprinted over there and up the ladder. Then howled with grief and rage. It turned out that boy was Watts' son. Alickee didn't know that, but he would have killed him anyway, maybe even more eagerly given his hatred for Watts.

Alickee had snuck off to the side with Tony so he could ambush the outlaws. While everyone's attention was on Watts and the boy in the tower, Alickee and Tony took aim with their blowguns, and thwip, thwip, thwip, the outlaws were hit and slapping at the darts. Martin and Jimmy and I rushed them, and Alickee and Tony ran to help. It just took us a minute to get them all tied up and sitting on the ground, away from the blazing cabin, and near the edge of the pit. The cabin was becoming a great bonfire throwing light and heat over the entire summit, spitting fiery embers every which way.

Meanwhile Watts stormed back over to where we stood over the outlaws, ready to kill someone over the death of his son. He'd thrown down his gun, but he was wielding a big Bowie knife. When he saw Alickee standing there, and Alickee saw him, it was like time stopped. Neither man could believe what he was seeing. Alickee saw a fellow Cherokee who had betrayed his people and kept company with rapists and thieves, the worst dregs of the white Intruders. And Watts saw a man who was already his enemy and who had just killed his son. A man he knew to be fearless and lethal.

Watts lunged at Alickee with his knife, which was probably the only brave thing Watts had ever done. Alickee wrestled with him for a moment but easily bested him and held his own knife against Watts' throat.

"For God's sake, don't kill him," Martin shouted.

Alickee grinned maliciously. "I'm not going to kill him," he said. "I'm going to let him live with the knowledge that I killed his son. And with this sign to all Cherokee that the man is a rapist." With that, he moved the knife from Watts' throat to Watts' ear, and with one stroke sliced off the ear.

That was the Cherokee punishment for a rapist, and Watts could never again be accepted among Cherokee with that sign.

"I never touched the girl," Watts yelled, clutching his ear.

"You're a liar, and for that you lose the other ear," Alickee said. And sliced off the other one.

Blood gushed from Watts' head. And Alickee stood over him and said some Natchez words that no one but him understood. Probably some kind of wizardry. Watts lay helpless and babbling while Alickee called on Natchez gods to curse him and his seed for the rest of his days.

Finally Alickee let him go, and he stumbled off with his hands over both ears, trying to staunch the blood. He climbed back up to where his dead son lay on the tower. He gathered the body and headed into the woods. I felt a stab of pity for him, more for the loss of his son than the loss of his ears.

The ears lay on the ground. Alickee bent down and picked them up and put them in his satchel. Something to add to his collection.

But where was Meley Jane? I felt a sick fear that they had already killed her.

I peered down into the pit, lit by the flickering light of the cabin's flames. It was shaped like a funnel and water had worn concentric circles into it like a giant corkscrew. At the bottom of the steep pit stagnant water pooled, covered with scum. The drainage was blocked by the bones and guts of animals. They'd just been throwing carcasses in there after they slaughtered the animals for their skin and fur. The stink was sickening, overpowering the smell of the smoke from the burning cabin.

Absolom was standing up to his knees in the nasty water, flies buzzing around him. They'd thrown the head of a horse down there, and it floated next to his leg, the long hair of its mane swirling in the green water. A snake, must have been a water moccasin, swam close to Absalom, and he screamed. Martin knelt at the edge of the sinkhole and threw down a rope, and the lunatic grabbed onto it. Martin pulled him out, the dog skittering up beside him with his nails. Then Martin bound him with the rope. He was filthy, covered with green slime from the pit, and still sobbing and moaning.

"Where's the girl?" Martin demanded, but the outlaws refused to speak, and Absalom just wailed and drooled.

Jimmy was walking around the summit looking for her. The enclosure under the watchtower had a door made of woven branches, almost like a basket. Jimmy pulled it open and cried out. In the light of flame and moon we saw Meley Jane, and next to her in the cage was Absalom's albino Bear. Somehow he had recaptured it after the Fourth of July parade. She lay nestled against the bear's soft fur, like a girl in a legend who's been taken in by the Bear people.

At first, neither one of them moved. Then they both crawled out of the cage, the Bear gigantic next to Meley Jane's small frame. Meley Jane tottered over to where we stood, holding onto the Bear's shoulder as if he was her bridegroom. We all scattered backward.

Meley Jane's dress was filthy, but a few green feathers still hung from the cord around her neck. The Bear's fur gleamed white, almost glowed, in the light of the flames. The shiny scars on the left side of his face and neck and shoulder also gleamed. He was beautiful and terrible at the same time. His one good eye pierced each of us, as if he saw every bad thing we'd ever done.

Meley Jane had a faraway, vacant look in her eyes. They lighted on me.

"I've been with the *Nûñnĕ'hĭ*, J.D.," she said. "It's just like what you told me. They brought me under the mountain, to their secret place, and they fed me and cared for me. They were so beautiful." She swayed a bit, like she was going to fall over.

"I'm going to kill the brute," Jimmy shouted. He was crying, the tears making tracks down his war paint. He rushed at Absalom with his knife drawn. But Martin grabbed him and held onto him while Jimmy struggled, just like that time at the ballgame when he was trying to rescue Charles.

Leathers chose that moment to make a run for it. But quick as you please, I pulled out the sling that Jimmy had made for me and winged him in the head with a sharp stone. He cried out and sank back down. I'd hit him right on the forehead, and I took some pleasure in the great lump that rose up between the H and the T of his brand. I'd put my own mark on him.

Then the Bear left Meley Jane's side and lumbered over to where Absalom and his cur lay trembling. The cur growled and showed his teeth but didn't dare to fight the Bear. The Bear lifted a heavy paw and raked Absalom across the chest with his sharp claws, ripping through his shirt and leaving five deep bloody furrows in his skin. Then he fastened his jaws on the dog's throat and shook it hard, flinging it from side to side, until it died.

The Bear lumbered back to Meley Jane. She dug her fingers into his white fur.

She turned to me again. "Finish him, J.D.," she said.

I felt the gaze of the Bear's one eye on me, how he saw right through me. He knew me. He knew my name.

"We can't kill him," Martin yelled in a strangled voice, still holding on to Jimmy. "He's Ben Cleveland's uncle. If you kill him, they'll hang you, and probably the rest of us as well."

"Justice requires blood," Alickee said. "What he did to the girl is worse than murder."

"I am the law here," Martin shouted. "The new law says jail, not blood vengeance. Will you sacrifice your grandson for vengeance?"

They both looked at me. Everyone was looking at me.

"I know what to do," I said.

I walked over to Absalom, put my boot on his bloody chest, grabbed a fistful of his hair, took my knife and carved a jagged line across his forehead while he screamed.

But before I could finish, Meley Jane came forward and took the knife out of my hand. She grabbed Absalom's hair and finished the job, hacking a ring around his skull. She held up the scalp like a trophy. Then fell to the ground in a faint.

The Bear nuzzled and licked her face. He waddled over to where the outlaws sat, slumped and shaking. He stood over them, squatted slightly and released a stream of urine that soaked all three of them. They shrieked like girls. I'd be willing to bet that their own urine mixed with the Bear's.

The Bear came back to where I stood, and for a moment he just looked at me, and I at him. Then he loped off into the woods.

"Get on out of here," Martin shouted at the outlaws. "Get out of here before we kill you all."

He cut the ropes that held them and they scrambled to their feet, ran to their horses, and galloped off down the mountain. Watts had already disappeared. Absalom lay on the ground, bleeding and groaning.

Jimmy was sitting next to Meley Jane, stroking her hair and trying to rouse her. Tony was opening the animal cages and freeing the minks and foxes, who scurried off into the night. When he opened one of the larger cages, he froze, then stumbled backwards.

"Another girl," he cried.

We all ran to where he stood. Crouched in a cage not big enough for her to stand up in was a little girl younger than Meley Jane, maybe seven or eight years old. She was a white girl, red-haired like Alfie, although she was so dirty you could hardly tell. We were still wearing our war paint, and we must have terrified her. She'd already dealt with enough monsters. Martin reached his hand into the cage and she snarled and bit it, like an animal.

Meley Jane had come to, and she pushed her way past us and knelt down in front of the cage. "Hey, sweet girl," she said. "Hey, little girl." Meley Jane smiled, which at that moment seemed the most impossible and maybe the saddest thing I'd seen that day. She beckoned with her hand, and the little girl crawled out. Meley Jane had sat down, and the little girl crawled into her lap. Meley Jane rocked her back and forth. "Hey sweet girl," she crooned, "It's alright now."

Meley Jane's face at that moment, it was the *I:gagadi.* It was *The Light that defeats the Darkness.* Because she was broken, and yet she pulled that love from somewhere inside herself.

At that moment, there was a crack of thunder and the sky opened up. It poured down rain like Noah's ark times. All the filth of that place was washed away, every rotten thing. The flames of the burning cabin were quenched and left us in a darkness broken only by the flashes of lightning. The smell of soggy ashes filled the air.

And in the crack of that thunder I heard the God-voice for the second time. *Digugotanv*, it boomed. *Judgment*. And I wasn't the only one to hear it, because Alickee heard it too. I could see it on his face, in the way he nodded at the sound, as if to say, *yes*.

If you don't believe in hell, you ain't never been to Barlow High Top. I saw then that the devil didn't live in the Leatherwood, he lived on Barlow High Top. But he doesn't stay put. He goes wherever he wants to. I saw evil and it wasn't some kind of book evil. It's disgusting, it's stomach-turning, the deeds the wicked do in the dark. And I knew I was puny against it, that I wasn't going to be David slaying Goliath with his slingshot. Goliath was going to stomp all over David.

Maybe part of why I became a preacher was to do battle with the devil I'd seen on Barlow High Top. Trying to kill the devil back in the Leatherwood, that was just the beginning. The devil is a shapeshifter. Sometimes he's hiding in a thief or a rapist like Joel Leathers or Absalom Cleveland. Other times he's hiding in a friend, a grandfather or a cousin, whipping a slave or rounding up Cherokee, stealing our land. Sometimes he's hiding in another Cherokee, like John Watts. And sometimes he's looking at me in the mirror. That's the hardest one of all.

That night, the rain washed the war paint off our faces and soaked us to the skin. Jimmy fetched some clean water from the creek and we helped Meley Jane wash herself and the little girl. I took some tassel flower and yarrow leaves from my medicine pouch and made a salve for the boils and bruises on the girl's skin.

We were all so somber we could hardly speak. We only had one more day to get back and stop the Colonel from hanging Carolina. But there was no way that Meley Jane and the little girl, or really even Jimmy and Tony, could do a ride like that in one day.

It fell to me.

In the dark, in the rain, I headed back down the mountain by myself. I got Gata from where we had left the horses, saddled up and rode again through the night and into the morning, all the way back to the Settlement.

Before I left, I grabbed Absalom's scalp and put it in my satchel. When I rode past the Chopped Oak near the Settlement, the one that was marked with all the scalps that had been taken, I stopped and added a mark. I was part of that tree now.

It was late afternoon when I reached the Settlement. The gallows was built and Carolina was tied to it with a rope.

"It was Absalom Cleveland," I shouted. "It wasn't never Carolina. Absalom had her in a cabin up at Quanassee, with a gang of outlaws."

"Is she alright?" Nathaniel asked.

"She's alive," I said. "Jimmy and Tony are bringing her back. But I don't know if she'll ever be alright again."

My father walked over and cut the rope that held Carolina. He lifted him up by the shoulders. "You're a free man," he said.

"I ain't never gonna be free," Carolina said bitterly.

Rachel was standing there, leaning up against Lydia, who was looking at her husband with pure loathing. Carolina ran to where Rachel was waiting, and they turned their backs on their owners and walked away, leaning on each other.

"Where is Absalom?" the Colonel demanded. He acted all self-righteous, like he had known all along who had done it and he was going to see justice done.

"In John Martin's custody," I said. "He'll be bringing him tomorrow. He'll turn him over to Sheriff Wyly." I didn't tell them about the scalping. Let them see for themselves, I thought.

The men stood awkwardly in the yard. There was relief but there was also a cloud of shame, because they'd been wrong and they'd almost hung an innocent man.

The next day, Jimmy, Tony, and Martin rode up with Meley Jane and the little girl, and Absalom all tied up. I was surprised to see that my mother was with them. Alickee must have fetched her to help with the girls. My mother hugged me while Nathaniel embraced his daughter, and her mother Betsy took her in her arms and wept.

"I'm proud of you, my son," my mother whispered in my ear. "You've done well."

Then all the womenBetsy, Lydia, Laughing Gal, and my motherdid something I'd never seen before. The women made a circle around Absalom. Martin had pulled Absalom off his horse, and he was a dreadful sight. His scalp was raw and bloody, and blood soaked through his shirt from where the bear had slashed him. Martin knew enough to get out of the way as the women surrounded the rapist.

My mother started singing, in a voice I didn't recognize. It was harsh and grating, almost like the green bird's cry. Betsy, Lydia, and Laughing Gal joined in, and it was like a forest of green birds shrieking, voice upon voice, building louder and louder. They called down a curse that knocked Absalom to his knees. He crouched and babbled as they battered him with a wall of sound, a wail to rend the soul. Their faces were twisted in pain, like they were feeling what Meley Jane felt **that** monster violated her. There was a power in their pain. It penetrated all of us, made us all feel what Meley Jane had felt.

There was nothing plain about my mother in that moment. She was the leader of the women, and she summoned a power that scared all of us. I saw that she truly was a Red Paint Clan woman, a woman of strong medicine.

The Colonel was aghast. "What witchcraft is this?" he shouted. But his voice was weak compared to the women's song. He could hardly be heard.

Finally they ended it, and stepped away from the lunatic cowering on the ground. Even I felt relieved when they stopped. They gathered around Meley Jane and the little girl, and led them away to my father's house, where they could doctor them and pray over them. Meley Jane never parted from that girl again. She named her Sarah, and everywhere Meley Jane went, Sarah went, for the rest of their lives.

When the women were gone, the Colonel tried to take charge. "Who scalped this man?" he demanded.

I stepped forward. "I did," I said. "And I'd do it again, I'd do it ten times, for what he done." I didn't tell them about Meley Jane's part in it, not then, not ever. "And what about you, grandfather? Have you not taken a Cherokee scalp or two? It was 10 pounds each for Cherokee scalps during the war. Did you ever collect on the ones you killed?"

"Don't you lecture me, boy," he thundered. "You have no right." But he had the look of a man who knows he's wrong. He seemed smaller and weaker and older, all of the sudden. Or maybe it was just that the way I saw him changed.

Benton was there too, and I felt his eyes on me, felt his judgment, the prim hypocrite. Sheriff Wyly and Absalom's nephew Ben Cleveland were also there. The Colonel had sent for them to take Absalom away. They had watched as the women cursed Absalom, and they heard me say I'd scalped him, but they didn't mount any objections. No one wanted to defend a rapist, not even his nephew.

But Absalom still got treated like a rich man. A poor man would have been hung. But Ben Cleveland and Sheriff Wyly had Absalom declared a lunatic by the court. He was sent to the asylum in Virginia, only because the Clevelands were wealthy and well connected. I hope they chained him to the wall. I hope they put a shackle around his neck just like he did to the Great White Bear.

The worst thing that happened when we got back was that the Colonel was true to his word about whipping Tony for going off when he told him not to. My father objected and said that he had given Tony the horse and if anyone ought to be whipped, it should be him.

But the Colonel wanted to make an example to his slaves. Instead of admitting that he'd been wrong, he went in the other direction, out of pride. He made Tony stand in the middle of the yard with his hands on the post of the scaffold he'd built for Carolina. And he gave him ten lashes with the whip.

Tony didn't even cry out. In fact, he smiled through the whole thing. Because we weren't just the Thunder Boys anymore. We were the Thunder *Men*, him as much as me and Jimmy. We'd saved Meley Jane and Sarah, and we'd saved Carolina. Tony had fought alongside Alickee and John Martin. He was a *Ditlihi*, a warrior. No one could ever make him less than a man again.

After Barlow High Top, all of our childhoods were over.

And Meley Jane? This is her right here.

[Mooney's Note: Wofford hands me the picture frame. The woman in the picture is dark-haired and solemn, clearly well-off, wearing a black cape over a brocade dress. It's hard to believe it's the same woman as the kidnapped girl.]

Meley Jane slowly got to where she'd talk to people again. She became very religious, and later she went to the missionary school at Tinsawattee with me, and I looked out for her. Sarah came too, and Meley Jane looked out for her. She had a good life. Ended up in Utopia, Texas. She sent me this daguerreotype, sometime before the war. She outlived so many of the Woffords. Except for me. I'm the last one left of that generation. The only one left to tell the tale.

Chapter 23

The Mourning Doves

Interview Twenty-three: James Mooney and James Daugherty Wofford
March 24, 1891; Tahlequah, Cherokee Nation

[Mooney's Notes: Wofford is looking at an illustration of a bird in an old leather book. In the black and white sketch, a large bird perches atop what looks like an altar. The bird is larger than the houses in the background, larger than the altar it stands on. Each scalloped feather is intricately detailed.]

This was my grandfather's book. Buffon's Natural History of Birds. Like I said, he fancied himself a naturalist. He studied birds, but he didn't know them as well as he thought he did. La Torturelle means turtledove. Or also mourning dove. Their songs are so sad. *Coooo-woo-woo-woo.*

[Mooney's note: Wofford whistles the dove's song].

But they mate for life. No one knows if that song is a love song or a song of mourning for a mate that's dead and gone.

In Cherokee we call them *gulë'-diska nihï* , it cries for acorns, because their song sounds to us like *gulë'*, acorn. You hear them most in autumn, when the seeds and nuts are ripe.

My last night at the Settlement that year was the night of the corn-husking. It was time to bring in the corn, both in the Settlement and at my mother's farm in the Valley Towns.

My grandfather decided we would start the day with a dove hunt, so Mama Peggy could serve the doves at the corn-husking feast. Flocks of doves swarmed the fields in late autumn, glutting themselves on grain and seed. When everything is dying, the feast of seeds begins. Birds roosted in the trees along the creeks and rivers and foraged in the wilting grass and cane, the last wildflowers, the purple pokeberries withering on the stalks.

The best time to hunt doves is at dawn, so we rose before sun-up that day, me, my grandfather, my father, my uncle, Benton, and Jimmy. They all brought muskets, but I brought my blowgun. So much easier. Doves are fast and hard to hit.

We walked to the corn fields along the Middle Broad. My grandfather had planted cotton in his new fields, but he still had a big corn crop, food for people and for livestock, and the main ingredient in my father's moonshine. We passed the cotton fields, the wads of white fluff still hanging, the last crop to be picked. The corn fields were heavy with ears that would be gone by day's end, piled in the barn for the shucking.

We fanned out among the rows of corn closest to the river, hidden in the tall stalks. It was cool and foggy, the mist rising from the water in the weak dawn light. The first bird sang to the rising sun, and when it took flight, the loud boom of my grandfather's gun rousted them all. The air filled with an explosion of birds, the flap and whistle of their wings and their shrill call.

We brought them down, almost too easy, like the passenger pigeons I killed on the trip to Kentucky. The sky would never be that full again, nor the harvest so plentiful. I killed at least a dozen with my blowgun, and when we were finished a pile of doves lay at our feet. They might have been sleeping, so peaceful they looked, sleek and gleaming in the rising sun.

We brought them to Mama Peggy to cook for the feast, then readied the wagons to gather the corn. On a bigger plantation, the slaves would do the harvesting and husking, but it took all the men at Wofford's Settlement to bring in the crop. There was a great coldness now between my grandfather and his slaves, after the false accusation against Carolina. Carolina and Tom and Tony did whatever work was required of them, but all of the Colonel's slaves had pulled into themselves. They went about their duties, but their faces were closed doors. Mama Peggy was still good to me and Jimmy, slipping us extra treats, because we were the ones who had saved Carolina. And she was grateful to my father for standing up for him. But to everyone else, she was cold.

There were three wagons in the cornfields that day. Jimmy and Tony and I worked together, filling my father's wagon with corn, while Benton worked one with Carolina and Tom and his new-bought slaves, Allen and Ben. It was one of those golden days of late fall they have back east, almost as warm as summer except the light strikes from a different angle, sideways and thick like honey.

Three boys can have fun doing anything. The stalks were taller than we were and we played hide and seek in the rows, jumping out to scare each other, throwing ears at each other. Then we'd get serious for a while and find the rhythm—bend and snap, bend and snap, lob the ears into the filling wagon. See who had the best aim. It was always Jimmy.

When we got hungry, we'd peel open an ear and bite into the sweet kernels. Fresh raw corn is good, the way the milky fluid bursts when you sink your teeth in. If you push your nail against the kernels, or squeeze, the milk squirts out. Ripeness was a thing we were learning.

By the end of the day, we'd delivered several wagonloads to the barn, and there was a long, tall mound of corn to be shucked. We set to shucking while the women prepared the feast. Among the whites, it was only the men who shucked corn, I don't know why. They'd drink whiskey and they'd sing and they'd shuck. My grandfather always let the slaves drink at the corn-husking. And my grandfather, my father, my uncle, even Benton, sat in a ring around the corn-pile with their slaves and shucked. Me and Jimmy too, with a rare dram of whiskey for each of us.

That year, the men who were slaves sat on one side of the mountain of corn, the whitemen on the other, and me in between, the No-Man's-Land I always was.

The way you husked corn was you had a husking pin in your palm, and you slit and tore the tight sheath of the husk, pulled it back, stripped the silk, tossed the chaff in one pile and the clean new ears in another. There was more than one coarse joke about the stripping of the corn, and nakedness and silk and milk and swords and scabbards. The rough husks made your fingertips sore, and the corn milk stung like nettles.

There was a song my grandfather would always sing:

Your hay it is mowed, and your corn is reaped;
Your barns will be full, and your hovels heaped:
  Come, my boys, come;
  Come, my boys, come;
And merrily roar out Harvest Home.

[Mooney's Note: Wofford sings the song in his soft tenor.]

We all joined in, we sounded good together, basses and tenors mingling like men on a ship or in a war. For a little while, it seemed like the bitterness was forgotten, that some of the men owned the other men. That some were ready to kill the other, as quick and easy as shuck an ear of corn. But it wasn't forgotten, really. Not by Carolina and the people who loved him. The pretense that a Black Wofford was family and not property, that was gone. It wasn't the name that mattered, it was the blood and the skin and the money someone paid to own a life. The rift that opened in the Wofford clan after Meley Jane's abduction and Carolina's near-lynching only widened in the years to come.

I noticed as we shucked that Carolina had a green feather tied in his long, wavy hair, the same kind of green feather Meley Jane wore around her neck and left for us to find. It came from one of my grandfather's parakeets. *Good,* I thought. *Mama Peggy has set the birds free. Long may they roam.*

Night fell and the moon rose full and huge, and the guests arrived from all over the Settlement. I was already a little drunk and couldn't wait to see Alfie. It would be six months before I'd see her again, and I'd decided I would get her alone that night and kiss her one more time before I left.

The women had set long tables laden with food, and it was plenty warm to sit outside, especially with the big bonfire burning in the center of the yard. Everyone was there. Will and his wife Mary and their little daughter Martha Ann, the same age as Jimmy's youngest brother T.J. The blasted Hollingsworths, father and sons. Our neighbor William Deal with his Cherokee wife and small daughter Ailsey. Alfie's oldest sister Carrie, married to John Vaughan, and their new baby, while Alfie's poor mother was pregnant with another, and it wouldn't be her last. The LeCroys were there, Dorcas Shoe Boots LeCroy and her little son. Betsy Terrell was there, fussing over the food right beside Aunt Lydia and my mother, who stayed for the feast. Meley Jane trailed the women like a shadow, and little Sarah trailed after Meley Jane. Jimmy's sisters Charlotte and Sarah helped too, always careful and gentle with Meley Jane and Sarah.

My father's woman Laughing Gal was there, but she stayed with the men. She was in charge of the whiskey, not the food. She kept it flowing, for herself and everyone else. She sat like a man, with her trousered legs spread wide, slapping her thigh as she laughed at her own jokes. You could hear her laugh from across the yard.

The Wards and the Browns were there, and we'd invited John Martin. He arrived with his two wives, sisters, Lucy and Eleanor McDaniel. Black Watt Adair and his wife Rachel Thompson were there, and John Bell, who was married to Black Watt's sister Charlotte Adair. And John Ward and his Cherokee wife Caty McDaniel, Lucy and Eleanor's aunt. So it ended up there were almost as many Cherokee guests as whites, and no one blinked an eye at that. The Cherokee women flocked to Lydia and Betsy's side, and the Cherokee language rang out in Wofford's Settlement.

Alfie arrived in a wagon with her father and hugely pregnant mother, her little sisters, and their slave Easter. Alfie was wearing a white dress I'd never seen before, must have been one of her mother's, and a white ribbon atop her long red hair. She'd brushed that fiery hair out long and loose. She was a girl at a party now.

Easter helped Alfie's mother Eleanor and the smaller McCracken girls down from the wagon. It rankled me a little bit, that Alfie had taken so quickly to letting a slave do the things that she should do. And yet she looked like a fairy princess from one of her own stories, and I rushed to greet her. Almost tripped over my own big feet. Then realized that I had no idea what to say to this new Alfie. Jimmy and Tony ran up to say I was needed by my grandfather to carry out more chairs, and that was the end of that.

Alfie's father had brought his fiddle. We'd laid down boards on the lawn for the dancing, and when he started to play, the children were the first to dance, holding hands and tumbling about. Easter presided over the children, keeping them away from the bonfire. She was hardly more than a girl herself, and every time I saw her, I thought of her mother at the auction and felt a little sick.

There was a long table spread with platters of fresh roasted corn, and squash and pecans and apples. It was a feast for Selu, whether they knew it or not. The centerpiece was a platter of grilled doves. Mama Peggy was famous for the way she prepared them, crisp seared skin encasing the tender meat within.

There were four or five other tables for the dozens of guests. The Colonel sat like a king at the head of the first table, with Granny Mary on one side of him and Benton on the other. The heir apparent. Peggy brought grandfather a plate, two roasted doves set in a bed of late greens and purple muscadines.

"A toast," the Colonel cried. "To corn, to cotton, to Wofford's Settlement and this rich harvest!"

He took his knife and fork and cut into the doves and ate the perfect birds. "Most delicious," he cried. "Peggy, you have outdone yourself."

Peggy smiled down at him, and she looked over at Carolina, with the feather in his hair, and nodded and smiled. And

I knew then what she had done. I knew what he was eating. I looked over at Lydia and Betsy and my mother and Meley Jane, and Rachel holding baby Hannah in her arms. And I saw that they knew as well, and they were glad.

The sad thing was that those birds were Mama Peggy's children, too. She'd sacrificed the birds she loved for sweet revenge.

"Where's my portion?" Granny Mary complained.

"Oh, yes Ma'am, there's a portion for you, too, Mrs. Mary." And Peggy went and fetched a second special plate.

We watched the Colonel bite and suck on a bone the size of an infant's finger. And no one said a thing.

I sat at a table with John Martin and the other Cherokee and white Tugaloo landowners—Black Watt Adair, John Bell, John Ward, Sheriff Wyly, Devereaux Jarrett. The Martins, Adairs, Bells, and Wards were so different from my own Cherokee family, and it seemed like a path for me to be like them. I *was* like them—fluent in Cherokee and English, educated in white culture but still able to tell Cherokee stories and say Cherokee prayers. That's probably why Martin took me under his wing, and when they all moved from Tugaloo to Etowah and Coosawattee and New Echota, so did I. This was the Cherokee aristocracy of that time. For me, it was a way to not have to choose between the two warring sides of myself.

My grandfather knew the fathers of these men, going all the way back to his days in South Carolina. It was a point of pride to him that I was taken up by the wealthy landowners. He ordered Mama Peggy and Rachel to wait upon them, and they brought the finest portions to our table. Doves, not parakeets. I said before that it bothered me that Alfie took so quickly to being waited on, but so did I. I wanted to seem important. I wanted Alfie and Jimmy to see me eating with the wealthy guests. I even wanted my mother to see it.

We were halfway through the meal when three horses rode up. I couldn't believe my eyes. It was Charles and Agnes, and another Cherokee woman I didn't know. Charles was dressed in whiteman clothes, but he still had his topknot, and a large silver earring hung from one ear. Agnes was dressed like a white woman, as was her companion, except they wore moccasins.

All heads turned as they dismounted. The fiddling stopped, and a hush spread over the guests. I looked to my grandfather and to my uncle Nathaniel. They were very angry when Charles did not return with Jimmy and me. They never spoke his name.

Lydia didn't care. She ran to her son and embraced him and embraced Agnes as well. Nathaniel rose and we all watched him stride toward his son, his face a mask. Then he held out his hand and they shook, father and son, like a business deal had been sealed. Nathaniel wasn't one for a lot of emotion. But he took Agnes' hand and kissed it, and I saw Charles' face flood with pleasure.

"Kill the fatted calf," my grandfather shouted, "for the prodigal has returned! To your health, my boy!" And he raised his glass in a toast.

And that was it. The fiddling started again, and the chatter of the guests. Lydia put her arm around Agnes and led her and her friend to the group of Cherokee women, who crowded around them, eager to welcome their new sisters. Laughing Gal seemed to know them, because she left my father's table and went to greet them. It turned out she was related to the Downings, Agnes' mother's family.

I looked over at Jimmy, who was scowling and kicking at

the dirt like he always did when he was mad. It was going to take a little longer for him to forgive Charles. And Benton, well, he looked like he was sucking on a sour pickle. But then again, that was his usual expression.

I went to Charles and we embraced as brothers. I led him over to my table and introduced him. He had already met Black Watt at the tavern on the fourth of July.

Black Watt said drily, "I guess you've learned to be a Cherokee."

Charles just grinned, something he never used to do. "Do you know my wife's father Thomas Pettit? Her mother is Catherine Hughes and her grandmother is Nancy Downing." And of course that led to a long discussion of all of the ways that everyone there was related, because they all were. So many of the people who lived along the Etowah had come from Tugaloo. And before long, the men at that table, me included, would also be pushed west to the Etowah and New Echota.

Charles fit right in with Martin and Adair, and he went from being the black sheep of the Wofford clan to a man of some prestige. Benton, who prided himself on being the successful brother, was fuming. He was sitting next to my grandfather, but that turned out to not to be the place of honor. No one paid him a bit of attention.

Nathaniel was standing next to our table when Aunt Lydia approached him with Agnes and her companion.

"This is Charlotte Downing, my mother's cousin," Agnes said shyly. "She lives near the Chestatee. She has something to show you." She spoke English well, as did Charlotte, both of them mixed blood.

Charlotte pulled something from a pocket in her dress and held it out in her palm. It was a lump of gold, a couple inches long, jagged and lumpy but bright and gleaming. Unmistakably gold.

"We found this near the river. We wondered if we could trade it for tools or guns or horses."

The men at the table all rose and crowded around to get a better look.

"Where did you say you found it?" Martin asked. The gleam of the gold was reflected in his eyes, in all the men's eyes. It didn't matter if you were a good man or a bad man. Gold did something to people.

"May I hold it?" Nathaniel asked. She handed it to him and he rolled it around in his hands, not unlike how an *adawehi* rolls the conjuring beads.

"Oh yes," he said, "we will trade for this."

"What part of the Chestatee?" Martin asked. His home near Nacoochee wasn't terribly far from where the Chestatee comes down off of Blood Mountain. And I'd told him about the string of gold beads that Joel Leathers and Joseph Wofford had found at the Nacoochee Mound.

"We'd be glad to take you there sometime," Charles said.

But no one found any more gold until 1829. We had another decade of pretending to ourselves that we could stay. Georgia strung us along until the Gold Rush of 1829. "There's gold in them thar hills"—that wasn't California, that was Georgia.

Nathaniel and Charles kept speaking with Charlotte Downing, negotiating a trade, but everyone else's attention turned to the middle of the lawn, where my grandfather had led Granny Mary to start the first dance. "A Virginia reel," he called out to James McCracken. Will and his wife Mary joined the line, and Alfie's sister Carrie and her husband John, and Sheriff Wyly and his wife. And the dance began, others crowding around to watch.

I saw this as my moment to get Alfie alone. She was standing at the edge of the crowd, watching the dance like she was itching to join it. But I snuck up behind her and tugged on her hand. "Come on," I whispered, and the old mischief sparkled in her eyes as we snuck away.

"To the shoals," I said. That was the spot where we always played. And that was the place to get a girl alone on a moonlit night. The small falls glistened in the full moon. We could hear the music and voices in the distance, but we were alone.

"The stillhouse!" she said, laughing, and ran to try the door. We weren't allowed to go in there, but she seemed to want to out-dare me. The door to the stone building swung open and we went in. There were two huge copper pots hung over low fireplaces, almost like the saltpeter cauldrons in Kentucky. But they were connected by coiling tubes to barrels. The smell of the fermenting corn was strong and foul. Casks, jugs, and bins of corn meal were scattered across the stone floor. It was dark in there, but the moon gave us just enough light to see.

Alfie hopped up on a barrel like she'd been doing it all her life. Her hands gripped the rim of the barrel and she swung her legs back and forth. Her fancy white dress was bound to get dirty.

I hopped up on a barrel too. I was wearing the hag stone Alfie had given me on a cord around my neck, and I made sure it was out so she could see it. But neither one of us said anything about it, or the kiss at the top of Toccoa Falls.

"You ever been in here before?" she asked.

"Sure I have, with my father and Laughing Gal."

"Ain't you ashamed of her?" she said.

"No," I said. "Why would I be?" I knew why, I just didn't want to say.

"She dresses like a man," Alfie said. "And she drinks too much. So does your father."

"I drink too," I said. I didn't, not then, but I was a little mad and I was showing off. I grabbed one of the jugs from the floor, uncorked it, and took a big swig. I handed it to her, and she tipped it to her mouth, but so slowly she barely got a trickle. She set it down and wiped the back of her hand across her mouth like she'd drank a lot.

"My father drinks too much," she said.

"It's a thing men do," I told her.

"Can I tell you a secret, J.D.? And you won't tell nobody?"

"Course," I said. And I never did, not til this moment when I'm telling you.

"He beats her sometimes," she said. "When he's drunk. And then he forces her—you know. All those babies. It's too much."

"I'm sorry, Alf," I said. "I didn't know."

"She can play the piano," she said. "She can read. She's a proper lady. I hate him!" She started to cry and pushed the tears away with her fingers. "I can't live like that, J.D. Not ever. I can't."

I thought about my mother and Ebenezer, and I couldn't stand to think of Alfie with a man like that.

"You won't ever have to," I said. "Not so long as I'm around." I slid off my barrel and started toward her. I had told myself I was going to kiss her, and I wasn't going to chicken out.

Just then we heard steps crunching across the leaves outside, and I turned, thinking it was my father or her father, and we'd catch a hiding.

But it was Jimmy, looming in the doorway.

"Why'd you leave without me?" he said.

Chapter 24

The Road Home

Interview Twenty-four: James Mooney and James Daugherty Wofford
March 25, 1891; Tahlequah, Cherokee Nation

[Mooney's Notes: Wofford removes from a leather satchel a dried up, bulbous old root, a bit like ginger or ginseng root but darker.]

I left for the Valley Towns with my mother the day after the corn-husking feast. I would help her bring in her corn, and then I would go to Kituwah and spend the winter with Yonaguska.

That morning, Carolina came and found me, and he gave me this root.

"This here's High John the Conqueror," he told me, placing it in my palm and closing my fingers around it. "This root protects you from anything that come at you. You just carry it on your right side. Those Pony Club boys ever come near you, they can't break through it. High John is strong magic. And J.D.," he said, "I'll never forget what you and Jimmy did, and how my Tony helped to save his Daddy's life. How do you say brother in Cherokee?"

"*Tsosdadahnvtli,*" I said.

"*Tsosdadahnvtli*, my brother," he said. "If you ever need anything, you call on me." And many years later, I did.

Carolina put a piece of his strong heart in this root, and that's why I've kept it with me always. His hand and the earth have held it.

The bags I tied on Gata for the journey back to the Valley Towns were full to bursting. The Colonel had given me Buffon's bird book, as if that could make up for his shameful acts. Reverend Meeks gave me my first Bible. I had Alfie's hag stone, Jimmy's sling, my father's pipe, Carolina's root. I had Absalom's scalp. I had my medicine pouch. I had Tsali's tobacco and Alfie's fireweed, my mother's bundle of rattlesnake's master and sedge. I had my blowgun, my musket, and my flute. I could pray for someone or kill them or play them a song. I could shoot a bird or tell you its name in three languages.

I asked my mother if she would mind if we took a detour to Toccoa Falls.

"Shall we go to water together?" I asked her, the first time I'd ever done that. And we did. It was getting cool so we walked into the pool below the falls fully clothed. We plunged beneath the water, seven times under, seven times up. I said the same prayer that Tsali had said when we went to water with him:

"I will stretch out my hand.
Water, you slide, the white foam washes us.
It will cling to our heads as we walk the path.
We listen to your voice. You make us new."

My mother got out of the water and sat on the shore with a blanket wrapped around her shoulders. But I sat down underneath the waterfall, the water pounding on my head. I wanted to be cleansed. I could wash off the blood on my hands. But it was the blood in my veins that troubled me, that witch's brew of oil and water, innocence and guilt.

The events of that summer changed Wofford's Settlement for good. When the Colonel learned that Peggy had served him parakeets instead of doves, he sold Tony and Carolina to Charles, and Rachel and baby Hannah to Benton. He figured that since Benton and Charles hated each other so much, he'd broken up their family for good. But Charles let Tony and Carolina sneak back to the Settlement to visit, and if Benton knew, he turned a blind eye.

I was never close to the Colonel after that. I saw him for the hypocrite he was. In the end, it wasn't Cherokee vs. whites that tore the Woffords apart. It was slavery.

Within a few years, Charles was running a grist mill on the Chattahoochee, Carolina and Tony with him. Charles treated Carolina like the cousin he was. Nathaniel and Lydia followed Charles with the rest of their kids. But their marriage was never the same after Nathaniel's betrayal of Carolina. Nathaniel was never the best husband anyway. And my father moved down to Etowah with Laughing Gal. They all moved into the Cherokee world.

After that summer, I was either at Kituwah with Yonaguska or working for John Martin training horses, or at the mission schools, first at Tinsawattee and then at the Valley Town mission with Evan Jones. Still hedging my bets, still walking that line. Training to be a medicine man, training to be a Baptist preacher. That wasn't as unusual as you think. When the Keetowah Society formed out here, it was filled with Baptists who practiced the old Cherokee ways. Still is. I'll say any prayer that gets me closer to the holy. The things I've seen and things I've done, there's not enough prayers in the world for.

Jimmy and Tony and I stayed close until the Trail split us up. And even then, the connection remained. We would always be blood brothers, with a stronger tie than a name or a color.

By 1820, the Colonel and Benton were the only Woffords left in Wofford's Settlement. The Colonel died with only two people with him, Mama Peggy and Tom. The two people who hated him the most in the world.

What happened to Alfie? That's a story for another time.

As I sat under the falls, I half thought I'd see the Great White Bear again. I figured he had something more to tell me. But I didn't.

I listened to the water, tried to decipher the voices in the torrent, the whispers in its rush.

I thought then that the Unspeakable Road lay behind me, that it was the road to Kentucky or the road to Barlow High Top. If I had known what lay ahead, I might've never left those falls. I might have gone to live with the *Nûñnĕ'hĭ*, I might be there still.

But I didn't know.

I walked out of the water and my mother pulled a blanket out of my pouch. It was the buffalo blanket I got in Kentucky, the same one I'd later take on the Trail and wrap my Mattie Ann in. My mother dabbed at my face, the thick fur still smelling of the power of buffalo.

"Thank you, *Etsi*," I said. I took the buffalo blanket from her and dabbed her face a few times. It was the face of my people.

"*Tsisdu*," she said, smiling. "Tsuskwanunnawata."

I finished drying myself off, we mounted our horses, and rode toward the Valley Towns and Kituwah.

Toward home.

Epilogue:
National Anthropological Archives, Smithsonian Museum, 2022

The interview from March 25 was the last transcript. I'd been reading for days, coming back each morning to open another leather volume of Mooney's notes, staying in the archive until closing time. I was sad when I reached the end.

But then I pulled another box from the cart and found bundles of letters tied with twine. I recognized J.D.'s handwriting on the addresses, next to the broken wax seals that had held the documents together. With white-gloved hands I untied the first bundle and carefully opened the first letter.

> September 19, 1820
> Tinsawattee Mission
> Dear Jimmy,
> I have terrible news. Alickee has been killed. They're saying that it's John Welch who done it, but I know the truth. It was John Watts. And I'm going to find him...

I knew then that I'd only touched the beginning of J.D.'s story. What happened to Alickee? What happened to J.D. at the mission schools? How did J.D. become a leader in the anti-Removal movement and a detachment leader on the Trail of Tears? How did he part from Yonaguska? What was his role in the abolitionist Keetowah Society out west? How did he come to fight for the Union in Indian Territory in his

60s? And how did he become Mooney's informant at the end of his life?

All of this was yet to be discovered in the letters.

Appendix A: William Wofford Family Tree

Colonel William Wofford 1728-1823
m. (1) Sarah Mary Cameron
m. (2) Nancy Greenleaf
m. (3) Mary Bobo

Benjamin Wofford 1758-1836 m. Mary Hollingsworth	Nathaniel Wofford 1766-1846 m. Lydia Ann Hopper	James Wofford 1770-1795	Charlotte Wofford 1772- m. (1) Thomas Baker (2) Franklin	Ann Wofford 1774- m. (1) Thomas Clark (2) William Bright	Sarah Wofford 1775- m. David Gillespie	Mary Wofford 1776 m. (1) James Lewis m. (2) Weatherspoon
William Hollingsworth Wofford 1789-1826 James Daugherty Wofford 1802-1893 (with Nancy Natchez)	William Benton Wofford 1791-1858 Charles Wofford 1793-1850 Sarah Wofford 1800-1882 James Whitney Wofford 1801-1866 Meley Jane Wofford 1803-1875 (with		Mary Baker	Hiram Bright 1810-1881	Lydia Gillespie 1797-1867 Charlotte Gillespie 1802-1870 William Gillespie 1805-1897	

	Betsy Terrell) Charlotte Wofford 1805-1880 John Thomas Wofford 1808-1895 Thomas Jefferson Wofford 1812-1900					

Appendix B

Enslaved Woffords Family Tree

Rachel's Side	Carolina's Side
Tom (b. 1740? In Africa) m. Peggy (b. 1750?)	Red Fern (b. 1740?), Cherokee, brother of Lydia Hopper Wofford's mother Susannah, m. Izzy, a slave of William Wofford (note: these characters are fictional)
Rachel (b. 1776?) m. Carolina	Carolina Wofford (b. 1770?)
Tony b. 1802 Hannah b. 1811	

Note: Tom, Peggy, Rachel, Carolina, Tony and Hannah are actual historical persons. Their names are found in Wofford wills. I have speculated on their birthdates and relationships. I have a theory that Toni Morrison, born Chloe Wofford, is a descendant of Hannah. The only fictional characters here are Carolina's parents Red Fern and Izzy. I chose the name Red Fern because there was a Cherokee family called Redfern in Burke County, NC during the time the Woffords lived there.

Appendix C: Cherokee Watts Family Tree

Trader John Watts
("Forked Tongue Watts")
1720-1775
m. Wurteh, sister of Doublehead

Wurteh "Betsy" Watts 1744-1814 m. (1) Bloody Fellow (2) Robert Due (3) George Guess/Gist (4) John Benge	Chief John "Young Tassel" Watts 1746-1808 m. (1) Mary Johnson (2) Wurteagua Carpenter (3) Oousta White Owl Hanging Maw (4) Tsiyugi	Nancy Watts 1748-1787 m. George Lowery Sr.	Elizabeth Watts 1750-1795 m. Alickee Natchez
Tahlonteskee 1760-1819 (with Bloody Fellow) Chief of Old Settlers in Arkansas John Jolly 1763-1838 (with Robert Due) Chief of Old Settlers in Arkansas Sequoyah 1770-1843 (with George Guess) Lucy Benge 1772-1846 (with John Benge) m. George Lowery (Agili)	John Watts III 1782-1832 Also: Margaret Soup Mink Fish Tail Thomas Rattling Gourd Two Wood Peach Eater Elizabeth Jacob Oostooli Rachel Mary Polly	John Lowery 1768-1817 George Lowery ("Agili") 1770-1852 m. Lucy Benge	Nancy Watts Natchez 1772-1843 m. (?) Benjamin Wofford
			James Daugherty Wofford

Appendix D:

Speculative Family Tree for Alickee and Yonaguska

Trader Cornelius Dougherty
c. 1700-1779

Sour Mush Daugherty 1728-1820	Daugherty Daughter m. Natchez Warrior b. 1720
Yonaguska 1759-1839	Alickee Natchez 1750-1819

Note: There is no historical record or agreement about who Yonaguska's parents or Alickee's parents were. Legend has it that Yonaguska and Alickee ("Ah Leache") were close relatives. When Alickee ("Ah Leache") was (in real life) murdered in 1819, Yonaguska was called upon to revenge his kinsman's murder. There has been speculation in the past that Sour Mush Daugherty was Yonaguska's father, based on land records. The fact that James Daugherty Wofford's middle name was Daugherty leads me to speculate that he was a grandson of Cornelius Daugherty as well. It is historically true that Cornelius Daugherty helped the Natchez refugees settle with the Cherokee near where Alickee lived in "Notchee Town," so a Daugherty daughter marrying a Natchez warrior would make sense. The legend surrounding Alickee's ("Ah Leache's") murder and Yonaguska's quest for revenge was fictionalized in Robert Strange's novel *Eoneguski: Or the Cherokee Chief* (1839).

Acknowledgments

My first thanks go to Marsha Mullen, who is J.D. Wofford's five-times great-granddaughter, for sharing family history, documents and photographs with me and encouraging me in this project. The most important thing to me in writing this book has been to portray J.D. Wofford in a way that makes his descendants proud and that is pleasing to the Cherokee people.

Thanks as well to Tony and Carra Harris, Georgia Trail of Tears members, for reading the manuscript and teaching me about Cherokee plants, and for Michael Wren of the national Trail of Tears Association for helping me with research questions.

My next round of thanks goes to my colleagues and students at Reinhardt University. My colleagues Bill Walsh, Ken Wheeler, and Jeff Bishop all read the manuscript and gave me feedback and edits. Jeff helped me greatly with Cherokee history questions. Reinhardt's President Mark Roberts and my former Dean Wayne Glowka have been unfailingly supportive of my writing and my quest to build Reinhardt's Etowah Valley Low Residency MFA in Creative Writing.

Thanks to Beth Glowka and Treena Galloway, the best editors ever! Your comments and edits made the book so much better. So did edits from two of my MFA students, Andrew Diaz Winkelmann and Tiffany Jansen. Readers should check out Andrew's historical novel *The Guava Tree*.

Thanks to my daughter-in-law Veronica Mangrum for helping me format the maps. I couldn't have done it without you!

Thanks to all of my MFA family, both faculty and students. Summer Residencies with Bill Walsh, John Williams, Gray Stewart, Will Wright, and Laura Newbern have been food for my soul. Our students have been a loving and supportive community to each other and to me. You guys have taught me at least as much as I ever taught you.

Many thanks to Trey Gaines at the Bartow County History Museum and Joe Head at the Etowah Valley Historical Society for opening your doors to me and facilitating my research. Thanks to Stephanie Nardil and Sandra Bruce, Wofford descendants at Wofford's Crossroads Baptist Church, who shared their documents and knowledge.

Thanks also to other Wofford descendants who have shared information with me, including Dottie Cornelius and Martha Wellsandt. Thanks to Danny Smith for showing me the Wofford cemetery and property and giving me fantastic information on William Benton Wofford. Thanks to Kristen Hanna for helping me research Altha McCracken Wofford's line and to Cole Owen for his excellent book on McCracken genealogy, *From Yesterday…For Tomorrow.*

Many thanks to Dorothy Witherspoon for allowing me to attend the African-American Wofford reunion at Wofford College in June 2023. Dorothy's book *The Homecoming* is invaluable for African-American Wofford descendants. I was honored to attend the reunion and hear your stories.

Thanks to my mother, Paula Coffey, for reading the manuscript and for keeping the faith.

And lastly thank you to Doug Little for being the book's biggest fan and promoter and for being my anchor, my helpmate and my truest friend.